I0641384

The Repercussions of Us

Andrea Casanova

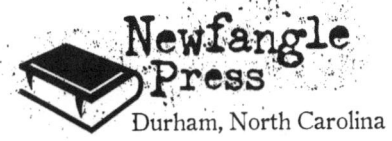

Newfangle Press

Durham, North Carolina

Prologue

We were almost done with the five-hour drive when the storms hit. The weather had been pursuing us the entire day. It was he and I together, racing against dark clouds in his black van. Raindrops spattered the windshield. We made a quick rest area stop, and that's all it took. The thunder caught up to us.

That was the storm outside the car. The one inside was worse.

I checked the clock on my phone. Checked it twice. If I didn't get to the dorm in time, I'd have to wait until the next day to pick up my keys.

The car in front of us was going thirty in a seventy-five zone. The storm was bad, but it was more of a fifty miles-per-hour bad. Definitely not a thirty.

My heartbeat raced beneath my fingertips. I tugged on my seatbelt, loosening it.

"Rain, stop it," he commanded.

I stopped. "I know, I know," I said. Rob hated fidgeting even more than he hated crying. "It's just that he's going so slow."

"Yeah, he is," Rob grumbled, but made no effort to pass.

I lasted a whole ten minutes without saying anything more.

"We have less than half an hour to get there," I said.

I saw the way his fingers wrung the steering wheel. It made the scars on his knuckles stand out—white marks which credited his moments of lost tempers and their only means of release. To me, the lacerated lines resembled the wires of an undetonated bomb.

"It's a five-hour drive. That means it takes us five hours to get there. You're the one who wanted to move five hours away from me."

"Just pass this car," I begged.

"Right. I get it. Even my driving isn't good enough for you."

"Rob…"

Rob was achingly beautiful. When he was happy, I was in heaven. When he was sad, I was devastated. When he loved me, I mattered. Simmering below this beautiful façade was an angry man. But it didn't matter. He was my first love, and it was easy to forget this side of him, especially since it hadn't been around in months. We had been good, and when we were good, we were a dream.

I took hold of his hand. My touch was always an elixir to his moods. It didn't work.

"I still don't understand why you have to move. Don't you like it back home?" he said.

My hand, tangled in his, clammed up like an animal in a bear trap. I could feel the storm brewing.

"I loved it because you were there. But I need distance from my mom. You know that, Rob," I recited. It had been months since we'd had this argument, but I still knew the script by heart, even if the lines were a little different each time.

"I don't get you. We had everything. You were doing great at the university there. We were happy, focusing on us, saving money. We were fine."

I cemented my lips shut, holding back the words I always wanted to say, even as I wondered if they were the words he needed to hear. *Sure, we were fine, but I wasn't. I need to leave, but not because we weren't happy. I want to test myself, to break free from my mom's house. School's a way out and a way toward becoming a writer.*

"You want to leave me," Rob surmised from my silence.

It didn't matter if I told him the truth. Rob believed what he wanted. No one would ever believe that a man who looked like him could be plagued with so much insecurity. *I guess that's what heartbreak can do to you*, I thought.

"I want to leave everything *except* for you," I tried, going off-script.

Silence fanned the tension. I broke first, because I freaked out when he went quiet. It was like a forest going still. So much could happen without warning when an angry man was too quiet.

"Rob?"

"What?" he bellowed.

I flinched.

"I'm sorry, okay? I can't pretend like everything is fine. I always said I couldn't do long distance, and you didn't care. You applied. You accepted. You decided everything without me."

I wanted to yank my hand away from him. I couldn't understand why he was suddenly backtracking from months of happiness. My heart and head were having an internal tug-of-war: *To apologize, or to argue, that's the question… should I keep suffering, or stand up against a sea of troubles?*

It was the one fight where compromise felt like betrayal.

"I told you this was important," I said. "This is what I've wanted for years. You're being selfish."

"Me?" he shouted, his widened eyes leaving the road ahead of us long enough to stare at me in disbelief. "You're the one leaving!"

"You're the one forcing me to choose," I said, meeting his stare, daring him to look away or crash the van.

He looked away.

The van went silent again, but, this time, he broke first.

"I don't want to break up over something as stupid as you moving, babe."

"It's not stupid that I want to move."

"You know what I mean," he growled.

Rob passed the car in front of us and accelerated, faster than even I would've gone in this downpour, fast enough that I wasn't sure if I felt relief that we'd make it on time or panic that we wouldn't make it at all. But even with his antics, I knew where we stood, where we were. We were in Act 1 of Shooting Stares, passing the scene where we held our pride like shields, and speeding along to the moment before the curtain call. It was the big forgiveness scene, the moment where I swallowed my words and refused to throw away the years we had together.

I wasn't sure if I could play that part anymore, but I knew I could write a better ending.

His reckless driving got us to the dorm right before the RAs left for the day. I jumped out of the car and ran inside to the registration table, showing them my ID. One of them talked my ear off about bus routes, setting up a meal card, and new student policies. I wanted to cut her off, but I didn't want to seem rude. By the time I made my way back to the car, I was sweating from humidity and anxiety.

My boxes were lined up along the sidewalk. Rob was sitting in the driver's seat.

"Let's just lug these upstairs and get showered. I'm too tired to do much more than that," I said.

He shook his head. "I'm heading home."

My mouth fell open. "Tonight?"

Rob nodded.

"You're leaving me," I whispered.

He shook his head. "No. You're leaving me. And if you need distance, then maybe I need distance, too."

I stood there, watching the black van drive away, hoping this was all a joke, wondering if it was the final act, or just an intermission.

Part One

How did I know it was over?

I was lying in bed with you, wondering who
was going to love me the way I loved you.

Trying to redirect my hands not to reach for
you

Forcing my eyes to look away when you
enter a room

Failing to convince myself that I wasn't the
one for you

Severed ties control my mind,

Malfunctioning signals from unnoticed cut
wires

Thoughts broken into fragments trying to
void you & us

Walked away from all we weren't

Still obsessing over what we were

How do you erase years spent together?

When one second pulled us apart.

~~We've hurt each other more than we've loved
each other.~~

1

No memories of him had been stitched into this twin-sized mattress, yet his absence created an indentation I couldn't help falling into. I turned over, prying my eyes open. The room, as lifeless and haunted as a cemetery, teased me with his ghost. He hadn't even stepped foot in here, but it was as if he had died on the floor, condemned to this shoebox of a room.

It was hopeless. He had left behind a scratch on my sight that couldn't be buffed out. My chest ached, fighting against stubborn heartbreak.

It wasn't supposed to be like this.

The thought echoed loudly, sending an avalanche of panic down, crushing me like an unlucky tree caught in the icy landslide. I needed to stop thinking about him.

I'd waste ten more minutes trying to hex myself to sleep. If I failed, then I'd concede to a nocturnal way of life. I'd pretend insomnia was a superpower instead of a curse. I'd use it to my advantage, spending the sleepless hours exploring my new town so that I wouldn't look lost on the first day of the fall semester.

I should've been parading around the room in my underwear at the sheer thought of escaping my mother's house. My music should've been playing so loudly that I was receiving noise complaints. It should've been a real turning-point-of-the-movie moment, but only a few hours in this tiny suite and the plain white walls and cherry-stained furniture were giving me a headache.

It's still a turning point. Just a tragic one.

I shut my eyes again and pulled my blanket up to my nose. If I were still a kid, maybe I would've felt safe by the stitched shield. Maybe then I wouldn't feel so alone.

The university had this unfair rule that all new students, even transfers, had to live in the dorms their first year. And while I was grateful to be paired with someone close to my age, my roommate hadn't arrived yet.

I found myself wishing I weren't stuck here. It wasn't that the dorm was rundown. I had my own room, a shared, small living space, and a bathroom. The beige couch didn't have any deep rips or suspicious stains. The floor tiles, unfortunately, were a sickly green and yellow shade, but a rug could cover that. Sure, the dorm wasn't like the ones on the northside campus that were basically apartments, but it was a step up from communal toilets.

It's not that the empty dorm made me miserable. I'd simply enjoy it more if I weren't alone, actively trying not to think of people who clearly weren't thinking of me.

Ugh.

My mind boomeranged to the man who stole my sleep. I couldn't help it. He wasn't supposed to give me a ride then just drop my boxes and me off on the sidewalk as if he were taking out the trash.

The emptiness caved in on itself, making the silence bounce like hydrostatic pressure, as if I were deep underwater and the mere act of existing was a struggle. I had put up a few things, like my framed Freddie Mercury poster. The brass mirror I had thrifted last summer rested nicely on my part-time desk/part-time vanity. Underneath my raised bed, I had thrown a red minifridge and laid out a teal rug. My things were in here, taking up empty corners, yet I failed to fill up the room enough to make it feel like mine.

I heaved out a heavy sigh, feeling the blanket transform from a fluffy safety net to a straitjacket. Hastily, I untangled myself and donkey-kicked the bed. Poor mattress had no idea its new owner was violent when stressed.

I sat up, disturbing the stifling silence. The dorm reverberated in anticipation for another, more exciting life to fill it.

Honestly, I also ached for someone to fill the emptiness.

"Alright, Rain. Enough," I snapped, slapping my hands against the mattress.

It was easier to surrender to the habit of talking to myself than to attempt to fix it. My swirling, murky musings funneled and gained clarity when I spoke aloud or wrote. A pen or a keyboard was a lightning rod for the storm of my thoughts.

"Maybe I should write?"

I would pull out my laptop and climb back into bed with it. Cast around for the perfect opening to pour out my emotions. Then, the floodgates open, I'd fill half a dozen pages with a torrent of thoughts about him, because I also had the bad habit of prolonging my pain.

My specialty, though, lay in plucking distractions out of thin air, and running free until life tricked me into dealing with my problems.

"That's it. Exploring it is!"

I crawled out of bed, throwing my maroon comforter to the side. I kept my black sweatpants on but traded my big t-shirt for a bralette and a university sweatshirt. I wasted no time grabbing the essentials. Keys. Wallet. Phone. Vans. AirPods.

I was out the door.

When it was daylight, the campus was the ideal brochure of manicured, cedar elm trees and mosaic brick towers. It was the type of place that was crowned in summer and dethroned in winter. At night, however, the desolation reminded me of an abandoned carnival, and the eeriness heightened the twinge of adventure.

Fortunately, I suppose, my dorm was in a good location, and after only a few paces, I was at the center of campus, stepping on a giant, stone walkway. It was drizzling, and the night sky was a black backdrop peeking through the overhanging limbs of trees. The only sounds were my footsteps and the patter of raindrops on leaves. Insects fluttered around tall lamp posts. Banners stitched with the ocelot mascot hung off the poles. The gold and green tassel borders were miniscule fingers wiggling at me.

"This is your new home, Rain. Your dream was to be free and now you have nowhere to go. Woohoo," I chimed sarcastically.

Dreams are wonderfully bright from afar. *But be careful what you wish for…*

Hugging myself, I continued walking, but every step felt like I was slipping. Visions of caramel eyes and locked hands began to landslide me into a black hole. I missed him, and I hated him for not being an easy thing to forget.

"This isn't working," I complained. Barely twenty minutes had passed, and my thoughts had already circled back to him several times.

I pivoted, changing directions down a street leading into town. The closer I got, the more the college town came alive. I passed a bar with a dancing lemon neon sign. Tipsy Squeeze. *Good name*, I thought. Fragments of music spilled from the patio. People talked outside, creating symphonies of laughter. Cigarettes passed like intimate handshakes.

I drank it all in as I passed by. I wanted to steal the random girl's smile as she leaned in to whisper to her friend. I wanted to project the same boisterous laugh I heard from my own throat so I could sound just as carefree. I wanted to bat my eyelashes at that stranger while clinking our drinks together because the possibility of more was enticing.

I shook my head, and depression rushed in to swamp the shattered reverie. I wasn't anywhere close to being like them.

The intersection was a building away when a hazy mixture of red and white light poured onto the opposite sidewalk. New Dawn Tattoos. Immediately, I gravitated towards its glass walls. The Open sign was missing the 'o,' and a guy was getting a tattoo on his back.

The longer I stared, the stronger the itch became.

A sudden roar of thunder exploded. I darted toward the shop, barreling through the door as the calm drizzle became a brutal downpour.

A bell chimed. The needles dragged, and, with a subtle wince, the guy lifted his gaze and fastened its hold on me.

Whoa.

Coming from a mostly Hispanic town, green eyes were rare, and his were radiant, like tree leaves alive with sunlight. He was sprawled on the chair, his naked torso pinned in place by the tattoo machine. His skin was lighter than mine, and he probably burned in the sun rather than tanning easily like me. My eyes traveled over his body, and I felt the heat of a blush creeping up my neck.

"Yeah?"

No hello. No hi. Just, "Yeah?"

Water dripped from my hair, landing like little raindrops on the floor. My lips tightened, remaining shut as I stared.

He arched an eyebrow, then talked without using his tongue. «Can you hear?» he signed, mouthing out the words as well.

My eyelids fluttered in surprise. *Nobody slips into sign language as casually as that. Not in real life.*

I had started learning American Sign Language in high school. Rob was my inspiration, having picked it up because of a childhood friend of his who was deaf. If Rob was invested in something, he usually expected me to be, as well. But my natural competitiveness had kicked in, and I had ended up taking four college courses on the language. I liked pretending I was fluent, but I still needed a lot of repetition and slow fingerspelling.

In class, I had learned that mouthing words was a bad habit since it could be confusing for some Deaf people, but as casually as he signed, I doubted he had learned how to do so in school.

I scanned his ears for an aid. His long, black hair curled right at his lobes, but no, nothing there.

"Can you speak?" he asked aloud now.

"Y-yes. I'm sorry. I—"

But then the artist giving the tattoo looked at me, and my words froze in my mouth. These eyes were brown, and friendlier, but my mouth wouldn't budge. Not even when he smiled and revealed two sunken dimples.

The artist tapped the guy sprawled on the chair, then signed to him, «Does she need help?» His sandy brown hair was styled up in a little wave, revealing ears that were also bare. *Weird.* Though, Deaf people didn't always need or want implants or aids. Some hated them.

"I want to get a tattoo," I blurted out, digging through my wallet for the scrap of paper that rested heavy on my soul. A receipt or a gum wrapper would be bigger. The words inking it in Aunt Rosen's handwriting tugged at my heart.

I love you, Rain
Rosen

Another quick motion of hands captured my attention—Brown Eyes signing to Green Eyes. I moved past the counter, trying to decode the movements.

«She doesn't look okay. Is she scared?» the tattoo artist signed neatly with one hand.

«Maybe she's scared of thunder,» Green Eyes replied.

I bit my lip. I didn't look scared. Did I?

Green Eyes cut me with the amused condescension radiating from his smile, and I realized I was staring too obviously.

"«It's ASL. American Sign Language,»" he remarked, interpreting as he spoke. "«He's Deaf.»"

"I know what ASL is," I ground out, averting my eyes, painfully aware of how awkwardly this was going.

The tattoo artist waved his hand. «Stop moving or I'm going to mess up. Do you want to do her? Or should I?»

The guy being inked returned his gaze to me. Any protracted moment of eye contact made my skin crawl. It never failed to feel like people were scavenging for a fault in me during the elapsed seconds. Usually, I'd turn, but this time, I scanned the face harboring those grassy-green orbs. He had a straight nose with a slight bump on the bridge. A scar severed the hair in his left brow. Dense eyelashes sharpened his eyes, and his lips were thin. The jawline, dangerous and unforgiving, could cut like a butcher's knife. When he clenched that jaw, it looked like he had popped a marble in his mouth.

«I'll do it,» he finally signed. Aloud to me, he said, "I can start on you once he's finished. I'm the other artist here." He pointed to the second station, where his Instagram handle was written on the wall.

I blinked. My brain acted jetlagged. *He'll be doing my tattoo?* My skin tingled in betraying anticipation. It had been so long since someone other than Rob had touched me, and stupidly, I wondered how it would be.

"That work for you?"

"Oh. Sure. I'll wait over here," I replied, jutting my thumb like a hitchhiker.

I couldn't walk away quickly enough.

In the front of the shop, there was a black, worn-down couch. My body sunk into the lumpy cushions.

Framed art hung on the burgundy walls. Each image was entirely different, except for the persistent motif of plants merging with other objects. Candles sprouted tulips. A radio had dandelions for speakers. A ribcage had two branches of wisteria for lungs.

All were painted except for the frame closest to me, in which fuddled, gray lines formed two hands holding a bouquet of flowers. The shading on the petals looked like smoke, and the grasp seemed gentle, as if the hands knew the bundle could get lost in the wind. The stems were barbed, tangling thorns and leaves. It was a juxtaposition of texture blending seamlessly in a world of contradictions. Jagged versus smooth. Petals versus thorns. Human versus nature. Returning my gaze to the hands giving a tattoo and the hands clasped on the chair's edge, my curiosity was piqued. *Which of them drew these?*

The ringing of my phone snapped me back to reality. Clutching the collar of my sweatshirt, I checked the screen.

Rob's name appeared.

I looked up at the two artists, just finishing their work, then back at my phone.

I slid the icon, ignoring the call, then turned off my phone.

I began detangling the wet knots in my hair. Using the reflection from the glass windows as my guide, I worked my way down my dark brown strands until they faded to a bleached, light honey color. I scrutinized my bare face. I had been cursed with transparency, and without makeup for armor, my feelings flashed like road signs. Warning! Heartbreak! Sadness ahead! Proceed with caution!

Feeling defeated, I left my hair alone, in tangles, and dug my back into the lumpy sofa.

No wonder they thought I didn't look okay.

I breathed in slowly, feeling my heartbeat beneath my eyelids. Lysol-saturated air branded my lungs.

"You ready?"

The voice startled me, causing me to jump. Noticing, he muttered, "Sorry," and stuffed his hands in his pockets. "What did you want to get?"

I rolled my shoulders, feigning normalcy. I handed him the piece of paper and my ID. "I want it on my ribcage."

His eyebrow shot up when he looked at my name, emphasizing the scar. "Alright... Rain," he said, punctuating my name with a wry laugh.

I narrowed my eyes. "Why's that funny?"

"Rain came in with the rain," he said, looking very proud of himself. "You want it to be scaled differently?"

"A little larger."

With a sweeping grin, he signed to his friend that I wanted it on my ribcage, adding another stupid comment, «Five bucks says she flinches.»

My brows wanted to arch, but I ran a hand over my face, choosing to appear vacant, not ready to disclose that I understood every word their fingers uttered.

"What did you tell him?"

"Just interpreting."

Liar.

The other replied, signing and making a face, «It's small. Don't be an ass.»

I glanced at his face. He smiled politely.

At least *he* wasn't a jerk.

"Give me a second," Green Eyes announced, returning to the counter with an iPad in hand.

It never failed—the excitement and anxiety. Even for piercings, I shook like a chihuahua. I waited, fidgeting, popping my knuckles. The fidgeting made me think of how much Rob hated it, and my hands stilled.

The guy who would be doing my tattoo had changed into a white shirt, so thin that I could see the outline of a ring which hung from a silver chain around his neck. The wrinkles of the newly applied bandage near his lower back were also visible. Whatever the piece was, it was big. Most of the tattoos I saw on him were large. He had a detailed, red rose on his right shoulder and a sparrow on his left. In the middle of his back was another, but with the way his broad shoulders made the shirt hang, I only caught a glimpse of inky darkness.

Not a drop of ink was visible on the other tattoo artist. He wore a gray, long-sleeved shirt and black pants, though, so any pieces might be hidden.

They talked with their backs to me. I craned my neck to get a better look, right when they both turned. I pretended I was rolling my neck.

The Deaf guy smiled. «I think she's checking me out,» he surmised.

I forced out a cough to disguise my laughter. I wasn't checking him out. Was I? *Not with Green Eyes in the same room*, my mind politely answered for me, and I felt heat creeping up my neck again.

«I'll go tell L,» mine responded. He dragged the shape of the letter down his shoulder, mirroring long hair. It had to be a sign name.

«Shut up,» the other retorted. They both laughed, and their expressions moved in a secret language I couldn't decipher.

"Here, sign this," mine said, handing me a clipboard. I scribbled my name and initials in cursive about ten times. When I handed the clipboard back to him, he added, "«You sure you're ready to get a tattoo?»"

Seriously? The tone was too condescending to ignore. Getting a better look at him, I could see that sweeping grin of his was nothing but a smirk. My desire to wipe it off his face overpowered me, but instead of reacting with the caustic words lacing my tongue, I yanked my sweatshirt off, copying his smirk.

He blinked slowly. Not in shock. Not in anything.

My spontaneity flatlined at his deadpan expression.

Okay. I expected a bigger reaction.

But then, the corner of his mouth twitched.

The other artist smirked. «You sure she's ready to get a tattoo?» he mocked.

«Shut the fuck up,» mine snapped. His gaze returned, searing my skin.

I had five tattoos. A crescent moon on the end of my collarbone near my shoulder. An outline of an open book on my left forearm. A quote on my bicep. A dainty flame on my wrist. Most infinitesimal and obscure were the two lines on my finger that most people missed but said one thing: I wasn't here for my first.

"I didn't know you had any," he said, walking around. He sat on a stool near the chair and threw a casual hand, gesturing for me to sit. "Where do you want it again?"

I rolled my eyes. Whatever. I'd get this tattoo and leave.

"Here," I told him, pointing to my ribs.

He glanced at the area and nodded. He wheeled over to some shelves, retrieving a tiny, sealed pool of black ink and a packet with a needle. His movements were methodical, like a doctor preparing for surgery.

He smiled, and I immediately noticed it was more genuine than before. This one reached his eyes, wrinkling the skin at the end of his brows. I wondered what ran through his head to cause it.

Aunt Rosen used to say I was gifted with feeling too much and that was why every emotion could be read on my face as easily as print on paper. I overthought and overanalyzed, falling into each and every mental rabbit hole, but this man looked like he had never tripped over a thought. A permanent aura of nonchalance floated around him. He moved like gravity didn't exist for him.

"What were you doing walking around in the middle of a storm on a Wednesday?" he asked while peeling the stencil. "We weren't expecting anyone to come in."

"It wasn't raining when I left," I answered, shrugging my shoulders. "Honestly? I was bored and restless."

He pressed the stencil onto my skin. "Check it out," he advised, jutting his chin behind me toward a large sheet of mirror nailed to the wall.

My reflection loomed in front of me. My body wasn't ugly. It was just a body. My shoulders were too wide. My chest could be bigger. My ribs poked out in a funny way. My waist curved in, but my lower stomach refused to flatten no matter how much I ran. My legs were strong and the only definition I had.

Looking at my body now, I hated it, taunted with moments I wanted to forget. The first time Rob kissed my collarbone and said he loved me. The times his hand reached for the blanket but landed on my hips. The many moments I felt like his hands were the glue keeping me together.

"It's fine," I mumbled. I walked back, watching the two speaking in fragments.

«She seems fine.»

«No, she looks—»

"«Stop talking about me like I'm not here,»" I snapped, using both my hands and voice.

"The hell?" Green Eyes laughed. "You sign?"

"«I've been studying American Sign Language for two years.»"

His friend gawked. «So, you understood everything?»

"«I guess I eavesdropped.»"

They exchanged a glance. I plopped on the chair.

"«Well, shit. Are you ready?»" my artist asked.

My mood continued to rollercoaster. I wasn't even sure that I wanted a tattoo anymore. But this one was for Aunt Rosen. Nothing could make it a bad memory.

"Ready!"

The vibrating buzz taunted my eardrums as the needles skated over my skin. I was entranced by the sight of ink depositing. Slow and steady, he drew the first line. Some artists had a heavy hand, but he seemed to work against the intense nature of the tattoo machine, actively making his touch light.

His friend leaned against the counter, knocking on the wood to get my attention. «I'm Travis,» he introduced himself, placing the letter 'T' on his cheek.

I smiled. «Rain, like how it's raining outside,» I said, immediately feeling pathetic. I spelled out each letter individually. In the Deaf world, a person had to fingerspell their name until a Deaf person created their sign name.

"I'm Noah," my artist said, signing a quick «NC» by his shoulder with one hand. "You in school?"

"«I'm a transfer. This is my first semester,»" I replied.

«What's your major?» Travis asked.

"«English.»"

«Ah, so does that say something profound?» he asked, straining to read the quote tattooed on the arm tucked to my side.

"«'Love builds a Heaven in Hell's despair,'»" I recited. "«It's a line from a poem.»"

I was eighteen when I got that one, figuring a line from my favorite poem wouldn't be a regret, and I didn't hate it, but I could hear how pretentious I sounded when I explained it now.

"Blake?" Noah inquired, lacking enthusiasm.

I gaped like a kid who had just realized someone else in the class liked the same things. To be fair, *The Clod and the Pebble* was a popular work, but guys my age didn't read poetry.

"Yeah," I breathed. "How did you know?"

"My mom used to read him to me."

"She has good taste," I said, still in shock.

Noah hesitated, his face eclipsed, but with a hard blink, he continued as if the shadow hadn't been cast.

"«What were you getting?»" I asked, letting my eyes wander to his bandaged side again.

"Touch-ups." His eyes flicked to my legs, hidden by the sweatpants. "You don't have any big pieces, do you?"

"«No, I don't,»" I said, feeling like I was making a confession. He didn't sound judgmental, but his attention on me was just too new, too difficult to get used to. A shiver crawled up my spine.

«Are you cold?» Travis asked.

Noah's lips swept to the side in a smirk. "Maybe you shouldn't have taken off your shirt."

"«Taking off my shirt was the quickest way to get you to stop being condescending,»" I pointed out.

Travis tapped my wrist. «We were expressing concern. Some people freak out, and you're jumpy.»

Ouch.

"I don't like thunder," I evaded. I did hate it, but the booming sky wasn't the culprit for my jitters.

Noah cleared his throat. Travis shrugged. They gave zero evidence of not believing me, but their lack of response said everything.

"«This place is amazing. I love the art,»" I added, changing the subject.

"It's my sister's. Dawn. Hence the name. Travis and I usually take night shifts during the week for her," Noah said.

«With that, I'm going to clean the rest of the place. I don't want to piss her off again,» Travis said, deserting us.

With just us two, the world balanced on a pin, and I felt too nervous to speak. I liked to think I was friendly and could talk to anyone, but my brain was kind enough to remind me of how I had spent the first couple of minutes here gawking at this guy, not uttering a single word.

"Is the art hers, too?"

"Mine."

"All of them?" I gaped.

He nodded. "This is our family's version of putting stuff up on the fridge."

"Whoa," I whispered in awe. "It's really good."

His boyish smirk faded. "Thanks. So, where are you from, Rain?"

"It's a few hours driving. You?"

"Here is home."

"Have you always lived here?" I pried, watching how his brows furrowed as he drew the words.

"We lived upstate until my sister moved here for college years ago. She dropped out and bought this."

My guard dared to falter. It was a relief to talk to someone who shared pieces of himself like it was nothing, and it was even nicer knowing he didn't know a thing about me. Another attractive amenity of this university was that no one from my high school had come here. In cutting myself off from my old life, I had tried to make it as clean as possible.

"So, family business, huh?"

"Sort of." He squinted his eyes the way a child would. Mischievously. Playfully.

"And you go to San Austin," I stated. "I'm impressed."

"Don't be. If there was a word for less than part-time, I'd be that."

"When did you start tattooing?"

"About five years ago, when I turned eighteen."

"You're twenty-three?"

"About. Birthday is at the end of the year." He dipped the tattoo machine in the pool of ink, muttering, "Just have to go over this line, and you're done."

"Oh. Great." *Home to the dorms, where loneliness preyed on my willpower.*

A minute later, the tattoo machine stopped. My skin, raw and hot to the touch, tingled when he sprayed the area, cleaning it.

I returned to the full-length mirror. The newest addition, vivid and inflamed, made my eyes water. My heart jerked at having Aunt Rosen's handwriting on me. Paper wasn't durable, and I knew the tiny scrap of her I kept in my wallet would fade eventually. Here, though, on my skin, she'd be as permanent as I was. We were connected again.

"Thank you. It's perfect," I marveled.

"Glad you like it." He wrapped the tattoo, dropping his eyes when I put on my sweatshirt.

"Cash, right?"

"Yep. Shop minimum. Sixty."

I dug through my wallet.

"Let me clean up a bit. We could give you a ride. It's still bad out there," he said, glancing out the window.

Lightning struck right on cue.

"I'm staying on campus. I can run it."

"Fuck, no. You're scared of thunder, remember? Let us take you up the road. That, or I'll wait with you until an Uber comes."

Which I had no money for, since I had just dropped it all on a tattoo and needed to save for my books. *Fantastic choices you make, Rain.*

"Here's to hoping you guys aren't serial killers," I replied, handing him the cash.

It was an ordinary exchange, made exhilarating by hands touching and Noah never looking away, but I was hopelessly enamored by it. His palms weren't sweaty or rough. They were nice, and I felt starved for touch.

When we let go, I noticed a piece of paper in my palm. *A business card?*

"I doubt serial killers give out their information. In case you like my work."

"Oh. Okay." I glanced at the digits that sat like thorns in my hand. I'd toss it later.

I waited for Noah and Travis at the front of the shop. Reluctantly, I turned on my phone. Text messages attacked my screen.

Why aren't you answering?

Look, I just want to talk.

Wtf. Your phone is off? Just let me know you're okay.

Please.

This isn't fair. I wanted to check in because I fucking love you.

That's how it's going to be? Fine.

I guess we're both being pretty fucking stupid.

"Ready?"

I jumped. Noah stood behind me. Immediately, I pressed the screen to my chest, hiding the texts from Rob.

His gaze slid to my hands. "«Let's go.»"

He and Travis communicated in their secret language of glances, and I grew irritated, feeling left out and judged.

My tongue and hands rambled. "«No. I'm fine. I walked here, and I can walk ba—»"

Travis grabbed my hand, shutting me up. «Stop. You're new here, and it's late.»

My gaze fell to my feet. Despite the pounding in my head whispering Rob's name, I signed a simple, «O-K.»

I couldn't tell if this was an act of rebellion or idiocy.

Outside, Noah and Travis went to an old, light blue pickup truck. Paint peeled off the hood and fuzzy pink dice hung from the rearview mirror. Travis beat me to the backseat, forcing me up front. As I climbed in, I noticed the rips in the seat being pulled together by black yarn. My fingers walked along the lines like a tightrope.

The ride was uncomfortable but short. The tattoo shop was right down the road from the university's main biology building, next to my dorm. Reality struck when Noah hit the brakes. My tattoo fever dream had ended. Awkwardly, I reached for the door, not saying a thing, but his fingertips touched my knee. We both looked down, and time stretched.

"If you need anything, you know where Dawn's is," he said, removing his hand.

I stepped outside and closed the door, but my hand lingered on the handle the way his fingertips had on my knee.

"Thanks," I said, meaning it, but wanting to express more. He had no idea what the tattoo meant to me, and he had no idea how wonderful the break from my dorm was. "Really. Thank you."

He leaned over, his eyes miraculously lucent in the night.

"Hope to see you around, Rain."

"Ditto," I stammered, turning quickly.

Inside my room, I cringed. *Ditto? Ugh.*

2

My favorite part of the day used to be when I stood in front of my closet, deciding what to wear. Bold colors. Stripes. Polka dots. Sequins. Tank tops. Shorts. But clothes had began to riddle me with anxiety after Rob made it clear they weren't just a form of expression. They were the impressions I left on people. They were the statements I made without saying a word.

They were advertisements for coming attractions.

I needed to stop overthinking, even if it meant being reckless.

I slipped on a jean skirt, wrapped my waist in a black belt with a gold buckle, and threw on a cropped gray sweater. I dusted off my combat boots and laced them up. I blow dried my hair. I decorated the shells of my ears with gold hoops and studs. I applied lipstick. I even accentuated my eyeliner with a wing.

When I looked in the mirror, I saw a lost girl with a clown's smile painted on. I was a weak illusion that people would see through.

"You look hot," my roommate called from the doorway.

I released a shaky breath. "I didn't know you were up."

Mikayla had moved in late last night, and this was our first real conversation. I didn't count the whole, "Hey! I'm Mikayla," and me replying with a sleepy, "Mhm." She looked exactly like her Instagram pictures. Long, red hair and bright, honey eyes to match, a slim figure sculpted by her life-threatening, adrenaline-junkie hobbies, and a condensed splat of freckles on each cheek like a globular cluster of stars.

"I feel naked," I admitted.

"You're in a sweater, Raindrop." She already had a pet name for me, and I didn't hate it enough to protest.

"And a skirt. They're both short. I should change."

Mikayla skipped towards me, flowing in her cow-print pajama pants. "You'll regret not wearing what you want. Might as well earn some stares."

My eyebrows rose and fell. Biased thoughts aside, I looked okay. My legs were my favorite part of my body to show off. My hair was flippy and smooth, a perfect salon blowout replication. My eyes popped with the eyeliner. There was no real, tangible reason to feel awkward.

"Wear it," she insisted. "I'm wearing my green overalls—and, oh! I found this crochet top."

I knew she wasn't kidding. Her Instagram was an exhibit of 70s fashion, and I admired her for it. Through the glimmer and glamor of knowing what she liked, Mikayla exuded a confidence not everyone could replicate.

I smiled. "How are you so comfortable wearing exactly what you want, when you want to?"

She flashed a grin back at me. "It helps that I carry a taser wherever I go."

I couldn't tell if she was joking or not, so I went back to obsessing about my appearance. "I don't know why I'm stressing out."

"Eh, it's a new school."

That definitely wasn't it, but I nodded anyways. "You're right," I agreed, hoping to convince myself that my nerves were as simple as she made them out to be.

I inhaled deeply, ignoring the tightness around my chest. "Rob would hate what I'm wearing."

She looked at me through the reflection. "Rob's your boyfriend?"

"It's complicated."

"Well, he's not here to tell you what to do, is he?"

I spun around. "When is your first class, anyways?"

"Oh. Not until three. I'm awake because of the hairdryer."

My eyes went to the neon green contraption sitting in front of the brass mirror. "Oh. I'll dry my hair at night from now on."

"At least on Mondays," she replied, smiling. "Look at that! Our first fight and resolution."

Another thing about Mikayla was that she was as eccentric as her style. I smiled.

"Glad we survived it," I said, reaching for my backpack. "Well, I'll see you. Good luck on your first day."

Mikayla shooed me away from the mirror. "Go have fun!"

§

After my tattoo stunt, I had returned to the dorm to be a hermit for the rest of the week, reading five books in four days. Now, with only minutes to spare before my British Literature class started, I regretted that I hadn't at least figured out where to get breakfast.

Alright, Rain. Go get that overpriced coffee and yogurt.

I stepped into the quad.

The quad, one of the popular spots on campus, was one long concession stand of tables for sports, clubs, fraternities, sororities, volunteering jobs, tutoring gigs, and any other activity or fascination imaginable. There was even a Quidditch team and a Renaissance music club. My first step into the throng was met by a dozen pairs of eyes. Guys surrounding a nearby table craned their necks to see me. They were a fraternity, Kappa Omega Ding Dongs, or something like that. My heart stopped, anticipating something bad to happen, but the arrays of sandy blonde hair quickly went back to their Greek way of life.

I gulped, put in my AirPods, and forced myself forward.

Even at 7:45 in the morning, there was a heightened vibration of energy. The possibilities of interaction were endless. I forced myself to meet the gaze of the next guy walking by. He had sunshine for hair and sky-blue eyes. He tossed me a smile.

Rob's remembered voice whispered in my mind, *You love the attention*, and dread filled my stomach like cement.

"No, I don't," I mumbled to myself, earning a wary look from the guy with blue eyes.

Yeah, not trying that again.

I avoided eye contact with everyone after that.

Following the flow of people, I noted the layout of the school and created a mental map. This campus was a stone maze, but it had some characteristic clues. The sight of the five flights of stairs to the library meant I should turn around. If the university was a body, then the library was its heart, the stairs were its veins, and the English building was its arm.

"There's got to be coffee by the armpit," I muttered under my breath.

After meandering through more people and more stairs, I found the English building on the other side of the quad, exactly where I would have started had I taken a different turn.

There went my time for coffee.

The brick was white, and the wooden doors looked medieval and misplaced. Chairs littered the hallways, providing nooks for students burying their heads in books. No one looked up at the sound of my boots, and I smiled, going unnoticed.

The lecture hall was on the third floor. As soon as I found it, I collapsed into the first empty seat. Whispered conversations strummed throughout the packed room. Everyone had a literature requirement to fulfill, so it made sense for the hall to be full, but for me, British literature was a passion. I had been obsessed with it since I discovered the Romantic Era in middle school.

As I waited for class to begin, I yanked out my notebook. The lined pages, once gold, now had frayed edges, and gray-blanched spots decorated the matte black cover. It was the last gift I had received from Aunt Rosen, and writing in it was the closest I could come to talking to her. I didn't waste the space. The notebook was too precious for me to dump my rambling emotions into it. I treated each page like priceless perfume, saving it for special occasions.

Last night, before I could fall asleep, I had wasted a page guiltily scratching out the same words which had kept me awake:

~~We're hurt each other more than we've loved each other.~~

I tapped my fingers against the sentence now, anticipating an emotional landmine explosion. The masochist in me was on a high because my stomach immediately convulsed. The romantic in me was dying on the floor. Whatever was left of me was sitting in this chair.

A guy took the seat next to me.

I ducked, shielding my face, and switched out Aunt Rosen's notebook for an untouched composition book. I grabbed my trusty, multicolored pen from the mesh pocket of my backpack and wrote the date in three different colors out of boredom.

The guy leaned in.

I propped up my arm. I wasn't in the mood to make friends.

His chest inched closer.

"Excuse me—" I began.

Oh, holy green eyes.

Noah's round laughter rose above the low chatter, turning heads, and it was like light breaking through the clouds.

"I saw you when I walked in. Should I sit somewhere else?" he asked, then proceeded to settle into a chair that looked comically small for him. He unwound a spiral notebook like it was a rolled newspaper and took out a pen from the pocket of his jeans.

I was still staring.

His eyes danced at me. "Well?" he laughed.

"Yes," I blurted out, because I had had no intention of seeing him again after taking off my clothes in front of him. Just thinking about it brought heat to my face. "I mean, no, you're free to sit wherever."

"Generous of you." His smirk creased one of his cheeks. "Interesting pen."

I stiffened. The trusty object suddenly felt as heavy as lead. "What are you doing here?"

"I am here," he responded, "because, like I told you the other night, I occasionally go to the same school as you."

Glancing at him, it was hard not to think of everything from the night we had met. Rushing in because of the storm. Sticking around because it was better than the alternative. Him, starting off bitter but sweetening, like wine. The gentle nature of his hands. And me, unable to get over the ridiculously premature feeling of kismet, all because he recognized my favorite poem.

I had told myself he was an intrusive thought. I had excused my outlandish behavior as a stress-induced, manic episode. I thought I'd never see him again, but here he was, not going anywhere.

"How's the tattoo healing?" he asked causally.

"Switched to lotion from Aquaphor."

"Huh. I usually recommend coconut oil."

I broke contact from his gaze and wrote my name on the other corner of the page, not knowing what else to do.

"Settling in fine?"

I sighed. "Yep."

Thankfully, our professor walked in, and our attention was redirected to the front of the room. The man wore glasses too big for his face and an orange plaid suit that looked itchy. He was also the only professor who didn't seem to feel that the first day of class was syllabus day. Instead of a calendar rundown, he launched into a lecture, going straight into the Old English period.

I jotted down notes. Noah's stare was like being under a spotlight. I did a good job at pretending it didn't affect me, throwing myself into color-coded systems and trying not to misspell any names from antiquity. At the end of the hour, my little, multicolored pen practically wheezed.

I took my time gathering my things. Noah took a noticeably longer time rolling up his single, spiral notebook. We stood at the same time.

"You're clearly going to fail this semester," he commented facetiously.

"*You're* going to fail if you keep staring at me," I chastised.

Oh, great, Rain. Was that flirty or just a completely awkward thing to say?

He chuckled. "It was educational. You write fast. Can I copy your notes?"

I squeezed past him with an embarrassed shrug, escaping with the crowd to the stairs, yet somehow, the crowd melted out of his way to allow him to walk beside me. He was incredibly tall, but to me, everyone was. Barely five-foot-two, I guessed Noah had a foot over me.

He held the main doors open with his long, scarecrow arm. Outside, the sun was powerful. I immediately squinted and made a visor out of my hands.

"Do you have another class right now?"

"Ummm…" I breathed, trying to stall long enough to come up with a nice way to separate.

"Do you want to get coffee?" Noah offered.

I tensed, bringing my teeth down on my lower lip. *Rain, just say no!*

"I don't have class until ten. I'm buying," he added, raising his brows in a pleading arch.

"No. Thank you, but no," I managed, walking ahead. *That was nice enough*, I told myself.

He caught up. "We have class together. We're going to be seeing a lot of each other. Hell, we already *have* seen a lot of each other," he laughed, not caring that I was trying to out-walk him.

"I'll get to know you in class," I said, pulling ahead.

"It's just coffee. You're not allowed to get coffee?"

"What?" I croaked, abruptly stopping.

My defenses shot up. Did he really say that? Why would he use those words? Sure, Noah might have seen some problematic text messages from Rob, but to word it that way...

"Why would you say something like that?" I asked, my voice accusatory.

He stepped in front of me, holding up his hands up to placate me. "They're just words, Rain. There's nothing stopping you. No class. No plans. No friends yet, right?" He dipped his head to my level, smirking. "Do you have something against coffee? Parents say it's going to stunt your growth?"

Amusement smeared his face like graffiti. Noah didn't know anything, and I was just a paranoid, emotional wreck. Inhaling deeply, I felt my throat expand and my lips form a tight smile.

"It's just coffee," he exclaimed nonchalantly.

I nodded, gulping. "Just coffee sounds nice."

"Great. There's a place nearby," he said, flashing a grin of perfect teeth that would've sent my mother, the dentist, over the moon. She was still upset that I refused to get braces to fix my slightly crooked two front teeth. *She always noticed the tiny things, but never anything that mattered.*

Noah led us around the building, where a giant café sign laughed in my face.

"You've got to be kidding me. I walked past this area at least two times this morning and didn't see it."

"Easy to miss," he lied politely.

I reached for the door, but Noah stepped aside to pull it open for me. Faking another smile, I walked through first.

The smell of coffee filled every pore of my body, awakening my cells.

My dependency on caffeine was sad. When Aunt Rosen used to drive me to school, we became Starbucks enthusiasts. Never mind the fact that we started our tradition when I was in fifth grade. My orders progressed from fruity drinks to coffee after a few years. She was an espresso type of woman, bold and straightforward. I, on the other hand, liked my coffee how I liked my desserts—cold and sweet. No matter the weather, I ordered iced drinks.

We joined the long line taking up half the store. Other patrons threw judgmental glances my direction. I wrapped my sleeved arms around my waist, covering my exposed torso.

Maybe something looser or longer would've been better.

"What are you doing?" Noah asked.

"Nothing," I said, though heat crackled on my cheeks. My skin was too tan to show the extent of my blush, but the feeling of embarrassment flamed inside me. "Sorry, it's just that everyone is so casual," I added, motioning my hand towards the people around us.

For the first time, I paid attention to what he wore. Both his loose, black jeans and faded, black and white checkered Vans had holes sprinkled throughout. The collar of the shirt was just as tattered, revealing the silver chain he wore against his skin. I pulled my eyes away from the peek of skin and was amazed to realize I knew the band logo on his t-shirt.

"I just noticed," I said. "I love COIN. The Dreamland album is great."

"Good taste," he praised. He dipped his head, placing his face inches from mine, then gently pulled my arms away from my midriff. "You look amazing. And before you tell me to stop, remember that there's no such thing as too dressed up. Besides, we look good together."

A laugh escaped my mouth, and the pit of my stomach flooded with warmth. *We.* His smirk became a grin, and, though I was tempted to smile, the pinch of happiness I felt quickly soured into churning guilt. I was wearing an outfit someone I loved would hate, accepting a compliment from someone who wasn't him.

God, what's wrong with me?

The line moved, and I fumbled for what to say next. I thought about what seeing him three times a week for a whole semester would be like. Every turn we made in this conversation would wander into uncharted territory. And I still missed Rob…

I chewed on my lip. *Think of something to say, Rain.*

"Are all your classes on Mondays, Wednesdays, and Fridays?" I asked, since it was the schedule for our literature class.

"Yeah. Just the mornings, though. I head back to the shop around one every day," he explained.

"How did you become a tattoo artist? Do you like it?"

"Love it. I've been sketching since I was a kid. I got into tattoos when I was a teenager and started doing them for friends. Very much under the table," he elaborated, talking with his hands. "I dragged Travis into it and have a stupid, cross-eyed smiley face on my leg to commemorate his apprenticeship. When I turned eighteen, Dawn opened the shop. We both apprenticed with her and her fiancé, Chris, and started doing our own work this past January."

"Wow," I gaped. "All that at twenty-two."

I barely had an idea of what to do with my life. Noah was ten steps ahead.

"How'd you get into signing? You surprised the hell out of Travis."

Don't talk about Rob. Don't talk about him or you'll never stop, my mind warned me.

"I'm from a border town. Everyone speaks English or Spanish, so in high school, when… someone I knew introduced me to it, I was instantly intrigued at something different. I picked up what I could from them, then studied it at my old college. What about you?"

"I switched schools in third grade and met Travis. Kids were dicks, saying rude shit all around him, so I figured I'd be his best friend. I was probably annoying, pointing to literally everything and asking how to sign the words. We stuck together after that."

More silence.

"What's your schedule like?" he asked.

"Most of my classes are on Wednesdays and Fridays. Our class is my only one on Mondays."

"That sucks. Waking up just for a fifty-minute lecture."

"It's okay. I enjoy the lectures," I admitted. "I mean, it's my major, so…"

He grinned. "Yeah, you mentioned that last time, too."

"Oh." I wanted to slap my hand on my forehead.

"How'd you choose it?" His voice, oddly gentle, was like the little push a kid needed to ride a bike for the first time.

"It's with an emphasis on creative writing." His brows rose. "Yep. It didn't sit well with my mom, but I couldn't see myself picking anything else."

"I bet."

To be honest, my mom's disappointment in me had been mitigated by the fact that I still wanted to go to school at all after what had happened with Aunt Rosen. Had it been up to Mom, though, I would've majored in something practical. She would've had me study dentistry and live a life like hers. Her dream was my worst nightmare.

"Let me guess, your major is art?" I asked.

"Business."

Would this man ever stop surprising me?

The line started to pass a display of to-go meals and snacks. My stomach threatened to growl at the mere sight of food.

Noah grabbed a breakfast sandwich. "Are you getting anything?"

"Mmmm," I hummed, scanning the options. I settled for a cup of fruit.

Noah bounced his weight from leg to leg as we waited for the couple in front of us to finish paying. He had a jovial, yet rebellious, quality about him. In high school, he would've been the class clown or the punk kid who didn't care about anyone's opinion of him. Maybe both. The old me would've thrived off his energy. Now, I stood there reticent and nervous.

"Hi! What can I get you?" The barista batted her eyes and smiled as Noah stepped up to the counter.

Noah was attractive. His body was decorated with tattoos, his hair was wild, and his smirk had just the right amount of challenge—safe enough to take the bait, but dangerous enough to give a reckless thrill for doing so.

Even if he wasn't your type, he was the kind of guy you wanted to check off a sexual endeavor bucket list.

Or maybe it's just me that wants to check him off a sexual endeavor bucket list. I shivered.

The barista's ogling shouldn't have surprised me, but it did make me feel as plain as the white walls of my dorm.

Her smile dropped when I stepped forward.

"Are you two on the same order?" she asked, giving me the side eye.

Before I could answer, Noah grabbed the cup of fruit from my hands, placing it by his sandwich. "We're together," he replied.

I didn't protest.

It was like the girl had been hit in the face with a water balloon. She recovered with a grimace, asking, "What would you like?"

"Medium iced caramel macchiato, please."

"Black coffee for me," Noah added.

Reaching for my cash, I swung my backpack to the front. As my hand fell on the zipper, Noah's hand clamped over it. "Here," he said, slapping his card on the counter. "It's on me, babe, remember?"

I froze, electrified by the word 'babe.' Having heard it uttered by only one other voice, it was strange to hear it wrapped in another tone. He tossed the word my way so casually. Was it for shock value or the real thing? Had a tender note of affection seeped through the syllable, reifying it?

Noah touched the small of my back, leading me to the side. Dumbstruck, I moved like a wind-up toy, not coming back to myself until he dropped his touch.

"The barista was being pretty blatant," I said pointedly. "Doesn't that stuff usually annoy you?"

"Actually, I'd prefer someone be direct. Words over glances. Less likely to be misconstrued."

"Her obvious staring wasn't direct enough?" I gaped.

His smile was teasing. "Nope."

It was oddly irritating. Not knowing what to make of his nonsense, I said, "Let me pay you back for the fruit."

"Hell, no. I asked for your company. I pay."

"But—"

"A cup of fruit and coffee is nothing. Well, if you count sugar water as coffee."

My pursed lips parted in a soft laugh. "If mine is sugar water, then yours is dirty motor oil."

"No, it's coffee," he argued playfully. "Genuine, engine-rumbling, heart-starting coffee."

Our order was called before I could reply. I couldn't take my eyes off him.

"Here you go," he said, handing me my coffee.

"Thank you."

We searched for a place to sit. There were a few empty tables and chairs, but the background lo-fi music sounded too clear, and no one was talking.

"Do you want to sit outside?" he asked.

"You read my mind."

Stale heat had replaced the cool breeze from the early morning. Summer was my favorite season, so Texas fit me well. Aunt Rosen used to say I was an iguana in another life because I loved being drenched in sunlight.

I walked ahead, picking a table far from the shade. Noah followed, uncomplaining. He was drinking me in with his eyes, and it was hard not to sink into nervousness. I pulled up my hair in a clip and reached for my cup.

"Thank you for the breakfast."

His lips twitched. "You already thanked me."

I looked away, popping a grape in my mouth.

"What are your plans while you're not in school?" he asked, speaking into his cup, slipping his tongue right between his lips before they touched the edge.

I shouldn't be noticing things like that.

I shook my head. "Probably work. I'll be applying to a bunch of places tomorrow."

"I was hoping you'd say that."

"Whyyy?" I drawled out my suspicion.

"Dawn needs front desk help. Someone to take calls, help clean. Stuff like that. Interested?"

"She doesn't know me," I averred. "*You* don't even know me."

"Stop by the shop tomorrow. Don't tell anyone, but the boss listens to me," he joked.

I didn't laugh. I had known this guy less than a week, spent only a couple hours with him, and he was already offering me a job.

"Why are you being so nice?" I blurted out.

His brows creased. "I didn't know being nice was a crime."

Guys aren't just 'nice,' Rob's voice rang in my head. *Guys are different from girls, and you're too naïve.*

My eyes remained cold.

"Look, my sister was here for me when I started school. She already had a life and helped me start mine. You're new here."

"You think I don't have anyone else?"

"Well, do you? Who?"

I grabbed my things. "I don't need the sympathy, okay? Thanks, but no."

"It's just a job, Rain," he insisted, but his words rang hollow. I pushed out of my chair, and he jerked forward, extending an empty hand to grab my wrist. "Wait. You're leaving?"

"You don't even know my last name," I said, jerking away from him. The moment stretched out like a rubber band about to snap. "I don't know yours. I'm not direct, okay? I'm never going to *be* direct."

He laughed. "You're being pretty direct right now."

I let out a shaky breath. "Until the next tattoo, Noah."

He didn't say another word as I stalked off. I was right. I had to be right. I had had my share of hidden agendas. Who was this nice without expecting something in return?

Frustrated, I reached for my phone in my back pocket.

Nothing.

Ugh.

I made a quick pivot. Noah, already heading toward me, grandly held out the device in my direction. I tucked a lock of hair behind my ears.

"Your phone is blowing up," he said.

Rob's name assaulted my screen.

"Fuck," I whispered.

"That's the first time I've heard you curse," he pointed out, smiling.

I glared.

"Rivas," he said seriously, "I'm not being direct with you."

"I. But—huh? How do you know my last name?"

He winked. "You filled out paperwork at the shop, remember?"

The earth could've swallowed me right then and there and I would've been eternally grateful.

"Did you catch *my* last name?" he asked.

"Not exactly," I confessed.

He took a step towards me and lowered his head until his breath tickled my ears. "If you read the card I gave you, you would've known it." He backed away slightly, eyeing me. "What'd you do with it?"

"I misplaced it," I lied. *Or chucked it in a random trashcan down my dorm's hallway.*

"I'm trying to be a friend, Rain. Come by the shop tomorrow if you want. No pressure," he said, throwing his hands up nonchalantly.

I studied his easy gait as he walked away. There wasn't a knot of tension in his stride. A sprout of hope grew inside me. *Maybe he could be a friend.*

He turned back around. "It's Colt."

I stared dumbly.

"My last name."

"See you soon, Colt," I breathed.

"See ya tomorrow, Rivas." He walked away, hands returning to his pockets.

I stood, my guard collapsing like a house of cards. I stopped thinking of bad outcomes and rising suspicions. Noah was nice, and I could use nice.

3

After a shower and trials of various outfits, I still didn't know what to wear for the interview. Was the attire professional, like any other job? Should I bust out my very professional and very itchy black blazer and matching slacks? Should I wear something to show off my tattoos? Then I would at least be showing off that I was familiar with tattoos.

The thought made me feel stupid. I wouldn't take a burger to a McDonald's interview.

In the end, my black and white striped pants went with a plain black shirt. I slid on some loafers. I straightened my hair and kept my makeup light. I switched out my long earrings and hoops for small, gold studs throughout my ear piercings.

Studying my reflection, I felt polished, put-together, and comfortable with my tattoos being visible on my arms. I grabbed my tote bag with my obnoxious pin collection and headed out the door.

It was almost noon by the time I arrived. I stared at the New Dawn sign, my stomach somersaulting at the thought of seeing Noah again. The fact that his truck was the only car in the parking lot didn't make things any easier.

You got this, Rain! It'll be a simple interview. It'll be over in five minutes tops.

I took a deep breath and swung open the door.

"Finally," Noah said loudly, his face buried in a sketchbook.

Panic rose in my throat, making my voice shake. "Should I have come earlier? You didn't say a time."

His eyes widened as he looked up. Then he smirked. "I thought you were my… first customer."

"Oh."

The door hit my back, pushing me forward. My steps were slow and careful, like prey in the sight of a predator.

His hands were stained from the charcoal. Up close, I could see a partial face haunting the page.

I pulled out my resumé, placing it by his smoky fingertips. He smudged the corners when he moved it aside, without looking away from me. His eyes were heavy and hot. Too intense. He couldn't lessen their intensity if he tried.

I looked away.

"I didn't say it yesterday, but thank you for this," I said.

"I like the get up."

It was like I hadn't said a word, and it nearly made me forget what I had just said. I dropped my head, hiding a smile. "Thanks. I wasn't sure what was professional for a tattoo shop."

"How dare you not wear a tie."

My eyes, looking anywhere but at his, caught sight of his shirt. Instantly, I recognized the band name splashed across his chest. "'My Thoughts On You' is my favorite of theirs."

The shock captivated his features. "Nice surprise, Rivas."

I shrugged. "We listen to the same stuff."

The shop's emptiness pressed us together. I felt awkward to be speaking to him, just the two of us.

"Am I too early?" I asked.

"Nope. Dawn and Chris, co-owner and tattooist extraordinaire, should be here soon."

"Okay," I exhaled, trying to feign normalcy. The only good thing about us being alone was that my apology wouldn't be ruined by an audience. I bit my lip and got it over with. "Also, I wanted to say sorry about yesterday. I was rude."

"You had your guard up. Don't worry 'bout it."

Guard up. Yeah. That's what that was.

"Sooo," he drawled, "how were the rest of your classes?"

"I only have Brit Lit on Mondays. My next class is tomorrow," I reminded him. "Like yours."

"There's that," he said, and, as an expert in the subject of awkward conversations, I recognized the tinge of desperation in his tone.

His fingers started toying with the silver chain around his neck. I fidgeted with my plum-painted nails. The silence stretched between us uncomfortably.

I didn't know how to act. It seemed like he wanted to get to know me, but I wasn't sure I was worth the effort. I was just… me. Even Aunt Rosen's voice in my head couldn't stop the negative thoughts from forming.

"I haven't—

"If I—"

We both started, stopped, and smiled at our word collision.

"You first," he insisted.

I sighed. *Here goes nothing.* "I haven't had anyone be nice to me in a while. Please don't ask why. But just know that if I seem cold…" I paused, making it a point to read his face for a moment. It held no judgement. "…I don't mean to be. I'm sorry."

He blinked.

Okay. I had just freaked him out. I looked away, ready to curse myself out for allowing myself to be vulnerable. "Well, okay. Your turn."

"Rivas, if I seem direct, I probably am. Not directly, though."

My face cracked into laughter. "Will I ever live that one down?"

"Eh, I still gotta tease you a few more times about it first."

The tension in my shoulders eased. "Any tips on how to win over your sister?"

"Dawn will like you."

"I hope so."

The door chimed. We both looked up.

A beautiful brunette came strutting in. Her legs, long and slender, were accentuated by her heels and skintight jeans. Her silky hair was pinned back without a single stray strand. Her azure eyes were as deep and intimidating as the ocean. She used makeup extremely minimally. Her nearly alabaster face didn't need the flare with which I masked my own.

I stood there, a ragdoll next to a barbie.

"Hey, babe," she said to Noah.

My lips parted. *Ohhhh.*

She walked around the corner and leaned in to kiss him. My eyes were riveted. Right before their lips met, Noah turned his face, and her mouth skimmed his cheek. His eyes met mine, and I couldn't tell if I wanted to fight her or run from the room. It was too intense of a moment.

Probably because it should've been reserved for this girl.

His arm hung around her tiny waist. "Jen, this is Rain. Rain, Jen," he said.

Her body perched against his. "Hi."

I took a step back out of respect. "Nice to meet you, Jen."

She didn't say anything, those indescribably blue eyes inspecting me like I was bug.

Noah's laugh broke the silence.

"Dawn should be here soon, Rain. I'm going to start on Jen's tattoo."

"Yeah, of course. I'll just wait here," I blabbed.

I couldn't fall onto the couch fast enough.

I wrote in my journal while I waited, a torrent of words filling the pages, yet somehow, none of them were about Rob. I lost myself in the scribbles. After a few paragraphs, time began to pass faster than my ink dried.

The door chimed. A woman with ashy blonde hair barreled through, clearly frazzled. A little girl hung on her hip.

"Someone didn't feel good," the woman announced.

A man trotted in behind them, happily carrying the girl's sparkly backpack and matching lunchbox. He grinned.

"It's our girl's first week of school, Dawn. She's not missing much."

"Good afternoon, Noah," Dawn said, then blew out a sigh through her teeth. "And Jen."

"Hi, Dawn, Chris, Ana," Jen said, from her position below Noah's tattoo machine.

Ana rolled her eyes and tucked her face in Dawn's neck.

"Hey, favorite niece," Noah called.

Ana poked her head out, scrutinizing me. "Who are you?"

"Hi!" I greeted, flipping on my public face like a light switch. It was like being center stage. Everyone was looking at me, but I focused all my attention on Ana. "I'm Rain. Noah told me about the front desk job. I brought my resumé."

"Rain is a type of weather. It's not a name," Ana said plainly.

"Anastasia!" Dawn scolded while everyone laughed.

"No, you're right," I agreed, smiling. "My mom wasn't as smart as yours. Anastasia is a beautiful name."

Dawn was trying to hide a grin. Suddenly, I knew this interview wouldn't be a challenge.

"Chris, take the heathen," she said, handing off their child. To me, she said, "I'll interview you."

"You got it," Chris said, peeling Ana away from her mom.

"So, Rain?" Dawn asked, shaking my hand.

"Yep! Rain Rivas."

"I see you waitressed for a year," she started.

"Yes. I can carry three pizzas without a spill."

"So, what you're saying is that you can handle inventory shipments."

"Yes. Yes, I can."

"Interested in tattooing?"

"Honestly? No. I love getting them, but my hands shake a lot."

"Good. I don't want to hire anyone who's trying to setup shop. Why do you want this job?"

"Because," I began, hesitating, "Noah said wonderful things about you."

Her fingers tapped on the counter. "Can you hang out for a trial run?"

"I sure can."

Dawn sat me down behind the desk, explaining how to answer the phone and what the shop's rates were. Ana kept trying to escape Chris' distractions to come investigate, so finally, I had to take matters into my own hands.

"Anastasia, come over here with me. I'm going to need help getting the hang of this place," I said, holding out my hand.

"Are you sure?" Chris asked.

"It's not a problem."

Ana ran over to me, smiling. Noah lifted his head, watching us.

The rest of the day consisted of getting through a six-year-old's inquisition. She couldn't stop asking me questions. It was all, "What's your favorite number? What's your favorite color? What's your favorite day of the week?"

I loved it.

Travis finished his last tattoo early and took off to meet his girlfriend, Lorie. Dawn, Chris, and Ana went home around six. Having landed the job, I stayed behind to fill out paperwork.

"I gotta admit, I'm amazed," Noah said while cleaning up his area.

"Amazed?"

"My niece spent more time with you than with me."

"Clearly, we get along better. Also, she liked my rainbow pen."

"I never said I didn't like it."

"But did you ever say that you did? No," I argued playfully.

Our banter as we closed the shop helped smooth over the awkwardness of his involvement with Jen, and I was trying to let myself be okay with it. In fact, if I didn't think about the possibilities of what might have been, this made things better. Being around each other would be easy. Uncomplicated.

"I should get going," I said, allowing myself to feel a little happy. "We have class in the morning."

"Let me drive you."

I frowned, ready to fight him on it, but relented when he added, "It's already dark outside."

We're friends now. A ride is fine.

"Just this time, Colt."

"Sure, Rivas.

4

My routine centered around not thinking bad things. I woke up, went for a run, showered, brushed my hair, colored my face with makeup, put on clothes I used to love, and distracted myself with reading until I needed to leave my dorm. If I could, I'd account for every minute.

This Friday would include a literature quiz, a yoga class Mikayla had talked me into, and work. I planned on curling up into a ball on the couch afterwards and having a movie marathon. Mikayla was sleeping over at a friend's apartment, so I'd have the place to myself.

Earlier this week, we had split the cost on a projector, which, combined with a laptop, acted as our TV. Mikayla wasn't fond of my habit of rewatching comfort movies, but I couldn't help it. It kept me from thinking bad things.

I smoothed my wet hair away from my face with a pearl headband. I had kept my promise and refrained from using my hair dryer in the mornings, so my waves thrashed a little wilder today. I grabbed a brown eyeshadow, buffing it around my eyes until my lids were a glittery smudge of twilight. I coated my lashes. For my lips, I chose a burgundy lipstick.

He'd hate seeing you like this.

The thought was as sudden and destructive as lightning, incinerating my self-esteem. I dropped my lipstick as if it were a cursed object.

Rob's voice filled my head. *Why are you wearing that? I hate it when you put on makeup. No, I'm not kissing you, I don't want to get lipstick on me. I barely recognize you when you look like that. You shouldn't need the attention, you already have a boyfriend.*

With him, having a good day meant being compliant. Maybe his comments weren't right, but they were always smothered in honey. *You don't need makeup. You're naturally beautiful. Don't cover up your best features.*

I had felt praised. When I stopped wearing makeup, I heard new words from him. *You're not wearing makeup? I love that. I love you.*

I bit my lip savagely. "I am not doing this to myself today."

I sighed, wishing Mikayla didn't need twelve hours of sleep a day to function. When she was awake, her vivaciousness spun at a hundred miles per hour, and I loved getting caught in her whirlwinds.

I retreated to my closet. The summer heat was still intense in the afternoons, so I resorted to a pair of denim shorts and an oversized white shirt. I slipped on my Converse, put my AirPods in, set the volume to full blast, and left.

The walk to the English building required no thought now. I mindlessly sauntered along cracked sidewalks and scrolled through my Spotify library. My morning playlist was a mess of indie and alternative.

An arm wrapped around me and hung off my shoulder. I recognized Noah's cologne from the hint of citrus. His iridescent eyes captivated me when I looked up.

"Hey."

I smiled back, stretching up to pop an AirPod in his ear.

I had felt safer around him since learning about the brunette. He had someone, which explained why he was unimpressed with the girl from the coffee shop, and why he laughed about my inability to be direct. Since then, my guard had nearly vanished.

We had grown into this weird friendship. Every time he wore a band t-shirt, he greeted me with this boyish, expectant gaze and lopsided grin. I found myself thinking of that expression a lot, in constant contemplation of whether it was teasing or sincere.

He adjusted his steps so we could be in sync. "You're two years younger than me," he said. "How did you find all the good bands first?"

"This song has been out for years," I teased.

"Then why haven't I heard it?"

"Guess your music taste isn't as good as you think it is."

He arched a brow.

"I read with random playlists going," I confessed.

"Oh yeah? What is the bookworm reading now?"

I rolled my eyes. "This is why I will pass Brit Lit and you will fail. Reading books doesn't make you a bookworm. It makes you smarter."

"I need the title, Rivas."

"Not giving it, Colt. Are you ready for the quiz?" I asked, redirecting the conversation.

He sighed, dipping his head. "Yes. Thanks again for emailing the notes."

"You're welcome." Noah's arm still hung off me. His fingernails were painted, courtesy of Ana, but he only ever let her use the black polish. It fit him.

"Can we do something after class?"

We both knew we'd get coffee, but he asked anyways. He liked the music I played and asked what I was reading. He was easy, uncomplicated. It was comfortable.

"Yes, but coffee needs to be to-go today. I promised Mikayla I'd go to yoga with her."

He cocked his head, letting his curls swing to the side. "You do yoga?"

"Mikayla can talk anyone into anything."

He chuckled. "When are we going to have some actual fun?"

"Sorry, I have a date with my book and a movie. That's my definition of fun."

"Huh. Throw in some Chinese takeout, and that sounds very similar to mine," he said, squeezing my shoulder.

I stopped walking. "You're not hijacking my night," I told him sternly.

"You won't even know I'm there. I have nothing to do, and I swear, if I have to watch Travis and Lorie feed each other popcorn one more time, I'm never going to be able to eat another kernel in my life," he protested, hands falling to his side in defeat.

"Switch to chips," I replied, stalking past him, even as I thought, *Maybe you should call Jen.*

"That's it?" His voice echoed behind me.

"We can't be late," I called back, smiling sweetly.

§

When I finished the quiz, Noah was sprawled on the benches outside with two cups of coffee.

"I have your sugar water," he said when I reached him. "What took you so long?"

"Not all of us are content with a C."

"C for Colt," he smirked, and it was hard to hide my answering smile.

"Hey, do you mind if we head to my dorm? I want to grab my gym bag so that I don't have to rush across campus later."

"Sure. Play that song from before, though."

We made our way, sharing AirPods and talking about nothing important. We were in the middle of a debate about movie recommendations when I saw Rob. Not the imaginary hiccup of him from earlier, but the actual, real-life him.

Rob.

He waited on the sidewalk outside my dorm, exactly where he had deserted me. I was yards away, still out of his line of sight, but once I saw him, I *felt* him. The dam I had worked so diligently to build broke from a single crack. A waterfall of emotions flooded me, the history of seeing him a thousand times before this, and the kaleidoscope vision of every Rob I had known projecting in my mind. *Lover. Friend. Mentor. Boyfriend. Ex-boyfriend.*

"What's wrong?" Noah asked, stopping in front of me as I became a statue. But the overwhelming grip of emotion had already choked me. My gravity had shifted, sucking me into a familiar orbit.

What is he doing here?

I hadn't talked to him since the day I moved in. The day he had said he needed distance and left me on the sidewalk with my boxes. He hadn't even tried. He'd given up. The anger I should've felt that day blossomed with a vengeance.

"I have to go," I said, not really looking at Noah anymore.

"What? Why? Rivas, you look like you've seen a ghost. Are you sick?"

"Yeah, I don't feel good." It wasn't really a lie. "I'll see you at work, okay?"

"Rain." His voice was commanding, but I was in a trance, immune. "Text me if you're not feeling better."

"Mmhmm," I replied weakly, my focus narrowing in on Rob.

His dark, shaggy hair tangled in his eyelashes, shadowing his face. His coal eyes sent vibrations down my bones. His slender body was a map I had memorized. His lips were a field I used to run to, and when they smiled at me, it took all my restraint not to catapult forward. My whole body missed him, so badly that an ache formed in the pit of my stomach and warmed my thighs.

That part of us had always been easy to navigate. It was the rest that gave me whiplash.

"Hi." It didn't feel like a big enough word, but it's what I said when I reached him.

He moved forward, cradling my face. His fingertips were like velvet. My heart lurched at the touch. He was familiar and gentle. I lacked the energy to stop him.

"I have so much to tell you," he murmured.

My eyes lifted. "What are you doing here, Rob?"

"Please, let me in. I'll tell you everything."

I glanced behind myself. Noah was gone.

"Okay."

§

I sat on my bed, watching Rob wander through my room. I had dreamed about him being here. Now that it was happening, it felt strange. He looked like a puzzle piece that didn't fit.

He took his time, noting my personal touches. He cautiously ran his index finger over the picture of Aunt Rosen and me tucked in the corner of my mirror. I was seven in that photo and obsessed with the movie *Beetlejuice*. Our hair had splotches of green from cheap, tinted hairspray. It was the first time I had put on eyeshadow, and I went crazy with it, bringing the dark purple color up to my eyebrows.

He swallowed hard. "You'll always miss her."

It didn't need an answer. During our relationship, we had both lost people we loved, and it had formed a bond I thought we could never sever.

"Why are you here, Rob? You left."

He frowned. "Maybe I'm here to explain myself? Fuck, I was upset."

"That makes leaving okay? And gives you the right to just show up unannounced?"

"What was I supposed to do? You haven't been answering your phone."

"You broke up with me," I balked.

"Is that how you remember it?" he asked, his voice sharpening.

I crossed my arms. "What do you remember?"

"I remember me fucking up again," he whispered, not meeting my gaze. "I can't handle people leaving. You knew that and still wanted to go—I didn't want to lose you, okay? It's just..." he paused, kneeling in front of me. His arms curled around my waist. "It felt like you were fine with losing me. I can't lose you."

He was sad. So, of course, I was devastated.

"I never wanted to leave you," I said softly, stroking his hair. He smelled of the woodsy cologne I had bought him for his last birthday.

"Can I stay? Please?" he asked.

I hesitated. "I have work."

"I can wait here," he said immediately.

I couldn't lose him again.

"Wait for me. We can talk when I get back."

Happiness sparked in the depths of his eyes. "Anything you want."

5

Work was hours of anticipation. I couldn't focus on anything. Travis tried to sign with me but got tired of repeating himself. Noah was oddly distant, not even asking how I was feeling after my fictional ailment.

Getting a ride from him after my shift ended wasn't really an option, so I snuck out of the shop while he was in the bathroom. The walk home didn't offer any clarity. Instead, each step caused my fragile heart to tremble. By the time I got back, I thought I'd fall apart at the slightest trigger.

The emptiness of my dorm made me panic.

Desperately, I ran to my room and saw a note taped to my mirror. Rob's terrible handwriting read:

Went for food. Be back soon.

See, Rain. You're freaking out over nothing.

As I waited for him to return, I made a nest in the beanbag chair and ambitiously grabbed my favorite book. The words would at least give my eyes something to stare at while my mind obsessed over what I should say or do.

The door opened. Rob came in, carrying a buffet of fries, burgers, and chicken tenders. I focused on how to arrange everything, not meeting his eyes, until the silence began to feel loud. I looked up, realizing he was waiting for me to make the first move.

I sighed, placing napkins on the empty side of the bed. "Rob, I don't really know why you're here. You know I love you, but I'm not going home. What is this?"

"This is me trying. I'm moving in with my aunt and uncle."

My eyebrows rose. "What?"

"Look, do you remember why I didn't want to do long distance?"

Only too well. I nodded. "Your first love. You were fifteen. She broke your heart. She left you for another guy."

"Well, I figured it all out. You and I will be living in the same city, so, nothing can go wrong. And *this*," he said, gesturing at his presence in my room, "is me saying that I'm not giving up."

My mouth fell open. I soaked in the information, waiting for it to stick, feeling it thaw my coldness.

"Say something," he begged, touching my knee.

My bottom lip wobbled. "I thought I'd lost you forever, Rob."

"I know, babe. I'm an idiot. Please give me another chance. Let me love you."

I held those beautiful, brown eyes with mine. My skin danced under his touch. He grabbed my wrist and pulled me to him. As he sank backwards on the bed, I let myself follow, finding his lips with mine. My body slackened against his, craving the peace behind reawakened memories. Feeling him was like falling back into a comfortably bad habit. The high was tangible, and I clung to it.

"You need to trust me, not control me," I whispered.

"I will. I do," he said. But his promise sounded hollow.

"You've said that before."

"I mean it this time."

Maybe he wasn't perfect, but I couldn't punish him for that. He loved the best he could.

I exhaled. "I believe you."

"I don't want to love you wrong," he confessed, as if he were reading my mind.

A tear fell from my eye and landed on his nose. With a small laugh, I brought my thumb to his skin, wiping it away. It crushed me that he thought his love could be wrong. It wasn't like putting on a shirt backwards. Love was complicated.

I entangled my fingers with his, marveling at our perfectly meshed fit.

"You don't understand. I need you, Rob."

"One more chance. Just one," he begged.

"I missed you," I whispered, arching to his mouth.

The night lengthened, like our kiss, and when our bodies intertwined, I believed in us again.

§

It was pitch black when my phone rang. Curled up in Rob's arms, I instinctively answered it before I was awake.

"Hello?"

"Rivas?"

Noah's voice made my heart stop.

"It's... really late," I said when I could breathe again. "What's going on?"

"You okay? You usually text me if you walk home."

"Oh! Yes, I'm fine. I'm sorry for not texting."

"You say sorry for everything."

"I'm sorry. I mean..."

He snickered, and I could almost hear his lopsided smirk. We were both quiet after that.

"Did you need something?" I asked.

"You're falling everywhere, you know."

It was too much for my sleep-fogged brain to handle. "Huh?"

"It's raining outside, Rain."

I let out a small laugh and Rob stirred next to me.

"I can't really talk right now," I said.

"Because he's there?"

My breath hitched again. "I..."

"I know, I know. I get it. Don't worry." His words slurred together.

"Rivas?" he prompted when I didn't respond.

"I'm trying not to say sorry," I said.

His laugh touched my ears. "I'll see you at work."

"Okay."

"Bye, Rivas."

"Bye."

§

The next morning, rustling paper was my alarm clock. I opened one eye and saw a blueberry muffin in front of my nose.

"Good morning, babe," Rob said, carrying a tray that also held two cups. "Got you a coffee. Black. Careful, it's hot."

I sat up, the grogginess of last night seeping into our morning. "Thank you," I mumbled, grabbing the muffin. "What time is it?"

"Almost noon."

My eyes popped open, and I stopped mid-bite. "What?"

He leaned over to kiss my forehead. "It's Saturday. You get to sleep in."

"I have work in less than an hour."

"Call in sick," he smiled.

"It's my first week." I jumped off the bed, but he twirled me into his arms, bringing me to his chest.

"I'm so proud of you. Do you know that?"

I gazed up, finding sincerity and admiration on his face. "You are?"

"I love you," he told me, and his words shimmered like stars.

I wrapped my arms around him. "I love you more."

We didn't have time for anything else, so I disentangled myself from him. I freshened up, skipping on the makeup and putting my hair in a messy bun. Outside of the bathroom and back in my room, I slipped out of my sweatpants and into shorts. I had just taken off my shirt when I heard Rob's strained voice.

"Rain."

I spun, grabbing a blue hoodie. "Yeah?"

"Rain." He stared at my chest.

I chuckled, tugging on a bralette. "You're such a perv," I teased.

He squinted, shaking his head. "What is *that* on your ribs?"

It took me a second to understand what he meant. "It's a tattoo," I said, "in Aunt Rosen's handwriting."

"Why didn't you tell me you got a tattoo?"

"Honestly? I forgot. How did you not see it last night?"

"Maybe because I was too busy prioritizing *you*," he snapped.

He must've seen my happiness crumble, because he looked away, muttering, "I'm just being honest."

I continued getting ready because it was all I could do. I turned, grabbing whatever shoes were closest. My combat boots. *I'm going to look crazy.* I tightened my laces and crossed the room, grabbing a book and my wallet and stuffing them into the tote bag that held my button collection. My favorite was the one that had a disco ball on it. It was stupid.

Just like this fight we're going to have.

The knowing didn't stop it. "What are you thinking?" I said.

"I'm thinking there's another reason you didn't tell me. When did you get it?"

"My first night here."

His brows bounced up in disbelief. "Wooow," he drawled, scratching his jaw.

Here we go.

"I'm sorry I didn't tell you."

"Where did you go?"

"New Dawn Tattoo. The shop where I'm working now."

"Let me guess—the artist was a guy."

"Rob, why does that even matter?"

He met my sad attempt at self-defense with an unwavering glare. "Why are you keeping things from me?"

"There's a lot you haven't told me too, Rob," I replied, motivated to hide the truth but terrified to lie.

"Was it a guy?"

"Do you seriously think I would do something with someone other than you?"

"*I* said nothing about doing anything with anyone."

Good job, Rain.

"Was it the same guy who called you last night?"

I knew my face had given me away before I said anything. "I thought you were asleep."

His victorious expression was too big for the small room.

"So, what did you do, huh?" he persisted, stepping closer. His gaze slithered up and down my body. "Let him put his hands on you?"

"What? No."

He coughed out a fake laugh. "You did, didn't you."

"Rob, not everyone wants to steal me from you."

"But you would run to anyone," he said, throwing a blow to my already bruised self-esteem.

My bottom lip wobbled, and I bit into it to stop the shaking. "Believe it or not, I'm faithful whether we're happy or fighting."

"I've heard that from women before," he scoffed.

"You're so quick to give up."

"How am I supposed to feel, Rain? We have a fight and immediately, you go out looking for—" but he stopped, turning his face as if he couldn't look at me anymore.

"Say it. What did I go looking for?"

His gaze fell back on me like a slap to the face. His intensity was frightening.

My voice carried, soft as a whisper. "You think I was out looking for someone else? Hours after we broke up?"

He said nothing.

"I cried, moved in, cried again, went out for the tattoo, and came back to cry because... what else do I do when we fight?"

He swallowed roughly. "The guy... he didn't—try anything?" he asked.

My head shook repeatedly as I found my way back to him again. I hugged him and held on tightly. "No. He didn't even look when I took off my shirt."

He stiffened in my grasp. "You took off your *shirt?*"

Ohh, Rain...

"I had to," I said, searching his eyes for hope, but they were already narrowed.

"He asked you take it off?" he asked specifically.

I could have lied and said yes. I could have said a girl had given me the tattoo. I had walked the tightrope between hoping he'd trust me and omitting the truth for the sake of precaution. Rob had expected me to be the bad guy for so long that there was no way I could be anything else.

"I took it off because he made a condescending comment," I said, but even as I spoke, I felt him pulling away from my embrace. "Nothing happened!"

He kept walking, leaving the dorm. Quickly, I pulled on the blue hoodie and ran after him down the corridor.

My fingers grasped his bicep. He tore himself from my grip.

"No! Rain, after the heartache I've been through, you knew what this would do to me, and you still did it," he seethed.

I tugged at his shirt. Reluctantly, he stopped. In a breath, I gathered my composure, hexing tears away as I stood in front of him.

"Rob, please. Nothing happened," I reiterated.

"Get out of the way, Rain," he demanded without glancing at me.

I clutched his chest, feeling like I was winning because he didn't push me off.

"Please. I'm sorry. Don't go."

Slowly, he unhooked each finger and placed my hands at my sides gently. He had this way of making me feel like a stranger for touching him, and I stood, disgusted at myself.

"My world stopped turning when I saw you here, Rob."

"I guess it can start again," he remarked harshly.

The earth should have trembled. Clouds should have dropped like rocks. The air should have turned to smoke. The whole universe should've collapsed in on itself. In my mind, it was a natural disaster threatening to end the world, but rays of sun licked the carpet and laughter from other dorms seeped through the walls.

The stupid world kept turning.

6

No new messages. Hours had passed since Rob left, and the pressure on my chest hadn't relented. Phone calls ended with me memorizing his voicemail. I even had the rings memorized. Five when he let it ring. One and a half when he ignored it.

I didn't want to think of him, but he was like a fog I couldn't see out of. With everything around me muted and hidden, it was just a matter of time until I crashed.

I told Dawn what had happened only because the red-eyed evidence of my distress was too obvious. I dreaded telling her it was a boyfriend problem, but when I did, her face didn't sour with judgment. She asked if I had eaten, and when I said no, she bought me a sandwich. It was enough to make me tear up again.

Noah stayed in his station, avoiding me. Even though I missed him, I wasn't sure if I could have had anything resembling a normal conversation without crying.

The end of the day came with no excitement or happiness. Numbed and tired, I went to get Clorox wipes. My hand was mid-twist on the cleaning closet's doorknob when a touch fell on my waist. It was feathered, but my senses were on high alert. I jumped at the contact.

Noah's mocking laughter fluttered around my ears like hummingbird wings. "Sorry, Rivas. I just needed the broom." My emotions must've shown on my face, though, because a second later, his brows were wrinkling with worry. "Shit. Are you sure you're okay?"

We were standing too close together.

"I'm fine," I lied, stepping around him.

"By your definition or mine?"

I counted points off on my fingers. "I'm not missing a limb. No one has died. I'm fine."

"Okay. Can I drive you home, at least?"

I wanted to say no, but I was too tired of fighting. I nodded. "Help me close up first."

The silence was so tense it felt like static. Every few minutes of wiping down surfaces was interrupted by glances toward the other side of the room, where Noah swept and mopped the white tiles. We made eye contact once, but I quickly looked away.

Afterward, I waited for Noah by the front door.

"Ready?" he asked, tossing and catching his keys.

I nodded, following him to his truck. I couldn't make small talk. If I tried, my heart would speak, and I knew it was better to leave that mess unsaid. I leaned my forehead against the side of the seatbelt holder, closing my eyes.

A turn or two later, Noah announced, "We're here."

I stretched, unable to stop a loud yawn. The door screeched as I climbed out. I waited as long as I could because goodbye was the last thing I wanted to say. His smile was unfairly patient.

I twisted my fingers. "I'm sorry I was weird today."

"You weren't," he said, voice steady and smooth, covered in a sweet, white lie. "Stop saying sorry, Rain. You did nothing wrong."

"Okay," I whispered, biting my tongue. I already wanted to apologize again.

He leaned out the window, his lopsided smile in place. "Anything you need, name it and it's yours, Rain."

It was enough to shatter whatever equanimity I had left. I wrapped my arms around myself and leaned against the truck. Noah had gotten out and his arms were around me. I burrowed into his chest, crying.

"I didn't do anything wrong. I hate him," I moaned.

"What do you need?" he asked.

"I'm fine," I said. I tried pulling away, but he wouldn't let go.

"Fuck, just let me get you inside, Rain."

"I'm sorry," I whispered. I didn't know why those were the words that came out of my mouth.

He grinned, his face begging me for a smile. "Are you really apologizing for crying?"

I dropped my head. "I guess so."

"Let me walk you in, and your roommate can take over from there."

I groaned and stood up. "Oh, no. Mikayla. What's she going to think about all this?"

"You don't have to say anything to anyone right now," he replied.

"Yeah, okay," I agreed, just to make him happy.

I scanned my student ID to get us into the building and dug out my keys from my bag. We rode the elevator in silence. I avoided his spotlight stare and led him down to the hall to my dorm. There was a handwritten note from Mikayla on the whiteboard.

Be back later tonight, Raindrop! Leftover pizza in my fridge. Hands off the breadsticks tho! —the best roomie everrrr

"She doesn't believe in texting?" Noah asked as I unlocked the door.

I shrugged. "She flip-flops." I peered inside the dorm, then back at Noah. "Do you want to come in?"

"Do you want me to come in?"

I bit my lip. "I don't want to be alone."

"Then you won't be," he promised.

"My room is on the left," I said, feeling stupid as soon as I said it. I threw my gaze around the dorm as I walked. Fortunately, it was mostly clean. No dishes or laundry lying around.

I realized how much of myself I was letting him see. There was my Freddie Mercury poster on the wall, my gold jewelry in a dish on my vanity, my laptop covered with animal stickers, my nail polishes lined up from dark to light, my minifridge and beanbag chair underneath the bed. Right by the ladder were my green, fluffy, monster claw slippers.

"Why are you smiling like that?" I asked, fighting off the heat climbing up my neck.

"I like your room."

That was too much.

"Get us some bottled water?" I said, pointing to the mini fridge. "I need to stay hydrated after all this crying."

He grabbed two and turned toward me with the little bottles in his hand. Something about my face must've stopped him because he froze in place. Then he gently reached forward to touch my cheek, wiping away tearstains.

Our eyes met.

All I could think, though, was *What if Rob is right?*

What if I had just thrown away the best relationship of my life?

All because of pretty, green eyes…

"Noah," I sighed, "I should shower and get some sleep. You should go."

"I don't want to," he said.

I was tired. Tired of guys who judged, who didn't listen, who seemed to think they could do whatever they wanted and leave me to deal with the fallout.

Not this time.

"You have a girlfriend, Noah. A *girlfriend*." I stressed the word and held up my hand to stop him when he tried to interrupt me. "You should go spend time with Jen. I should spend some time alone."

"You don't want to be alone," he reminded me.

"Maybe now I do," I said. "Can you please take no for an answer? Or are you only here because you want what you can't have?"

The passion in his eyes changed to ice. He turned and left the dorm.

§

Stepping into the hot water, the grime of the day slowly melted off. I watched the suds of soap dilute and swirl away across the green tiles. I dumped shampoo on my head and scrubbed. I ran a washcloth over my body. When I got to my legs, I lathered soap in my palm and smoothed my fingers across my skin.

Suddenly, standing required too much effort. I sat on the shower floor, bringing my knees to my chest. The sobs came, loud and unexpected, like the first thunder of a storm.

Crying in the shower from a broken heart. I thought I was better than this.

Stop. Please, stop.

But I couldn't.

I stayed there, crying and letting the water run. I'd be in the middle of putting conditioner in my hair and would stop abruptly because the world didn't feel right. Whenever my tears restarted, it was as if I hadn't just run myself dry. My eyes were two infinite wells.

When too much time had passed, I forced myself out, changed, and pulled my hair into a damp ponytail. I wiped the fog on the mirror, seeing a stranger in the reflection. My face had puffed up like a fish. My eyes had sunken into the swollen skin like rocks disappearing into wet sand.

"This a new record for things you've messed up in twenty-four hours."

I gargled some mouthwash and swapped my contacts for my gold-rimmed Harry Potter glasses. Noah would've either teased or complimented them. He had stayed because of what he had seen, which should've been more reason to kick him out, but I didn't want to be alone.

God, what must he think of me.

I shut off the bathroom light and went to my room. My empty room.

I locked my door, crawled into bed, and went through my first aid kid. I took two Tylenol PMs. I plugged in my phone and turned on the string of lights I had recently put around the bottom of my bed. Against the soft glow, endless notifications flooded my phone. I checked for Mikayla's name. As of five minutes ago, she was heading back to the dorm. I replied with a sleepy-face emoji. A message from my mother said she'd call in the morning to catch up. I sent a thumbs up, even though I had no intention of answering her call. I pushed the phone under my pillow and stared at the ceiling.

What now?

Life didn't feel like my own without him, but forgiveness couldn't blanket over what happened. I had felt it when it happened—the new thorn of anger I couldn't pluck, the one I'd have to accept like a scar to the soul.

Curling on my side, I whispered, "I know I hurt him too, but why did I have to become smaller for him to love me? They say you learn the secrets of life when you die, Aunt Rosen, but it's a lie. You would've found a way to tell me them."

I stopped, finding even more pain in the one-sided conversation.

As if by instinct, I started analyzing every little thing I had done wrong. *I should've told him about Noah and my job when we got back together. What was I thinking?*

I pushed the palms of my hands into my eye sockets, frustrated at Rob, at Noah, and at myself.

Rain, stop!

It sounded just like Aunt Rosen's voice, blunt and loving.

Love should stop when you realize it's wrong. I should have been able to pour water over us like we were a fire and throw dirt on the ashes and let that be the end, but nothing could erase the warmth I felt for him.

I fell asleep praying an intrusive thought: *Please, let us come back from this.*

I didn't care how irrational it sounded. The world had done crazier things than bring us back together.

7

Sleeping it off hadn't worked. I woke up with a heart ready for another dose of breaking. I needed a friend to help me through it. Rob was a gaping wound, but Noah was the salt rubbed into it, and how was I supposed to handle both alone?

At noon, I rapped against Mikayla's door. She yanked it open, then retreated back to bed. "I am catching up on sleep," she groused.

"Well, I need you to be Mikayla in all caps right now," I said, gripping my mug of instant coffee as if it were trying to escape.

She popped an eye open and slid over, patting the bed. "Come on."

I sat on the mattress. She threw an arm around my stomach, and I put my mug on her desk. She used it as a bedside table, putting it in the corner of her room and leaving the floor plan open. She liked the extra room for yoga and spontaneous dance parties.

"What contingency is harshing your mellow?" she asked, and I smiled. She was eccentric, lively, and the nicest person I had met, other than Noah. *Noah. Ugh.*

"Hey," she said, alert to my emotional withdrawal. "What's wrong?"

I stared at her, chewing the inside of my mouth. "Can I trust you?"

"Duh. You're the only person who doesn't judge me when I put on the Spice Girls."

"They're an unguilty pleasure," I defended.

"You already have something to hold over me," she said, tugging my arm. "Spill it, Raindrop."

Her pet name for me wasn't enough to make me smile. I looked down. Suddenly, my throat tightened, yesterday and three years of bad days lodged in there. Tears welled in my eyes.

Mikayla sat up against her pillow. "Are you in trouble?"

"It's nothing," I choked out, regretting the words immediately.

I needed to recount the past without tweaking the details. No camouflage. No red herrings. No twisting a fight for the sake of keeping a relationship.

I spilled.

§

Rob. A single syllable. A simple name. A person I loved so deeply. An end to me.

He and I had years of history. Ours wasn't a simple, teenage love where we went to prom and talked on the phone until the sun came up. We weren't aged in innocence. We were bound by things we didn't share with anyone but each other. We were a tumultuous mix of fire and smoke—whoever burned, suffocated the other.

We met when we were sixteen, when I had a lonely space I needed to fill. When you're a teenager and you lose the one person who made things right in the world, the world stops being a kind place.

If my loneliness were a dark cave, then Rob was the full moon in the night sky. When I found him, I reached for him before he put out his hand to me. As soon as his eyes landed on mine, I was filled with relief. Someone had finally noticed me. Someone cared. I was special just from the light he shed on me.

We met because we were the last two students waiting to get picked up after school every day. Somewhere between awkward introductions and nervous laughter, I discovered I could fall for someone just by the way he looked at me.

Time passed and our feelings grew—wild and stubborn, like the flowers bursting through sidewalk cracks.

One afternoon, both of our parents were late picking us up again. We walked around the back of the school to kill time. He was slouched against a wall when I got the nerve to kiss him. He kissed me back like he'd been waiting to do it since we met.

We didn't fall in love. We were always in it. We started in the middle, right in the chaos of it.

We used to be so good.

He was my best friend before he became anything else. We shared the most messed up, broken pieces of ourselves with each other. I told him the fractured pieces of my story. I told him about my mother, whom, in my most twisted moments, I wished dead, because at least then her negligence would be excusable. My mother had prioritized everything on her list of important things above me, and when I realized how little I mattered, I resented her for having me. Why have a kid if you couldn't handle being a mother?

I also told him about Aunt Rosen. She had come to live with us when I was five. Everything good about my childhood had come from her. I was so unbelievably happy until I turned ten and she got her diagnosis—cancer.

In turn, Rob told me about his own wounds that wouldn't heal. His parents had little interest in raising a child and had sent him off to spend every summer with his aunt and uncle. The girl next door he met there had become his first love, then left him for another guy. The meaning of love had changed for him after the fear of losing it was instilled into his mind. He lived his life bracing himself for the next loss. When we met, he was already worried about how we would end. It made his love paranoid and reckless. Possessive.

We were together for six blissful months before doubts began to bud. I was already head-over-heels, stomach-aches-when-we-aren't-together, I-care-about-every-little-opinion-you-have in love when we had our first fight, over me texting a guy in my class. Then there was the one about me wearing shorts and a lowcut top to hang out with my friends. From then on, it became only too easy for us to square off. We relished how our emotions depended on each other. It didn't matter if it was a good day or a bad one— I loved making him happy or miserable, because, somewhere along the way, I had come to feel that the bigger the reaction, the more it meant he cared.

Words became weapons, and once we started fighting with weapons, we didn't know how to resolve wars without them. It was easy adapting to volatility when reconciling felt like being rescued from everything that was wrong in my life. He could cut my heart into pieces, and I'd be happy it was he who held the knife, because he'd have a thread and needle behind his back to stitch me up again.

Aunt Rosen used to say, "Your heart doesn't make the best decisions. That's what your head is for. Both have to agree for it to be right." The problem wasn't my heart. Denying my love for him would be like denying breath in my lungs. The problem was my head, where the battlefield had unreliable banners and stubborn soldiers.

Rob knew my desperation to leave my house but acted surprised when my life was packed into boxes. I had expected him to find room in the cardboard and come with me. We both had things to run from. We could move here together. He could find a job, since college wasn't part of his plan. Weekend sleepovers would've happily stolen my freedom. I'd discover Rob's new favorite takeout place and it would become our Friday night tradition. We'd be even better than before.

He turned away. He didn't fight for me. Which meant that, after everything we had been through, I still wasn't enough for him.

Years of knowing him, learning him, and loving him for us to end. The love that had gotten me through the day for years had vanished in a single moment, because of a bad minute.

So. What now?

§

"Say something," I said to Mikayla, wiping away my tears.

She hesitated. "Are you sure you want me to?"

I nodded.

"You and Rob aren't an intense, misunderstood romance. He's not the toxic guy that changes. This isn't one of your comfort movies. This is real life, and you aren't together. You shouldn't be."

I gaped.

"Oh, Raindrop," she whispered, shaking her head. "It was an era for you. A lovely, painful, abusive era for you. And now it's over because he doesn't know how to love."

"How can you say that?" I cried. "He's hurting, too. How can I blame him? We were kids when we got together."

"You *were* kids. You're both older now. He needs to act like it. I doubt this was the first time he treated you like this—"

"It is," I interjected, feeling a weird desire to not portray him as the villain. "He was the family I didn't have. He was my source of love and support for years."

"There are wounds that don't bleed, Raindrop."

"I know," I replied, needing her to stop.

"Pass me my laptop. I'm showing you."

"Mikayla," I groaned. "We're not researching this together."

She crawled over me, retrieving the laptop from the desk herself. "I know this seems stupid, but humor me, 'kay?"

I rolled my eyes.

She typed away. "Ah! Here," she said, shoving the laptop onto my lap. Bold letters screamed at me, *See if You're in an Abusive Relationship. Find Out!*

"This is a load of crap," I said, repulsed. "It sounds like something from a school nurse's pamphlet wall."

"If it's a load of crap, then you have nothing to worry about. If not, then we'll deal with it. C'mon, I'll fill it out for you," she said, grabbing the laptop back. "Does he call you names?"

"No."

"It doesn't have to be profanity. Does he call you stupid?"

I stared at her. She answered the question without any real validation.

"Is he patronizing?"

"Sometimes."

"Dismissive?"

"No," I answered instantly. I had always found Rob's intense focus on me romantic.

"Does he invade your privacy?"

"Rob saw me without my clothes on, Mikayla. What sort of privacy could he invade?"

"Well, you know. Read your journal or text messages. What about if you're fighting? Does he use the silent treatment?"

"Who doesn't?"

"Lots of people don't, Raindrop. Does he swear or yell at you?"

"Mikayla, this is pointless."

"Does he make you feel like everything is your fault?"

"If we're fighting, of course he's going to tell me it's my fault."

"That's a yes. Does he use sarcasm to hurt you?"

"He uses sarcasm because he's sarcastic!" I exploded.

Mikayla, unfazed, checked the 'yes' box.

"Does he try to control you?"

"I don't want to do this."

"Does he put you down? Does he dictate personal choices, like what you wear? Do you feel beat up, emotionally? Does he keep you away from your friends?"

Her voice droned on, my silence the only outward answer, even while inside, my own inner monolog kept saying, *Yes, yes, yes, yes…*

"This wasn't the first fight that left you feeling this way." She had stopped reading from the screen. It was a statement, not a question, so I stayed quiet.

"And I doubt this is the first time you've tried to talk to him about it," she added. "It's not your job to teach him how to love."

A sob broke out of me. "If not me, then who?"

I could deal with being alone. I had been lonely for years before him, but the thought of him returning to nights without someone to talk to—it killed me.

"You can't be with him," she declared.

My heart split apart. "Not anymore," I said aloud, wiping my face.

"I'm sorry. I was probably supposed to be making you feel better."

"No, I needed it." I looked away, picking a random spot on the carpet. "It still doesn't feel real."

Mikayla hugged me. It was a small gesture, not even a tight embrace, but it felt like I hadn't been held in ages. When my guard fell, it was like dropping a mirror. Fragments of myself shattered.

"Let it all out," she soothed, bringing me closer.

"God, this is all I've been doing. I've cried nonstop. I'm sorry." I choked on a sob. "I'm so stupid, thinking we could work. I fell asleep praying we could get through this."

"It's not love. Not the pure kind at least."

We were quiet for a moment.

She grabbed my hand. "Do you want to talk more?"

"No, I'm okay," I said, not knowing if I was telling the truth.

Mikayla huffed, crawling off the bed. "Okay, then it's my job to put a cork in your tears. Please tell me you're not the type who gets so sad they can't eat."

In the middle of a tear etching its way down my face, I laughed. I missed having friends. Under Rob's thumb, I had cut off people for reasons too minor to remember. His friends were mine but were distanced out of "respect" after a while. Pieces of my life were plucked like weeds to fit his image of what we should be. Watching Mikayla throw on bell bottom jeans and a cardigan, I realized that having friends again was the first positive thing resulting from the breakup.

"C'mon!" she said, dragging me out of her room.

"Wait. I need my phone," I told her, remembering I had left it off and charging.

"Hurry. We're hitting up a breakfast buffet."

"Okay!"

§

Her "breakfast buffet" was nothing more than the dining hall on the opposite side of campus that we never frequented because of the distance.

"I still don't understand we had to go to this one. I would've been happy with Frosted Flakes," I said.

"Because you needed to walk through nature. It's what you do when you're sad. It makes life tolerable," she reasoned.

I was about to argue that a tree couldn't fix a broken heart when she added, "Also, there's a waffle bar and a mountain of donuts here."

She tapped her bag. "I'm snagging us some donuts for later," Mikayla schemed. "Oh, you also have to get an orange juice. It, too, makes life tolerable."

I smiled, grabbing a tray and a plate. My eyes were set on jumbo waffles and a bowl of strawberries.

Mikayla found me again right as I swiped my student ID. "Follow me," she said leading us to a booth tucked away in the corner. Before I could slide in, she blurted out, "Wait!"

Jittery as usual, I jumped up. "Why?"

Her grin promised a plan as outlandish as her clothes and vocabulary. "Wait 'til I dress the table."

I exhaled loudly.

Mikayla took out a lace tablecloth and flipped it across the table. She grabbed my tray, set it next to hers, and put a lunchbox with donuts in the middle.

"Now we can begin!"

I had no idea what she was up to until we were both huddled around her tote bag. Slyly, she uncapped her water bottle and poured the contents into our orange juices.

"Mimosa?" she asked, sipping out of hers to make room for more of the cheap champagne she had smuggled in.

"You're a genius."

"I know," she smiled. "Hey, just so you know, you can cry on me whenever you want. I'm not going to judge you. We rarely know how deep a hole we're in until we try climbing out."

"Thank you," I said, meaning the words a little too much.

We ate. We drank. We ate some more. And my smile and laughter stopped being faked.

Part Two

Sometimes a safe place gets mistaken for love.
But what do you do when a warm bed turns
into
Cuts + love + bruised skin. I thought I
was better than this.

        I didn't know. I didn't feel it.
The rope around my waist, the way the knife
behind your back matched mine
I thought the jokes hit my stomach
I thought the butterflies made a home
I thought my imaginations were scribbles on
a treasure map

Cuts + love + bruised skin. I thought I
was better than this
Than burning myself to cinders so heat
kissed your lips
Than cutting down all of my olive branches
so you could feel peace
I thought the cuts + love + bruised skin
Were flints of passion, were passing comets
of miscommunication,

I thought we were fates drawn in the
constellations.
But we are what we hate.
We are the mistakes I revisit before my
pillow holds my head.
We are the regrets I'll cry about when I
see my child fall in love for the first time.
We are the cuts & love & bruised skin.

Love you don't get from your family you
find somewhere else.

8

Class was emptier now that Noah made a habit of skipping. It had been days of my green-eyed blackout. At first, I gave him the benefit of the doubt—I wouldn't know what to say, either, if the roles had been reversed—but then he kept not saying anything. I gave Travis our class notes, expecting a text. Nothing. I went into work, hoping he'd be there to smooth over any awkwardness. Nothing. I sent him messages. Nothing.

Days feel longer when you're fighting with someone, but they feel frozen when you don't even know what you're doing with them.

Trying to drown out my anxious thoughts, I raised the volume on my AirPods and swung open the door to class. Lately, I had opted for a random spot in the middle of the room, because having Noah's vacant seat next to me made me lonelier than usual. There should've been the same two-seat gap, but today, one of the seats was filled. Noah sat there with his sketchbook in his lap.

He tossed out a lopsided grin when he saw me. I had to actively grind my teeth and remind myself that I was still upset at his silent treatment to avoid smiling back. I rolled my eyes, concentrating on the music blasting into my eardrums and pretending I was in a music video. I aligned my steps with the tempo of the song and sat as far from Noah as I could.

I ended up sitting next to a blonde girl, who eyed me curiously.

I gave her my best smile. "Hi. Can I sit here? The guy I usually sit with is being a jerk."

"What a bastard," she exhaled. "Which one?"

"Pretty face in the back of the room, with a sketchbook. By the doors."

She pretended to pop her back, sneaking a glance. I almost did the same.

"Hey! So, did you get my text asking about our paper?" she said, faking small talk, then moved her backpack to her side, whispering, "You can sit with me whenever you want."

I had never been so grateful for instant girl code loyalty.

"Thanks."

We pretended to be deep in conversation. She laughed at whatever I said and nudged shoulders with me like we'd been best friends forever. In reality, we barely got around to exchanging names and talking about our majors.

Our charade got cut short once the lecture started. I took notes in my usual plethora of colors. In the middle of a poem that our professor was reading, I heard Noah cough. I only knew it was him because it also sounded remarkably like my name was lodged in his throat.

English class was supposed to be a safe haven—a place where my life paused. Today it was a prison cell. Nothing helped the time go by. Manacled by desk scuffs and pen taps, I tallied the minutes instead of noting important writers and their works. Noah was rows away, but he may as well have been right behind me, kicking my chair.

When class ended, it was as if a starting pistol had been fired, signaling a race to be anywhere Noah wasn't. I threw my notebook into my backpack, crushing loose papers, and exited through a different door to throw him off.

Outside, I popped in my AirPods and took a longer route to the library. I didn't look around. Halfway up the stairs, I risked glancing up. Unfamiliar faces soothed me. Relieved, I kept walking.

Someone to the left matched my urgency. "Rivas!"

Noah's voice tripped me, almost making face plant into the concrete. My peripheral vision caught sight of his curls.

He reached my side, inspecting me, curling his hands around my shoulders. "Hey, are you okay?"

"Screw your freakishly long legs," I grumbled, pausing the music on my phone.

He laughed. "Can I buy you coffee?"

People meandered around us. I straightened, taking an extra step up the stairs, and just like that, we were closer to eye level than ever before.

"I don't drink coffee anymore." The lie felt blatantly false, even to me, so I added, "Noah, I have to go. I'm meeting Mikayla."

"I'll walk with you. Gotta make sure no other creep gets in your way."

His smile, like his laugh, was careless. He expected us to be our normal selves, but I didn't want to act like things were okay.

I turned around, not offering anything but a silent agreement.

"What's up?" he asked.

"Nothing."

"Hey, thank you for the notes," he said, shoving a stack of papers into my hands.

I blinked at my own handwriting. "You're welcome."

"Get this—your color code system works."

"Hmm."

"Yeah, I can recognize Wordsworth now."

I scoffed.

"Wordsworth is… wordsy," he drawled.

I refused to succumb to his joke. I threw a wall between us with the bricks of my terse responses.

"He can be."

"Yeah, so you agree?"

"Sure."

His brows raised. "Okay. What's up? You didn't sit with me and you're acting weird as fuck. C'mon, Rivas. What's wrong?"

I tucked a lock of hair behind my ear. "You ignored my messages. You didn't reach out when I gave Travis the notes. Days of radio silence kind of sucks, Noah."

"Shit," he breathed, scratching his jaw. "I didn't know you'd take it bad." He dipped his head the way he usually did to win my smile.

I couldn't give it to him. *His apologies are just as lousy as Rob's.* I rolled my eyes and took another step.

"Wait." His hand shackled my wrist. He must've seen from my expression how the sudden touch affected me, because he dropped his grip. "Shit. Sorry," he mumbled.

"Nothing's changed, Noah. I'm still dealing with my stuff. You've still got… complications. Or is there anything you want to tell me?"

He hesitated. I nodded, thinking about everything. *I'm not anything to him.* Yeah, it hurt, but I knew where I stood now.

"I have to go. I'll see you at work," I said, before I could start crying again.

§

I found myself adrift in a deep, post-breakup sea. On low-tide days, I woke up, went to the gym for a run, showered, studied, went to class or work, and spent time with Mikayla in our dorm to distract myself. On high-tide days, I woke up to memories, daydreamed alternate endings, and found leaving my bed impossible because my heart kept me chained to it. The nights were always the same. I covered my mouth and cried.

In Brit Lit, I kept sitting with the blonde girl. Unfortunately, I couldn't remember her name. Sarah? Tara? At work, I kept to myself. I wasn't rude, but I was distant. Whenever Travis or Noah came to the front to socialize, I kept my responses short. I pretended Noah's "apology" didn't sting like a fresh tattoo.

A week passed, and the summer heat weakened. The arrival of my birthday would usually signal a seasonal drop in temperature, which in Texas wasn't much. Back home, I used to climb into Aunt Rosen's bed whenever there was a cold front, and we'd sleep by the window, feeling the breeze and planning out my birthdays. The important ones, like sixteen and eighteen, had the most extravagant ideas. Sixteen sundaes for my sweet sixteen. It was the first time I took my sugar addiction too far and felt sick the rest of the day. Eighteen was different. We were supposed to get matching tattoos, but Aunt Rosen couldn't. I went alone, getting my crescent moon tattoo and sending her pictures. At twenty-one, we were supposed to try making twenty-one different cocktails. There would be nowhere to send a picture.

She would hate me spending my birthday moping.

"I promise I won't," I said while doing my eyeliner. On days like this, makeup was a psychological barrier against crying.

I had to do something, for Aunt Rosen's sake. Mikayla wanted to take me out, but I just wanted to eat pizza and watch *Beetlejuice*. Our compromise was her buying alcohol and sneaking the contraband to our room, me picking up pizza after work, and us watching movies on our projector.

I was in the middle of slipping on a black dress over a white, long-sleeve shirt when I heard Mikayla.

"Good morning! Are you excited for tonight?" she hollered, springing my door open and twirling inside. "Hot commodity! You look great."

"Thanks," I mumbled, moving past her to my desk and digging through my jewelry.

"Wait!"

I nearly dropped the jewelry dish. "Mikayla, I swear on everything I love and hate, if you do not stop scaring me, I will kick your ass."

My threat elicited laughter. "You only cuss when you're angry or upset. I love it! Here!" She pulled a sparkly, purple box from her overall pockets.

I shook my head. "I told you not to."

She placed the gift in my hands. "And I said I was still going to. Don't worry, it's small enough to be guilt-free."

"Sure," I muttered, inspecting the glittering mess. It was my first gift, presumably my only one. Well, the only true gift. My mom had already wired me a hundred dollars as a present. As a college student, I was grateful, but as a daughter, I felt a pinch of disappointment.

"If you don't like it, I'll email you the receipt," Mikayla promised.

Inside the box was a set of ornate, book-shaped earrings. I couldn't help laughing. It was the corniest thing I had ever gotten.

"What?" she asked genuinely. "You said you were an English major, and you have non-schoolbooks in your room."

"Mikayla, this is perfect. I don't know how to thank—" I began, but was interrupted by the body-slamming hug she gave me.

"Happy early birthday! I can't wait for later."

I laughed, reaching out to fix her frizzy bangs. "You're just happy you'll have a new, legal drinking buddy after midnight."

She scrunched her nose. "Possibly."

"You're awful," I sighed, putting on my earrings. "Thank you. I love them."

"See you later!"

§

Five minutes into my shift, Dawn shoved a cake on the counter and said, "Cake for everyone." The blue icing was highlighted by white cursive letters spelling out, "Happy Birthday Rain!"

"It's today?" Noah muttered from behind the counter, looking like a deer in headlights.

Dawn smacked him. "It's tomorrow, you idiot. But the shop is closed on Sundays."

Thankfully, they didn't sing to me, which helped me not be so mortified. Feigning a happy-go-lucky expression, I ate a slice of cake with Ana. Her lips were stained blue from the icing, so I purposely smeared some on my lips to match. Dawn took our picture. Chris pressured me into having one taken with Noah and Travis. I painted on my best smile as they draped their arms around my shoulders. I waited for Noah to talk to me, but he sat as far from Ana and me as possible.

It was awkward for me, to say the least. But once work picked up, I could relax, even sneaking glances at Ana's iPad while she watched *Moana*.

At closing, after Dawn and her family had left, Travis came to the counter. He was waiting for Lorie to pick him up. «Ready to join the twenty-fun club?» he asked, helping himself to a bite of cake.

«Do we get t-shirts with that?»

His mouth quirked. «That can be your present.»

«No presents under any circumstances. Unless it's coffee.»

«That's not enough,» he argued. «And not fair. I didn't know you had a birthday coming until I walked in today.»

I smiled. «If Dawn hadn't taken note of it, no one would have known.»

«Not big on birthday festivities?» he asked, sincerity shining through his eyes.

«Not really,» I replied. «I'd skip the day if I could.» I stole his fork and took another bite.

«You know what? Me too. I hate it. Lorie still makes people sing to me at restaurants. It's awkward as hell when I sign thank you to them.»

I couldn't help laughing. «She loves you.»

«Yeah, she loves my Deaf ass so much she forgets I can't hear. What good does singing happy birthday do for me?»

My laughing doubled. «It's the sentiment that counts.»

«Nah, I just hate the attention, so if you want to skip it, then you have a cup of coffee waiting for you on your next shift.»

Dramatically, I placed my hands to my chest. «That's too much.»

The noise of a tattoo machine caught my attention. I turned my head to where Noah was busy touching up one of his tattoos. When I turned back, Travis was scrutinizing my expression.

«You two are being weird,» he said, keeping his hands close to his chest—the equivalent of whispering in the Deaf community.

«We're fine,» I lied.

«Did something happen?»

I shook my head a little too quickly and stole a glance at Noah. Deep in concentration, not feeling our stares, he worked. A lock of his hair hung across his forehead. His brows knitted together. Only one thought rang through my head—*I miss him.*

«If nothing happened, go talk to him.»

«He's busy.» I checked my phone for any new, oh-so-important notifications. It was a cheap way to end the conversation. Travis, however, waited until I locked the screen again.

«For a week, I've seen you two avoid each other. You forget—the Deaf man sees everything.» He shot me an impish grin.

A flash of headlights raked across the shop as Lorie's car arrived.

«I expect you two to be on good terms before I see you again,» Travis continued, wagging a finger at me sternly. «I'll know because Noah will tell me.»

«What?» I gawked. «Wait. Did he say we weren't on good terms?»

«Darn,» he said, exaggerating a finger snap as Lorie walked in. «Time to go.»

«Wait,» I insisted. «What did he say about us?»

«It's what he didn't say,» Travis corrected. «Free coffee until Halloween if you make the first move with him.»

«Halloween?» That was five weeks of glorious, free caffeine.

Travis nodded.

«You're on.»

§

Dawn had left me with more than half a cake to carry to the dorms. Maybe it was silly, but I treasured the cake as much as my outlandish earrings.

I read while Noah finished up his tattoo. He put music on while we cleaned, and I was grateful for the noise. In the silence between songs, I thought of how to get back to where we were before the Rob incident.

We listened to four songs without saying a word. All I came up with in that time was pushing myself on him, just like he had done in the beginning. He had sat next to me without asking in Brit Lit, so I waited by his truck without asking. Since I had a cake to carry, I hoped he wouldn't reject the idea.

Through the glass, I saw Noah triple check the equipment and the lights. Some comfort flooded my veins when he came out, flashing me a lopsided grin, but as soon as we got close to each other, we turned into puppets, not able to move our own strings.

Our mouths fell dumb. His hands went to his pockets. Mine clutched the plastic cake box. His brows rose.

I shrugged. "You're going to give yourself a headache thinking so hard."

He smirked and unlocked the door. "Get in." He took the cake from me, and I slid into the truck.

Noah being quiet was like my favorite song being banned from every streaming platform. Halfway up the road, I caved.

"How have you been? You haven't been speaking to me."

He blew out an incredulous laugh. "Are we talking about this? Like, actually talking about it? Or are you going to run away again when I try to fucking apologize?"

I turned my body to the window, muttering, "Don't cuss. I don't like it when you cuss."

"The last I checked, you forgot where you sit in class, and you supposedly stopped drinking coffee. Which I call bullshit—I've seen you drink your sugar water like it's nothing. And you don't even leave the counter at the shop to come talk."

I crossed my arms. He parked in the bus lane and took out the keys from the ignition. Apparently, we weren't going anywhere until this was resolved.

"I was giving you space," I said under my breath.

Noah undid his seatbelt, angling his body to me. Reaching over, he uncrossed my arms. I gave way like a weak branch. His fingertips skated down my arms, landing on my knuckles. I watched his precise movements. Slowly, his hand hooked onto mine. I didn't react. I was simply frozen, feeling everything. He was warm and rough. Our faces glowed red from the traffic light above us.

I had an overeager, ingenuous heart. His came out like a party trick. It was dangerous for us to touch like this. To look him in the eyes was a disaster waiting to happen. I did it anyway.

"Shouldn't you be with Jen right now?" I asked, my voice quick and heavy, like a guillotine. Our eyes held. If he could read the words buried in my eyes, he'd know I was asking another question behind the verbal one: *What are we doing here, Noah?*

He let go of my hand, placing it gently on the plastic covering the cake. "Jen and I aren't like that. We never were. We've only ever been an on-again, off-again kinda thing. I don't even want *that* with her anymore."

"You need to be telling *her* that, Noah."

"I did."

A beat passed. His honesty snuffed my anger.

"When?"

"After what you said the other night. Sometimes the truth hurts, Rain, but you were right." His eyes glistened with sincerity.

"So... are we okay, then?"

He shrugged. "I'd kinda like to hear how you were cool with us spending all that time together the way we did when you still had your own... 'complications,' I think you called it?"

"You don't get it," I said, dragging my palms across my face.

"Rain, don't cry."

My makeup was ruined, but at least it wasn't from tears. I was too frustrated. I put my hands down, scowling.

"Look, when I moved here, he left me on the sidewalk. Just... drove off and left. I thought we were finished."

"I don't want to come between you and him," he said.

"You have nothing to come between. We broke up."

Shock stretched over his features. "You did?"

The red from the traffic light switched to green. No cars were around to honk. The color of his eyes melted away. They were too transparent now, seeing right through me.

"Are you sure this time?" he asked.

"A jillion percent."

A smile broke out on his face. "As long as it's a jillion."

My shoulders slackened. He took my hand again.

"I care about you, Rain. I'm shitty at showing it, but I do. I was avoiding you and letting you avoid me in return. I'm sorry."

I lowered my gaze, staring at our touch. My index finger slid over his knuckle. Our movements were shy, scared of crossing a line.

"I was mean to you. I don't know how I would've reacted if I were in your situation. I'm sorry," I said.

"Remember when I said you have stop saying sorry?"

I gripped his hand harder and tugged him towards me. "What? I can't be sorry also?"

"Nope," he quipped. His smile was like sunlight on me. We finally felt normal again.

"Rivas?"

"Yeah?"

He squeezed my hand. "Fuck, I missed you."

"It was just a few days," I said, even as I thought, *I missed you, too.*

"It felt like years. What are you doing tonight?"

"Date with Mikayla."

"What about tomorrow?"

I eyed him. "What would I be agreeing to?"

"A surprise."

"I swear, if someone else gets me a present—"

"It's not. I promise. Wait. Who got you something?"

I dropped his hand and bunched up my hair, exposing my book earrings. "Mikayla, and maybe Travis."

"Travis?"

"He may have promised me coffee for a month if I made the first move and talked to you."

"What?" he seethed, pinching his brows together. "He bribed you?"

"Technically, it's a birthday gift, not a bribe. And I did want to talk to you. I just didn't know where to start."

He blinked in utter wonder. "I can't believe him. If it's not him, it's Lorie. And if it's not her, it's Dawn. Everyone in my life meddles."

"Is that a bad thing?"

"Your family doesn't meddle?"

His question banged against something hollow in my chest.

"No, not really."

"You're lucky," he said.

"I'd argue the opposite. Text me tomorrow? I promised Mikayla I'd celebrate tonight with her and if I'm late, I won't hear the end of it."

"Fiiiiine," he said, drawling out his defeat.

§

I made it through *Beetlejuice*. I drank terrible cocktails and shots of whiskey. I flailed my arms while Mikayla and I danced to the playlist she had made, feeling strangely proud of myself, until my mind began imagining that I was dancing with Rob instead of with her. God, he had never even danced with me, yet now I pretended that he swept me off my feet.

My happy filter dimmed. I told Mikayla I was tired. I shut my bedroom door and wandered down cyberstalking lane, heading to social media to see if Rob missed me.

His profile had been thoroughly expunged of all our fleeting moments of happiness. It was as if we never were and had never rescued one another. Choking back a gag, I continued scrolling through his content. Not one photo suggested I had ever been a part of his life. His profile sent a single, unambiguous message: *I am fine without you.*

My pupils became sensitive to the sight of him. It was as if he were the sun, and I was stupid enough to keep staring directly at him.

"Fuck," I cursed, turning my phone off before the tears found me again.

I cried. I cried uncontrollably, because every day ended with the ugly truth—Rob wasn't here, and I hated myself for wishing he was. Falling into my pillow, I pretended I could call Aunt Rosen in the morning. I'd ask her when this would stop hurting and if eating ice cream and screaming sad songs really worked.

9

Morning didn't bring some miraculous acceptance or sanative relief. Instead, the sun brought a steady drum of knocking. Grousing, I stumbled out of bed with my eyes half closed, dragging my feet. As I groped for the doorknob, I heard the dorm room door open, along with a zap. Yes, an electric-sounding, comic-book-letter-bolding ZAP!

Wait. Mikayla. Oh, no, no, no.

I jolted into action, running into our small living area. Mikayla held a pink bar of lightning in her hand like a pistol. It was a taser, and she had it pointed directly at Noah, who had his hands up.

"Mikayla!" I screeched. "What the hell?"

Turbulent off adrenaline, she snapped her face towards me. "This guy needs to take a hint!" she proclaimed, turning back to Noah. "Back off, creep! I'll fry you like bacon."

"Oh, my God," I gasped as she let loose another zap. "Mikayla, that's not who you think it is! Noah, say hi to my crazy roommate."

Noah muttered, "Hi," at the same time that Mikayla said, "Tattoo dude?"

"Yes. *Noah*," I emphasized.

"My bad," she mumbled.

"You talk about me?" Noah asked, grinning like an idiot.

I ignored him and snatched the tiny but powerful contraption out of her hand. "You almost zapped him!"

"The guy showed up early in the morning pounding on our door! A zap would've been justified!"

"Justified? What happened to you being a pacifist?"

"*This*," she said, taking the taser back and waving it in the air, "is our security system, okay, Raindrop? Tattoo Dude would've been fine after he pissed his pants."

I sighed, hesitantly turning to Noah. "I am so, so sorry."

"I apologize," Mikayla huffed, adding a soft, "partly." She crossed her arms. "But can you really blame me for bringing in some backup after... well, you know. College campuses aren't always safe. Stuff happens."

My hands fell heavily on her shoulders. "I get it, but next time, ask who it is first, like a normal person."

We contended in a stare-off. After a few seconds, she surrendered. "Fine."

"Thank you," I exhaled.

"I'm going back to bed. Nice to meet you, Tattoo Dude," she said, retreating to her room like a grumpy bear to a cave.

I looked at Noah. "I don't think you'll argue with me for saying sorry once more."

"Remind me to never surprise you again, Raindrop."

I groaned. The nickname would be the bane of my existence.

His gaze traveled up and down me. "Do you need to change?" he asked. "Though, I have to admit, I like seeing you in your pajamas."

I was in my usual—sweats and a hoodie. However, my sweats were a pistachio green and the matching hoodie had cupcakes stitched in the corner.

"I hate being cold as much as I hate surprises," I told him, ignoring his teasing grin.

"Duly noted, but it's too late to cancel on me now."

"So, where are we going?" I asked.

His eyes had a devilish glint. "Do I need to explain to you what a surprise is?"

Shaking my head, I decided to go along with the madness today. My silent promise to not stay in and wallow would be upheld after all.

I moved aside, throwing my arm to the wind. "Wait on the couch. I need ten minutes."

Noah trudged in happily, plopping on the cushions and propping his legs on the coffee table.

Ten minutes later, I had washed my face, applied my signature winged liner, and smeared a mauve color on my lips. I wore faded jeans and a pink and red checkered cardigan. Not bothering to wear something underneath, my cream bralette slightly showed. My hair fell however it seemed fit. I grabbed my white converse and stood in front of my mirror. Not exactly what I imagined I'd be wearing on my twenty-first birthday. I thought I'd be more... together.

"Alright, I'm ready," I announced, walking into the living room and grabbing my tote bag with its pins.

Noah jumped to his feet. "Here," he said, pulling out a new pin. He smoothed his thumb over the surface, smiling before handing it to me.

"A skull?" I asked, wondering why the little, mocking image resonated with me. The icon reminded me of the prints at Dawn's shop.

"With roses for eye sockets," he noted lamely, stuffing his hands in his pockets. "Thought you'd write a metaphor into it somehow."

I stared at the white-boned face and blooming petals in awe. I should've instantly known it was his work from the glances I had sneaked at his sketchbook. His art was as poetic as anything we learned about in British Lit. He mixed in nature with whatever he drew, and I couldn't help admiring the way his imagination worked.

"Or it can just be a skull with flowers," Noah added, obliging my silence.

"It's your art. I love it. Thank you," I said when I could speak.

"Come on," he urged, uncomfortable now. It made my smile grow.

§

The white, Victorian house had a wraparound porch and a chimney. To make it even more picturesque, there was a tire swing hanging off a large tree by the side of the home.

"Remember when I said my dream house was the *Gilmore Girls* house?" I said, craning my head out the window as Noah parked the truck.

He chuckled. "How could I forget?"

"Noah, this is basically it. Where are we?"

"This is where I'm obligated to be every Sunday."

"Huh?"

"Family time," he said, mimicking Dawn's higher tone.

"You brought me to your sister's house? My boss's house?" I gaped, wondering why he thought this would be appealing.

"Yep!" he chirped, jumping out of the truck and walking around to open my door. He must've seen my expression because he looked at me with confusion clouding his eyes.

"Rivas—" he began as I also started to speak.

At the same moment, another, high-pitched voice squealed, "Rain!"

I strung my lips into a smile and turned right as Ana threw her small arms around my legs. "Hi, Ana!"

"*Feliz cumpleaños!*" she yelled, flashing a prideful grin.

"*Gracias,*" I replied. "I'm thoroughly impressed with your Spanish."

"In French, it's *joyeux anniversaire,*" she added.

"Impressive," I laughed.

"You speak Spanish?" Noah asked.

"A little."

"I swear, I know nothing."

"She's Hispanic. Her last name is Rivas," Ana said, her attitude overpowering me. "You're too self-absorbed, Noah," she chirped.

He swung her up into the air like a ragdoll. "Do you hear how she talks to me?"

"Stop!" Ana screeched.

"I mean, she's not wrong," I teased.

"Did your mom order from the café like I told her to?" he asked, placing her down after a quick hug and kiss on the check.

"Mom listened to your instructions. Don't worry," she answered, sounding way too grown up. She slipped her hand into mine.

I eyed him. "Instructions?"

"Uh-huh," Ana hummed. She tugged on my hand, whisking me away and into the house.

Some houses were cold, with a vibe like a museum. Mom's was like that. She decorated with obligatory family photoshoots and bland, framed art. Our living room sofa had firm cushions that no one sat in and matching throw pillows that weren't soft.

This house was nothing like that. Blurry, imperfectly shot, candid photos and Ana's fingerpaintings were hung at random intervals along the walls. The green sectional had red blankets draped over it. Toys were left in the hallway. I almost stepped on a plush penguin with marker-drawn eyelashes.

I loved it.

"Pssst! The food's this way," Noah pestered.

He leaned against the wall. I stood for a moment, hopelessly captivated by him. He had a beautiful life, a family that treasured his time, and friends who went to bat for him. I had no idea why he had chosen to invite me in. My own family was a shambles. Dad had left us when I was born. My mother had cried over him for the first five years of my life, cried over her parents dying the next six, then cried over Aunt Rosen for the rest. Her fragile heart had gotten in the way of a lot of things, including us having a relationship.

"I can't remember the last time I had a family meal." I whispered the thought, then snapped my mouth shut when Noah's scarred brow rose. I shook my head and regained my composure. *Get a grip, Rain.*

"This house is wonderful," I exhaled.

"Thanks!" Dawn said, descending the stairs. "I'm happy you could come over." Her platinum hair was tied in a bun, and she was in a big t-shirt and leggings.

"Noah, come help out with the drinks." Chris' voice rang out from deeper in the house.

I trailed behind them to the kitchen. The marble island was filled. Pancakes, eggs, scones, toast—the breakfast spread was enough to feed a second family.

My mother had constantly lectured me about dressing to look like you're at least 'trying.' But watching Chris work on the other side of the island, pouring orange juice and champagne into four glasses, his flannel pants and sweatshirt officially made me feel overdressed.

"Happy birthday, Rain," he said, handing me a glass.

"Thanks."

He poured orange juice in a Snow White cup, then pretended to pour some champagne into it from a closed bottle. "Here, Ana," he said with a wink.

"To you turning twenty-one," Dawn said, ushering us to raise our glasses.

I blinked, uneasy at being the center of attention. "This is for me?"

"The drinks are," Chris answered. "The food is because my soon-to-be wife ruined our original breakfast."

"What? Ana, you said your mom listened to my instructions," Noah gaped.

"She did, but she almost killed us first," Chris laughed, tears coming to his eyes. "She tried making Rain a homemade breakfast."

"What the hell were you trying to make?" Noah interrogated his sister.

Dawn stiffened. "Eggs, okay? I forgot to oil the pan. I may have accidentally burned a towel. It's soaking as we speak. Not a big deal, alright?"

"God, you're stupid," Noah exclaimed.

"And you have never in your life offered to cook, so shut it."

"I left my card to order the food!"

"I was trying to make it special!"

Taking a sip, I hid my grin.

Noah loaded my plate with a bit of everything. He brought me French toast, bacon, and a side of fruit. He refilled my glass as soon as it was half empty. Whenever I moved, he said, "I'll get it," and waited on me like I was royalty.

I had no idea how to feel.

Ana told me about the fact that she was going to be the maid of honor for her parent's wedding next month. She had refused to be a flower girl because it was too simple of a job. She wanted to stand up there with her mom. We talked a lot about the upcoming big day. Dawn handed me an invitation, claiming there was no point in mailing it to me. Chris said he was excited to hear Noah's best man speech. Noah's face said he was dreading it. The conversation was easy. By the time we left, the drinks gave my vision a carefree haze.

We sat in his truck. I flicked the fuzzy dice hanging off the review mirror. He flicked my arm in return.

"Where to next?" I asked, giddy without the usual stream of anxiety flowing through my brain.

Noah turned the key and tipped his head to the side. A lock of hair draped across his face. "Where do you want to go? I'm yours today."

"Hmmm. Let's go downtown. I have birthday money I need to spend."
I hated to admit it, but it would make me smile to spend Mom's money on
clothes she would hate.

"Your wish is my command."

§

An hour later, I skipped down the sidewalk with a bag full of clothes.
Noah was a good sport, never rushing me and encouraging me to try on
whatever I wanted.

The walk to the dorms dried out the alcohol in my system. My liveliness
from earlier had burnt out and my steps dragged in the fumes. I didn't know
if it was the alcohol betraying me like a hangover or the fact that I was
exceptional at ruining a good moment, but I found myself thinking about
Rob. He had done tricks like this before. Whenever we had fought, he would
shower me with gifts or kind gestures, just like Noah had.

Those wrapped apologies had always felt hollow. It was like someone
shredding your favorite copy of your favorite book—the one with all your
handwritten notes and annotations—then replacing it with a new, empty
copy. Sure, it was good to have it back, but it would never be the same. Even
so, I had always been a sucker for Rob's big apologies—it was easier to
simply accept my role in his big forgiveness scene than hurt him further.

"Hey, you didn't have to plan this big breakfast for me to forgive you,"
I said.

"I don't know what you mean," he said.

"Noah, it's okay. I don't need these over-the-top gestures to say sorry."

He looked at me with his eyebrows pulled, probably wondering why I
couldn't just say thank you. "Rain, it's not like that."

But it was. In that moment, I didn't understand why the guys in my life
were so great at delivering aggrandized apologies, or why I was always on
the receiving end of them.

I looked around, the physical sidewalk blurring before me as I caught
cracks of emotions I usually tried to step over. My life was a plat of wreckage
after a storm. Sure, Rob was one corner of destruction, but even before him,
I had been surrounded by broken things.

My family was a joke, and I barely had any friends. I had heard people
say how the absence of those things could add brilliance to your life. It could
make someone interesting, compassionate, determined, or self-reliant. In my
case, it had led me to spiral downward. *Something must be wrong with me.*

At my door, I dug for my keys without saying a word. My emotions
were teetering on thin ice, and his spotlight gaze doubled their weight. Tears
were close to slipping through. I put the key in the lock, hoping he'd just say
happy birthday, goodbye, and not ask to come inside.

When he didn't, I whispered, "I'm fine now. You can go."

"What?"

"I had a lovely time with your family. You should go."

"What's wrong?"

I shut my eyes. "You should go."

"No. Why? What happened?" he demanded.

I sank my teeth into my lips to stop them from trembling.

"Rain?"

"I'm going to fall apart now, okay? So, go," I said, my voice breaking on the last word.

"Everything was just fine an hour ago."

"Well, now it's not. I can't keep talking. I don't want to freak you out. Please, Noah. Go."

He ran a hand through his hair in frustration. "I can't, okay?" It sounded like an admission. "Tell me what's wrong."

I covered my face. "I really need you to leave."

His hands pried mine away. "And I already told you I can't. I'm not going anywhere."

His touch, albeit gentle, pinned me down. I turned my face toward the hallway just to have a tiny escape. "You should go. If I start to cry, it'll be a waterfall."

"I could fucking care less right now about the quantity. I'd be worried about a drop." He let go of my hands to run his thumb across my chin. "What happened?"

I shook my head. "Nothing."

"Seriously? You're about to cry in my hands. Just say if it's about him."

Instantly, my sadness morphed into anger. I pushed him away. "What the hell, Noah?"

Shrugging his shoulders, he took an extra step back. "It was an easy assumption to make. So, it's not about him?"

I struggled with myself, remembering the internal monolog that had triggered this conversation. "It's not *just* about him," I said, exasperated but unwilling to lie to Noah.

"Then what else is it?"

"Can we please not talk about it? Vulnerability isn't your thing."

He swallowed roughly, looking hurt. "That's what you think?"

"It was an easy assumption to make."

"Try me."

"You're going to walk away if I do."

"Let me prove I won't."

I sucked in a breath. *Fine.*

"I don't have friends that count as extended family. I don't have a niece who sounds more grown up than I do. I don't have brunch at my sister's gorgeous house once a week. I'm an only child, and it's better that way, because I'd hate someone else growing up the way I did. My parents weren't a real couple. Not in the way it counts. I highly doubt I'd be able to recognize my father in a lineup. But my mother still held onto whatever pieces of him she could.

"God, my mother—let her have one reason to be miserable, and she's a victim for the rest of her life. She was upset over my dad leaving until she could be upset over my grandparents' death. Then, my Aunt Rosen, the one part of my family I wish every kid could experience, gets breast cancer. One day Aunt Rosen's telling me to be patient with my depressed mother, and the next, she's gone. I guess life didn't have any patience for her. What the absolute fuck is that?

"So, you know what I do? I turn to someone I thought could love me. It's not a secret. I loved the wrong person. He used to give me the most wonderfully orchestrated apologies whenever he hurt me. I stuck around because it's incredibly easy to stay in a bad place when the rest of your life feels just as terrible.

"So, there you have it. This wasn't how it was supposed to be. Aunt Rosen and I were supposed to make twenty-one different drinks together. We were supposed to do so many things. Now, she's dead. And I'm... alone."

The emotional grenade I had dropped between us wiped everything out. In the fatal silence, he studied my face, but made no move towards me. I couldn't shelve my feelings now. I slid to the ground, welcoming the breakdown.

Seconds of tears and silence passed.

"Can you please say something, even it's goodbye?" I asked.

"I suck at this."

I looked up, confused. "What?"

"I brought Travis a bottle of vodka when his grandfather died," Noah said by way of explanation. "I'd rather him be drunk than have to offer him any real condolences. If he was sober, he'd have realized what a terrible friend I am because I don't know how to be there for people."

I shook my head. "Sometimes, all you have to do is listen."

He sat down next me, reaching beneath his collar to fidget with the silver chain he always wore. At the end of the chain was a simple, silver ring.

Without thinking, I reached out and slid the ring on my index finger.

"It was my mother's wedding band," he said softly, gauging my reaction. I stopped playing with the ring and let it rest on my knuckle.

"She and my dad married young—too young to know it was a bad idea," he continued. "Alcohol was the love he couldn't leave behind. When I was eight, he drove them off the road. Mom was gone instantly. He... lingered for a while, before complications took him, too. It gave me time to hate him.

"Dawn and I went to live with our grandparents. When Grandma asked if I wanted something of my mother's, I asked for this," he said, grimacing at the story of his own life. "Yeah. I kept the ring that bound her to the piece of shit who took her from us."

I let go of the ring, but he grabbed my hand, keeping me there.

Our eyes locked, and for the first time, I saw a more complete picture of Noah. Ever since we met, he had seemed like the kind of guy that nothing bad ever happened to, but I understood it now—his calm, cool demeanor was his defense mechanism. There, sitting in the tiny hallway, my heart recognized his, and the similar scars covering it.

I wiggled my arm to hook underneath his. He nestled me closer.

"I wish you were never lonely, Rain. You're not the only one carrying baggage."

"I know, but sometimes it feels so heavy I can't even take the first step."

"I can carry you," he said, wrapping an arm around me.

Then, under me.

"Wait. No! Colt, what are you doing?"

But it was too late. I was in the air and against his chest in seconds.

"Put me down!"

He ignored me. "Put the damn key in," he ordered, squeezing my sides.

"Okay!" I yelled, half laughing. "Colt, I can walk."

"Shh! I'm not about to risk being tased again," he scolded.

I dipped my head, peppering soft laughs on his neck. "I'm still sorry about that."

"Yeah, your big-ass smile proves it," he smirked, opening the door to my room and setting me down.

"You know, Noah, I wasn't bombarding you with my past to make you share yours," I said, all seriousness again.

"That's not why I did it. It kills me knowing you've been hurt," he muttered.

I offered him half a smile. "You've been hurt too."

"But you still love everyone, even people who've hurt you."

"And you don't?" I scoffed.

"Not anymore," he said seriously.

"Does that make it hurt less?"

"I don't know."

I hesitated a minute, thinking about everything, then neutrally asked him, "Do you have to go?"

He matched my tone. "Do you want me to?"

"No."

"Can I sleep here?"

"Yeah."

We climbed into my bed. With it being so high, it felt like we were perched in a treehouse, escaping the real world. I curled on my side. Noah lay on his back. Slowly, we inched closer, dozing in and out, mumbling things like, "Is this okay?" and, "Come here." I ended up curled around his arm, and his shoulder became my pillow.

I slept better than I had in weeks.

10

Mikayla had promised me a Saturday evening of binge watching our favorite shows, which was interrupted before it even began by a knock at the door. It was Noah, carrying a bag of Chinese takeout. He looked surprised to see Mikayla, and even more surprised when my redheaded whirlwind of a roommate squealed her delight and relieved him of the bag, opening it and diving into a carton of noodles.

And that was how we ended up there—Noah and Mikayla squished on the tiny couch, stuffing their faces, and me on the floor, arguing that we should've gotten another order of chow mein.

"You two are awful," I complained. "I got one chopstick-full bite of noodles. All I've eaten are steamed vegetables and rice."

"Here," Noah said, giving me a few pieces of orange chicken from his takeout box.

Vexed, I swatted his chopsticks away. "I wanted noodles."

His smile made the soy sauce in the corner of his mouth lift and smear. "I'll order more next time."

I grumbled and tossed him a napkin.

"We still have a few egg rolls," Mikayla offered.

I shook my head, leaning against Noah's legs. His bony knees were better than getting stuck with the awkward middle seat on the couch. A happy bubble of comfort had encased us ever since our sleepover. His touch conveyed a serene warmth even through the barriers of clothes and blankets, and it was easy to feel spoiled with him as a built-in space heater. Having both him and Mikayla, my anxiety thinned, fading away like white noise into the background.

I chewed, watching Mikayla laugh over something Noah had said. *I swear, Noah can charm the bitterness out of anyone.* One evening hanging out and my roommate was under his spell.

Mikayla and I clicked. Our personalities swished well together, like champagne and strawberries. Then there was Noah. Our magic was in our platonic friendship. Sure, he was attractive, but my heart didn't race when his body molded against mine. Instead, it slowed, syncopating to the beat of his.

Plus, his reasons for sleeping over were honest and uncomplicated. He loved living with Travis and Lorie, but their dynamic was unbalanced. "I go from being the fun uncle in one family to the third wheel in another." I was his cure for loneliness. If Noah wanted anything else with me, he would have said otherwise. He was direct. There was no way we would be more, especially since his loud chewing was making me regret having him over.

"What are we watching tonight?" he asked through a mouthful.

"*Gilmore Girls* or *One Tree Hill*," Mikayla answered.

"Aren't you two done rewatching that crap?"

I feigned a heartbroken gasp. "That *crap*? It's early 2000s TV gold."

"Chad Michael Murray is a god," Mikayla said with a seriousness that provoked a fit of uncontrollable laughter from me.

Noah, eyes lit and flickering like a candle with amusement, pleaded his case while ignoring Mikayla's scrunched, freckled face. "It's outdated and unrealistic."

I threw my arms up as if saying, "Exactly!' but laughing made speaking impossible.

"Dude, that's the point!" Mikayla countered for both of us.

Noah's scarred brow furrowed in defiance. "I'm not watching that shit again."

"It's because you like him with Brooke," I said.

His eyes bulged. "Peyton doesn't even like him! She just wants what she can't have."

"Guys," Mikayla said.

I was about to lose it. "She loves him!"

"Hey, friends!" Mikayla said, raising her voice. Her wiry bangs settled on the side of her face. "I have an idea." She smiled, playfully holding an idea behind her back.

"Which is?" I asked.

Her eyes sparkled, and I knew before another word was spoken that she craved the rush of adventure.

"Let's go out."

"What? Why? You promised we could binge our shows," I whined.

"Tipsy Squeeze? I'm down," Noah agreed, then smirked at me.

He said yes just to be annoying!

"We don't work tomorrow, and I haven't seen you tipsy in a week," he continued as I gaped at him. He winked. "We'll have fun."

I frowned down at my sweats. "It's already eight."

"Okay, Grandma, do you have to wake up early for church?"

"Mikayla," I pleaded.

She stood and placed her chopsticks on the coffee table, buzzing with energy. "We go for a few drinks. We see if Lucia and Monica want to come. We dance and have fun. Come on, Raindrop!" She said each point like she was tossing me bargaining chips, but to me, each was a tally mark for staying in.

"We can walk it to Tipsy Squeeze," Noah planned aloud.

"Perfect! We buddy system it to-and-fro, avoiding the designated driver luck of straws," Mikayla beamed. "I gotta change."

I stuck out my tongue as she twirled to her room. She saluted me before slamming her door shut.

"I wanted to stay in," I lamented.

"You'd never leave your dorm if we didn't force you to."

"That's not true!"

Noah rewarded me with another smirk.

"Fine. Then I want my own personal order of noodles next time," I relented.

"Let's make it two," he conceded.

"Are you going out like that?" I asked, glancing at his torn, black jeans and matching, hole infested, black shirt. The light thread of his silver chain poked through all the black cloth like a weave of glimmering stars.

"You forget, we live in a college town. Though—" he said, pausing to swallow another bite of orange chicken, "—I'm excited to see what you come up with."

Dramatically, I let my shoulders drop and pushed myself up from the floor, mumbling, "I'll be back."

My closet was a mess. The tiny space overfilled with textures, checkered patterns, and slips of earthy greens and browns. My shoes hung in pockets over the door to give me more space, but it was hopeless. Nothing fit.

I combed through my options with frequent yanks and shoves. The clothing hung with potential, like knives in a box. The sharpest blade was a floral corset top that I wore for about five minutes before feeling too exposed. The dullest butter knife was an oversized, rust-colored sweater with a black lace trim across the collar.

To be safe or to be me.

Impulsively, I grabbed the corset top and a pair of jeans. I added my white boots and leather belt. My makeup was the bare minimum. I left my hair undone, bringing a clip inside my small, black purse.

It's time to be me again.

When I walked back out, I found Noah pacing. His face, lit by cellphone light, perked up. His green eyes went from sage to a rich emerald, and for the briefest moment, I was in awe with him again, the way I was on the night we first met.

Oh, holy green eyes.

His smile broke my concentration.

"Has Mikayla come out?" I asked, pulling on my boots to distract myself from his face.

"She just left."

"What?"

"Yeah. She told me to tell you that she'll meet us there with her other friends," he said with a nonchalant shrug. His gaze fell but his lips lifted. "I like the boots."

"Thanks," I said.

"You know, we don't have to go out if you don't want to. We could stay here."

Noah and me alone in the dorm together? I shivered.

"Mikayla would be bummed if we didn't show up," I replied lamely.

§

Tipsy Squeeze took their name literally. If there were bars in Alice's Wonderland, they'd look like this. The bar and tables were purposefully unleveled, sloping up and down like mountaintops. The stools had lemon slices painted on them. There was a mirror ceiling throughout the whole place, except for the bathrooms.

Past the door, we were met by music and the throng of bodies. A few steps in, and it became a challenge not to bump into anyone. The crowd was thicker than I expected after walking by on that first night.

"Hey," Noah said, leaning down to yell into my ear. Whiffs of orange from his cologne floated around me. "Mikayla's by the back wall. What do you want to drink?"

"Whatever you're drinking."

He ran his hand across the width of my back. Carefully, he nudged me forward, saying, "You got it."

"Yeah," I breathed, but I lingered, watching him walk away. Only Noah could simultaneously be so intense and casual.

I spotted Mikayla quickly. Monica and Lucia circled around her, looking like twins with their blonde hair and matching black dresses.

"Hey!" I said, popping my head between them. As soon as their speculative gazes landed on me, I knew that Noah and I were the subject of their conversation.

"Nice to meet you, Rain," Lucia chirped.

"I was just telling them that your *friend*, Noah, is tagging along tonight." Mikayla said the word 'friend' like it curled.

I stared at them without saying a word.

Monica caved first. "He sleeps over?"

I threw an I'm-going-to-kill-you look at Mikayla.

She waved my anger away. "Is it supposed to be a secret? You come and go with him all the time."

"She does *what* with him?" Lucia grinned, poking my side.

"It's not like that," I insisted, pushing her hand away.

"You're really just friends?" Monica asked.

"We're good friends. Nothing more," I said.

"Nothing less," a lower octave voice dropped in. A beer was placed in my empty hand. "I'm Noah."

"Hi!" Lucia beamed. "It's possible we were just discussing your comings and goings with Rain."

"Just the fact that you sleep together," Monica interjected.

"Not like that," Lucia rushed to reassure.

"Unless Rain is holding out on us," Monica interrupted.

"Or unless I asked her to keep *us*," Noah said, dipping his head in my direction, "between *us*, right?"

Monica's jaw fell open.

"You're not helping," I told him.

Under his breath, he said, "Who gives a fuck what I do with you? You don't complain."

His words turned me to putty.

Mikayla wrapped an arm around my neck and chimed her glass against my beer. "Enough of our analysis of the universe's plans. I'm taking Monica and Lucia to dance with me. Give you 'friends' some space." She whirled away, leading her posse of girls closer to the DJ booth.

Noah reoccupied the empty space. "So, which one does Mikayla have a crush on? Or is it both of them?"

"What?" I shrieked.

I stared at my roommate and her friends. They were dancing and spinning each other. Yet, as soon as my attention focused on them, subliminal clues revealed themselves. Lucia's bashful expression whenever Mikayla's hand lingered. The sway of Monica's hips against Mikayla's.

"How'd you catch that?" I asked, completely dumbfounded.

Noah took a victorious gulp of beer. "I'm an expert at reading the signs."

"Signs of what?"

An obnoxious smirk swept his face. "Attraction. Lust."

"Okay, okay!" I blurted out, wanting his words to stop. They were like a struck match to my own attraction. He had the potential to burn my tallest towers down.

"Don't be so shy, Rivas," he teased. Under the hue of a blacklight, his magnetic draw was ten times stronger.

"I need a shot," I declared, desperate to escape this one-sided tension. "Tequila."

His mouth quirked. "You drink, I drink."

One shot became two. Two beers became four. I danced without hesitation. Songs swished around. The night flew by with the uncanny knowledge that it would someday be a memory I would miss. My brain was swimming, and when I realized I couldn't understand the words he was saying, I wondered if I should sober up.

"Huh?"

Noah laughed. "Do you want to go outside?"

I was about to nod, but a song came on, "Pretty Please" by Dua Lipa. Suddenly, Mikayla was there, clutching my hand and dragging me to the dance floor.

"This is my *song*," she squealed. "I'd literally strip to this one."

When the chorus struck, lightning did too, because what was a made-up, drunk dance between us became a synchronized movement of hips, turns, and twirls. The song was sultry, lending itself to a flirtation I usually pushed away.

And then, guilt slammed into me.

He'd hate you right now.

Just like that, Rob appeared in my mind, like a curse I couldn't break free from. A chill hit my chest and shoulders. I dropped Mikayla's hand in the middle of a spin.

You love the attention.

You shouldn't be desperate for anyone else's eyes.

"What's wrong?" Mikayla yelled, her voice high above the music but low under the flashbacks.

"I'm tired," I lied.

"Well, energize up! We're dancing on a table."

"What? No!" I shrieked, but once she got a hold of me, she didn't let go. She pulled me up, ignoring my countless protests. Standing on top of the table, she grabbed my hands and placed them on her hips.

"No wallowing! Forget whatever you're thinking. He would've ruined tonight."

"How did you—" I began.

"I see it on your face, Raindrop."

How was I supposed to override my own brain?

"I'm going home."

"No!" she insisted. "We're having fun! Don't let him win."

Don't let him win. I cringed at the words.

"Besides, Noah is looking at you."

"I used to be fun. And happy," I sulked, intending for the words to be a hushed, perturbed thought, but the alcohol loosened my lips.

"Then dance with me. Be yourself!"

Here's hoping 'fake it till you make it' is real.

Mikayla still held her drink. Without asking, I stole the glass of red liquid, draining it in one gulp.

"I didn't taste a drop of alcohol," I said, laughing.

"Hooray!" she cheered, taking the empty glass and setting it aside. Smiling, I took her hand and began dancing.

The blur of alcohol was a fickle fog, obscuring and revealing my thoughts of Rob. One moment I was doing great, perfectly distracted by keeping my balance. The next, I was swaying on my feet, willing the drinks in my stomach to stay where they were and to let me exist without thoughts of him.

Singing to each other, we lowered ourselves with each guitar chord, then rolled our hips up. In a swift move, Mikayla turned me to face the crowd while she hung on the side, singing off-key to a group of strangers.

Eyes clung to the peaks and valleys of my body. A force inside me pushed me through another step, but I was terrified of being looked at. My joints tightened and my throat was closing. Frantically, my gaze swam, flying over people. Until...

Noah. He leaned against the bar, watching. His eyes, naturally hooded, deepened in the dim lightning. His gaze had lost its usual composure. The veil had dropped, and beneath—it was not platonic.

My heart reacted, beating unevenly. My throat dried under the heat of him looking at me.

I wanted his hands where his eyes looked. I hallucinated a fantasy, responding to his gaze as if he could touch me without being near me. When he looked at my neck, I brushed my fingers across it. When his eyes traveled down my chest, so did my hands. It was a game. Of what, I wasn't sure, but I knew I was winning when I saw his mouth drawl out the word, "Fuuuck."

Mikayla spun me again, twirling me back into reality. The song, losing its magic, faded. I hugged Mikayla and leapt down from the table before she could make me dance another set with her.

Noah stood right where I had last seen him. His smirk was indecipherable. I went to him, feeling my face turn red.

"Don't make fun of me," I pleaded.

He found my hand and tugged me closer. His lips tickled my ear. "I liked watching you. Let's go?"

I nodded, unable to speak.

He didn't let go of me while we meandered through the crowd. As we squeezed by a group, he rubbed his thumb against the back of my hand. The minute gesture created a frenzy in me.

We pushed outside through the doors. Without the loud music, I could hear how breathless I was. Even though the breeze cooled my skin, every inch of me felt hot. I couldn't tell if it was the drinks or Noah that was making me feel this way, but I didn't hate it. Honestly, it scared me how much I liked it.

I turned toward the patio with a smile on my face, remembering my first night here and how badly I had wanted to be a part of the throng. *And now*

I am. I looked across the people there and realized one of them was staring back at me from just a few feet away. His coal eyes, wide with surprise, were staring at me out of a face framed by dark, shaggy hair.

It was Rob. The real one.

A sudden jolt of fear sprang me into action. "Shit," I cursed, instantly panicking. "Noah, I have to go," I uttered.

"What the hell? I thought we were—"

His voice cut off because Rob was approaching us, eyes as piercing as daggers.

"What are you doing here?" Rob growled at me. His eyes were riveted on Noah.

"What am *I* doing here? What are *you* doing here?" I said, answering his question with one of my own.

Rob started to say something, then stopped, shaking his head in blatant disappointment. "Did I not mean anything to you? Was our whole relationship a joke?"

My stomach dropped. "Are you serious?"

"Who is he to you?" he demanded, pointing at Noah.

"He's a friend."

Rob looked at me with disgust. He looked at me like I had cheated on him. It was like tar being poured over me—I couldn't escape the grime.

"Guys like that don't have friends. He's the guy who called, right? The last night we slept together?" When I didn't have a response right away, he turned, shaking his head. "I can't believe I ever missed you."

He was already striding off. I saw his black van parked under a streetlight a few yards away. I moved to chase after him, but Noah was still holding my hand in a tight grip.

"Noah, I'm fine. Go," I begged, an ache slicing my throat. He stared at me, his brow furrowed. "Please."

Noah let go of my hand. I nodded my thanks and turned to run.

"Rob, wait! You have to stop. I don't want you to leave like this," I called as I chased after him. "I'm trying to have a life here," I said, gasping out tears, trying to keep up with him.

"Trust me, I can see that," Rob called over his shoulder.

"I'm not doing anything wrong! You're the one who keeps showing up unannounced, like a stalker, and all it takes for you to leave is for me to have a friend you don't like?"

We were at the van. He reached for the car door, and I grabbed his arm, because it was still a natural response for me to reach out to him.

Rob wrestled with the door and his words. "You're really delusional, you know that? We're broken up. Do whomever you want."

Something inside me cracked. Anger and adrenaline filled the empty fissure.

"I am not this slut you make me out to be! We could've been happy if you didn't always feel the need to suffocate me! I couldn't breathe. You were too much. Why couldn't you just trust me? You thought I couldn't be friends with someone who has a dick without wanting it!"

"Now you can have as many friends and as many dicks as you want," he said.

He pulled on the door harder, not caring that I was hanging onto his arm. I threw bottled-up emotions into the air, and they burst like fireworks.

"Fuck you, Rob. I don't deserve to be treated like this, but you keep doing it over and over again."

In the heat of the moment, he yanked open the door, pulling it open and knocking me off it. My knees clashed against the concrete. My hands caught myself too late. My shoulder slammed into the ground. My hair settled around me like a veil.

And Rob did nothing.

My heart finally heard what my head had been trying to tell it for months.

"We're done. Don't come near me again, you goddamn asshole!" I yelled, gathering myself. I stepped forward, wanting to hurt him back, but something wrapped itself around my waist—Noah's arms.

My fists pummeled the door. "I hate you!" I sobbed, destroying and repairing my heart a thousand times over.

Rob revved the engine and lowered the window. "You can have her," he said to Noah. "Good fucking luck."

11

My anger dissolved into the tears on my face. The heartbreak was finally silenced. The shock of what had happened put everything else on hold. In a trance, I watched Rob's van drive off.

"I'll kill him," Noah muttered.

Noah's arm was still wrapped around me. As if hypnotized, I said, "He didn't touch me."

"No. He just let the skin tear off your knees," he snapped. "You're bleeding."

"I can walk back by myself."

"I'm not leaving you, alright?" His voice became gentle, as if slowly coaxing consciousness back into body. I nodded, straightening my spine.

We walked in uncomfortable silence. Noah kept an arm around my shoulder. I didn't know what to say. I hardly knew what to think. I would've felt ashamed if I felt anything. It would've meant I still cared.

When we made it to my dorm, Noah grabbed the keys, unlocking the door for me.

"Do you have any band-aids?" he asked, nodding to the bathroom.

"They're in my room," I replied as I walked inside. "Come on."

Even after everything that had happened, I found myself remembering how tempting the thought had been of doing more than just sleep with Noah tonight. I looked away as a blush took over my face.

"Band-aids," I said, pointing to the closet. "They're over there in the blue box."

I crawled onto the beanbag chair, feeling sick. I drank a whole water bottle. The fight had sobered me up, but I drank the water anyway, figuring it could help avoid a hangover. Noah crouched in front of me, carefully applying Neosporin and Scooby Doo band-aids to my knees, his curls trailing down across his forehead.

Aunt Rosen, I thought to myself, *how can such a gentle man and such an angry one exist in the same universe?*

He stole a glance at me. I tried to guard my expression, because I knew my emotions were printed plain as day across my face.

"Are you over him?" he asked.

"It's been over for a while now," I sighed.

"That's not what I asked. If you're thinking about getting back with him, Rain—"

"Why would you even think that?"

He frowned. "You cried over him. Tonight."

"It's not because I want him back. I'm not even sure it's because I miss him."

"Then what are the tears for?"

I didn't know how to make him understand, so I stretched up toward my desk, wincing from the scrapes on my palm, to grab my favorite book— *The Prophet*, by Kahlil Gibran. It was easy to find the right page and the line I had underlined again and again on it.

"'To know the pain of too much tenderness,'" I read to him. "'To be wounded by your own understanding of love; / And to bleed willingly and joyfully.'" He was waiting for an explanation, so I gave it to him. "Despite the red flags—the rules, the possessiveness, the temper—my gut instinct was to love him," I continued. "Isn't that sad? I'm not delusional. I'm just a hopeless romantic. Or a hopeful one."

He waited for me to say something more. When I didn't, he asked, "Why do I feel like you reading this… is the closest I've gotten to you?"

I couldn't return his gaze. The incident with Rob had cracked me open. Speaking to Noah like this, with so much vulnerability, was me bleeding out. I didn't necessarily want to be this open, but I couldn't stop it.

I flipped to another page and continued reading. "'Yea, the guilty is oftentimes the victim of the injured, / And still more often the condemned is the burden bearer for the guiltless and unblamed.'"

"Has he ever hurt you?" he asked.

"Never physically," I said.

"Has love always wounded you?"

"Yes. No. I don't know, Noah. To love is to let go."

"What if I want to hold onto you?"

I had been certain that Noah couldn't make my heart race. But here we were, the promise of either disaster or paradise. I didn't know how to like anyone without falling headfirst. I had loved too much. He had never loved.

"Noah," I breathed. "Maybe you shouldn't."

"I want to," he insisted. He moved closer. Our chests touched. I wasn't sure what we were doing anymore, but it was out of my hands and into his. "Be honest, Rain—is this one-sided?"

"I've been trying not to think about us," I said.

"But you do think about me like that."

Reluctantly, I nodded.

"I think about you more than I want to admit," he confessed.

Then he kissed me.

Our lips only broke apart to fall deeper together. His mouth, reckless in the words he had said, kissed me with a slow intensity. He leaned in, running his tongue between my lips. My fingers stretched across his stomach. His breath shuddered, blowing warm air against my mouth. My stomach flipped. My legs tightened.

Finally, he twisted, parting, but still holding my face. "We're not done talking, Rivas."

I expelled a laugh. "You're kidding."

"You drank."

"I'm not drunk."

"I don't give a shit."

I removed my hand awkwardly and angled my body away from his. *So, he doesn't want this?* I hadn't thought about him this way until he said something, and now, there was a gaping hole through my chest because he had stopped kissing me.

I forced myself to look at him. Unspoken words pricked me like thorns.

"What?" he asked, snaking his arm around my waist. Like a hook, he reeled me in. My body molded to his perfectly. His large hands ran up my arms. "It doesn't mean I don't want you."

The butterflies in my stomach swarmed like wasps. "You kissed me," I briefly recounted.

"Who wouldn't kill to kiss you?" His voice was low, like a cello, and the sound vibrated around me.

"You're not stupid, Colt. You read girls as quickly as I read books. You work in a tattoo shop. You're a great artist. You buy me coffee and tease me about what I drink. We like the same music. You look like *that!*" I said, exasperated and mortified.

Noah laughed, bringing his bottom lip between his teeth. "I look like what, Rivas?"

Noah was the epitome of male attractiveness. He was impatient and childish. He could be friends with everyone in the room but would keep returning to you. He made you feel special like that. His honesty was brutal and intentional. His moss-colored eyes were addictive, and I had no idea why they wanted to gaze into mine.

His smirk baited me to continue. The challenge in his face was more intoxicating than the drinks at the bar. I didn't want to hold back and become another stranger in my own skin, but telling him I wanted him? I didn't have confidence like that.

Be bold, Rain. Be the you that's still in there.

"You look like a Calvin Klein model!"

It was out there now. I couldn't shake this unsteady feeling. It was like stepping off a ledge blindfolded. I prayed for water to land in, but hitting the ground and not feeling a thing was a decent plan B.

His gaze dropped to my lips. "Do you know what you look like?"

I inhaled deeply. "Tell me."

"You look like someone I've been desperate to draw. You're beautiful, Rain, and it's insane you don't see it."

My heart drummed as rapidly as a hummingbird's wings against my ribcage.

He held my face. "You don't know how long I've been wanting to do this."

I leaned into his hand, feeling vibrations through his fingertips. He was tempting. Comforting. A paradoxical touch I wanted everywhere.

"You win the compliment contest," I said finally.

A laugh bounced off his lips. "You're different with me," he said, his tone somewhere between a question and a statement.

"So are you," I replied.

Noah outlined my lips with his thumb. I watched him study my face, fraction by fraction. He smiled when I brought my index finger to the scar on his eyebrow.

"What happened?"

"Baseball to the head when I was in little league."

We stared at each other and broke out laughing.

"You should say you were in a fight," I teased.

I was in the middle of laughing when he grabbed my hand, inspecting my ring finger.

"What do these mean?" he asked, his grip centering around the middle of my finger where I had two lines tattooed.

"Honestly? I thought they'd look nice if I ever got married. Or if I didn't," I explained, shrugging.

He nodded. "What do the others mean?"

I looked down at my covered body, remembering what I had where. "The book and quote are self-explanatory. The moon was Rosen's idea. She was supposed to get one also. The flame was clearly to show off how tough I am."

"Yeah. Once I saw that, I knew not to mess with you," he smirked.

I wiggled out of his grasp, sitting cross legged in front of him. Before I could ask it, he answered my next question.

"I have my mom's hands tattooed on my back," he said, taking off his shirt and twisting to show me. Up close, the work was detailed and hauntingly beautiful. "The rose on my shoulder is because there were always flowers on our dining room table." He stretched, showing his side. "Waves because... nothing. The star..." He continued the tour to the other half of his torso. "Eh, I was eighteen." He faced me. "You already know about the cross-eyed face on my leg commemorating Travis' apprenticeship."

His body was taut. Lean. On display. He didn't care. He kept an unperturbed expression.

My nerves betrayed me through my shaky breath. I wanted him, but my feelings for him were smeared in guilt. It had been only a few weeks since Rob and I had slept together. What would Noah think? Would I be the girl who moved on too fast?

"I don't know what this makes us," I murmured.

"Do you need an answer?" he asked, gently drawing circles on my leg.

My gaze lowered.

"I want easy," he said.

I had never tried easy, but I knew I wanted something different.

"I'm not sure I'm what you're used to," I admitted.

"This could be fun," he persisted.

I sighed heavily, looking at him. Noah held possibilities in his green eyes. Maybe it wouldn't be love, but I could be happy to feel a carefree touch instead of a suffocating chokehold. Noah, despite walking through the minefields of my past, wanted to be here, and I liked being wanted.

Aunt Rosen, love and happiness aren't dependent on each other, right?

I didn't know if I'd regret this later, but I decided to ignore the red flags ahead. We were good as friends. We could also be more.

"As long as we don't end," I said.

Noah's brows scrunched in confusion. "What?"

"We can't end what doesn't start, right? I don't want to lose you if we don't work out."

"You won't," he promised. "We aren't together unless we choose to be. It's as easy and simple as that. No pressure. No strings."

"No strings," I repeated.

He planted a kiss on my lips. "We should sleep."

"Like I'll be able to now," I muttered.

His eyes widened in amusement. "Because of me? You're already that into me? Hell, Rain, I haven't even fucked you."

My lips parted. "You are… impossible."

God, his grin was annoying. He loved the affect he had on me.

I shut my eyes.

"Can I hold you?" he asked. It was the uncharacteristic softness of his voice that made me open my eyes again and look at him. "I'll sleep better," he continued. "Sometimes, I feel like I'm drifting into space, like I'm about to disappear."

The casual cadence in his voice slowed and ebbed into an enchanting intensity.

"Are you always this honest?" I asked.

He blinked up at the ceiling. "Why not? You've been honest with me."

"I miss being held," I admitted, turning over and scooting into his chest.

He rested his hand on my hip, curling his thumb across me. "Your skin is so soft."

My stomach tightened when his arm blanketed me.

"If I'm your anchor, you're my gust of wind," I mumbled, then immediately felt stupid. "I don't know why I said that. I mean, you said you felt like you were drifting."

His breath brushed my shoulder. "You speak beauty with your words. Bless me with them whenever you want, Rivas."

I smiled in the dark. "I bet you could also. You see nature in everything, just like the poets."

"Mmmm. If I'm your peace, you're my chaos."

I turned my head, completely taken aback.

He grinned widely. "Don't worry. I meant it as a good thing."

I relaxed in his embrace and let his words grow a garden of happy feelings in my heart.

"You just have to be good at everything, don't you, Colt?"

"Rematch tomorrow."

12

A cacophony of telephone rings and feet hitting the floor stole my sleep from me. The sheets were still warm. They reminded me of the night before and its blissful, unexpected end.

Noah was stumbling around the room like a zombie. I sat up, feeling for his phone.

"It's over here," I mumbled, waving it in the air.

Without looking at me, Noah grabbed it and silenced it. "Thanks. Sorry, it's Dawn."

"Oh, right. It's Sunday."

"Yeah," he groused, collecting his clothes from around the room.

I studied him. His shoulders—his whole back—were tense. His movements were jagged and unlike him.

When I was kid, I'd had days that simply started *heavy*. I'd open my eyes and already want the day to be over because I lacked the energy of keeping it together. On the days I told Aunt Rosen how I was feeling, we'd skip the day. She'd pull me out of school and help me paint lies so white that my mom would let me stay home.

I had a sudden, childish thought. On a whim, I went for it. "Hey, do you want to—"

I hesitated.

"What?" he snapped.

Instinctively, I jerked backwards. I retraced my steps in my head, wondering what I had done wrong. I'd done nothing but find his phone. Unless last night had already become a regret for him? I shivered and wrapped my arms around myself.

He sighed, rubbing his forehead. "What were you going to say?"

"Are you mad at me?"

His face smoothed, devoid of emotion. "No. Why would I be?"

"You just seem it."

His expression slackened until the Noah I knew was smirking at me. "Good thing I'm not. Going to Dawn's feels like a chore today, alright?"

"Alright," I said.

But I wasn't alright. Not really. After last night, my emotions were like exposed nerve endings at his mercy to either stimulate or destroy. I was emotionally polarized, with no middle ground to stabilize myself.

Stop freaking out over nothing, Rain. He said he's not mad. He's. Not. Mad.

I crawled over and climbed down from my bed. "I'll walk you out."

My feet hit the ground and wouldn't move further. I didn't want him to go. Not like this. He said he wasn't mad, but something was off, and I felt the urge to keep him right here until I was sure he was fine.

His hand touched the small of my back. The slight protectiveness in his touch sent a wave of calm over me. I reached for his hand, plucking his fingers like they were guitar strings.

"Noah? Do you want to skip the day with me?"

"Skip the day?" His lips twitched into a smile. "No one's asked me that before."

"You woke up in a bad mood. I'm starving and I hate eating alone. Besides, I heard getting lost in someone is the best way to forget about yourself."

"Who said that?"

"Me."

For years, I had run away by running into someone. I just had never been honest about it before.

"Is it really that simple?"

I slid my hands up his arms. His skin called to mine, coaxing my touch to stay where my excitement bloomed.

"With me, yes."

He pressed his forehead against mine. "No talking about anything serious," he bartered.

"Of course. That's rule number one of skipping the day."

"What's rule number two?"

"What do you want it to be?"

His laugh tickled my nose. "What usually happens when you do this?"

I smiled, flooded with memories. "I haven't done this since my aunt got me out of school for a fake doctor's appointment. We'd eat junk food. She'd watch TV. I'd read."

He thought about it for a second. I held my breath.

"Have any alcohol left over from your night with Mikayla?"

I tilted my head at him. "It's barely nine."

He crouched down to my height, grinning. "It's adult junk food."

I bit the inside of my cheek.

"We have nothing to do, Rivas. This was your idea."

"There's vodka in the back of my fridge," I confessed.

He kissed the side of my mouth. "Troublemaker. What would your RA say?"

I shook my head, checking my phone before we wasted the day finding the bottom of a bottle.

My mom's name ruined my phone's background picture.

"My mom called," I gaped.

Noah twisted off the bottle cap and chugged for three seconds. "Ugh," he groaned, fighting against the harsh taste. He collapsed on the beanbag chair, holding up the bottle. "That's one way to wake up. Your turn."

I stared at my phone, wondering why she'd randomly call. We operated strictly by text, or we gave each other a heads up before calling. Via text.

"Are you going to call her back?"

"No," I decided. I sent her a text, nothing more.

It was enough to make me need a drink. I tried to copy Noah's long gulp. It was a spectacular failure. Noah tried to conceal his laughter while I coughed hysterically.

"God, Colt."

"You're too soft." He swigged again, winning the unofficial drinking. I didn't know how he could handle it. My throat was still burning with pain.

"I'm going to get ready for the day," I said, grabbing a pair of leggings and a sweatshirt. "Then, we can go get food."

"Why are you going to change?"

"I'm not walking around in my pajamas."

"That's not far off from what you're already in," he pointed out.

"It's an improvement," I replied tersely.

My mom was weirdly strict about clothes. Perhaps it was just instilled in our culture to dress up for things, but I couldn't stand the thought of staying in the same clothes.

"If I stayed in my pajamas, I'd want to be lazy."

He cocked a brow. "So, we're going to productively skip the day?"

"Well," I began, putting my tongue between the gate of my teeth. "Like I said, I'm hungry, and you're going to need food at some point."

"Fine."

I was almost out of the room when I paused at the doorway, looking back at him. Unfairly confident, he stared back, always ready to challenge me.

"I like you in those things," he said, his eyes traveling over me.

"Leggings?"

"They hug you good."

I narrowed my gaze. "You're trying to mess with me."

"No. I'm being direct."

Desire pulsed through me. Last night was amazing. My journal was going to hear about it for entries to come. My tensions loosened whenever we touched, while the rest of me heightened. Between the sheets, in the breaths between us, in the middle of the night, I did the same to him, and I wasn't sure I'd ever get over it.

I shivered. "Ignoring you," I sung, leaving him.

In the bathroom, I saw that his toothbrush was next to mine. He had left it after coming back last night, and I couldn't deny how much I liked it being there.

When I came back, Noah and I curled up on the beanbag chair, squishing together to fit. We took turns sipping on vodka from my favorite mug, which was shaped like a beehive. I told him about my childhood obsession with the insect after finding out that they died after using their stinger.

"They couldn't all be suicidal," I said, and his laugh got lost somewhere in the curve of my neck.

We talked for hours, trading anecdotes from our childhoods. While I had obsessed over bees, Noah had been the kid hunched over a sketchpad.

After some begging, he let me flip through his drawings. With each turned page, I found myself deeper in awe of the whimsical edge he saw in everything.

"I just draw what's in front of me," he explained.

"With a twist," I replied, smiling at the sight of a boat sailing in a glass of water.

He ran his hand under my shirt, tapping his fingers against my hip. I tried to ignore what his touch did to me.

"No faces?" I asked after skimming through several versions of his truck, with branches for wheels and flowers instead of rust stains.

"I like to practice with easy subjects, but there are a few."

I slid the sketchpad back onto his lap. "Show me."

He took us to the bottom of the stack, where fragments of eyes, noses, and lips were scattered across the pages.

"Everyone shows emotion differently. I like figuring out the small giveaways. Sometimes watery eyes look rounder. Sometimes, thinner. It's a puzzle."

"That's why it feels like you're studying me when you look at me. Because you are." His gaze had always felt so intense.

"Maybe."

I stared down at a picture of Ana with sunflowers for freckles. "I love this one. I can't believe this is what's in your head. Do you have more?"

"Later," he promised, placing the sketchpad on the floor.

Our sips of vodka had gotten smaller. He took the mug from my hands. "What to hear some poetry?" he asked.

"A rematch already?"

His smirk was my only answer.

I straightened my posture. "Okay, let's hear it. Woo me."

"Your eyes, when they're watery… it looks like they have a radiant cut to them. Like they're diamonds."

I made a face. "So, you like it when I cry?"

His lips quirked. "I like it when you laugh. Whenever you're really laughing, your eyes water almost immediately." The liquor made him more honest and careless. "When you cry, I hate the world a little more."

Time suspended when he looked at me this way—with appreciation, like he'd be perfectly content staying here, becoming a statue, with his thumb brushing across my jaw.

I crawled over him and retrieved the mug, needing to wash away what I was thinking.

"What? I can't say things like that to you?"

"You didn't use to."

He pushed my hair back. His palms rested against my neck. "So? I thought you were beautiful the moment I saw you. I'm just explaining why."

I pulled out my phone, deflecting. "I'm ordering food."

"The sting of you is worth the honey?"

I turned, eyebrows raised and smile blossoming. "That was awful!"

He feigned a shot to the chest. "Hey, I tried."

"Don't," I laughed. "Should we order delivery or pick up?"

"Delivery. Let's stay here."

"Okay."

The world took its time turning on its axis. I chose the music we listened to, taking requests periodically. He sketched while I wrote. Between the songs and scratches of paper, I had never felt so at peace doing nothing with someone else.

The pizza arrived in the middle of my rambling prose and his sketches of bees trading their wings for open books.

We ate, exchanging glances with every other bite. We were too buzzed to talk, but once the bread soaked up most of the liquor, I asked, "Is Dawn going to be mad?"

"Yep."

"Then you didn't spend the day with me, okay?"

"Fair enough. I'll blame it on Travis."

I shook my head. "Poor guy."

"What's next?"

"Sleep? I don't usually drink as soon as I wake up. Ugh, and I need to brush my teeth."

"Let me go with you. You make me feel like a slob."

"You said it, not me," I teased under my breath.

He tickled my sides as we walked down the hallway.

In the tiny bathroom, Noah towered over me. We looked at each other through our reflections. Hyperaware of one another, we stood together closely. I bent over to spit out the toothpaste and felt him shift forward against me from behind. I straightened, leaning my head against his chest. He brought his hand up to my waist. My lips parted. His gaze darkened with need. Crescent moon impressions from his fingernails stamped my skin. The air thickened. The clothes we were wearing seemed to conduct electricity.

I let out a rushed breath and left the bathroom quickly. He trailed behind me without saying a word.

Back inside my room, I climbed up my bed. He drained the last sip of vodka before following.

"You haven't had enough?" I asked.

He grinned, making his way towards me. "Of you? No."

I scooted over, giving him space, but he shook his head. Before I could say anything, he rolled on top of me, eclipsing my body with his. His chin tickled my collarbone. I slapped his chest, laughing and coughing out the words, "Colt! Stop!"

With a wicked grin growing on his face, he pushed his hands under my sweatshirt. I twisted until his weight pinned me completely.

"Noah Colt, this isn't fair!" I huffed. "Please."

"Fine," he whined, freezing in place, his hands still on my skin.

Awareness sank in. His body rested between my legs. His eyes bore into mine, seeking permission. I shifted my legs wider and felt him hard against me. His fingertips, like blades of grass, passed over me, bending to my curves. When they reached my chest, my back arched to him.

"Noah," I breathed, fear creeping in. "Don't."

"Shit, I'm sorry," he whispered, untangling himself from me and sitting up.

I placed my hand on his shoulder. "No, that's not— I mean, I like this, but— Noah, I'm being the responsible one today. Like you were yesterday. I don't want you to do something you'll regret just because you're drunk."

He barked out a laugh. "I'm nowhere near drunk, Rivas. You made me drink a boatload of water and eat half the pizza."

"I simply said you *could* eat half. Each slice was of your own volition."

Electricity buzzed between us. Were we dancing around basic want and need? Was it a powerplay, each of us hoping the other would be the first to cross already blurred lines?

My heartbeat raced. *He knows how to say no if this isn't what he wants...*

I dragged my nails down his arms, then pressed back into the pillow, making him chase me. He inched forward, pressing his mouth over mine. My hips filled his hands. My breath came out in tantalizing pants. He ran his fingers through my hair, and moans hummed from my throat.

I stopped kissing him in a quick and hurried exhale. I turned on my side. He adjusted his arm so I could lie on it. He dug his thumb under my pants, running along the string of my underwear, then hesitated. A second passed. I jutted out my hips.

"How the hell do you feel like this?" he groaned, giving in and pulling me to him.

Our bodies collided right as my tongue got lost between his teeth.

There was no way he couldn't feel my warmth seep through my clothes just like the sensation of him was inevitable.

I ran a finger along his waistband, partially following his lead, mostly losing myself in the moment.

We held each other by the reins out of our clothes.

He backed away.

"What?" I asked.

He glanced at the small space between us. "I don't think I can handle not touching you."

"Then, don't."

"What if I touch you and don't want to stop?" he murmured on my lips. My whole body flared up in goosebumps. He lowered and kissed my neck. "Would you let me have you whenever I wanted?"

I grabbed his face. "You can't say things like that."

"I think you like it when I say those things."

"Maybe," I whispered. I couldn't meet his eyes.

"Maybe? I need to know. How else am I going to figure out what you like?"

Rob had never bothered to ask what I liked. He had always simply assumed he was doing everything right. I was caught off-guard to have someone be this open and straightforward.

I could get used to this…

He leaned in to kiss me, pressing the words upon my lips. "You have to tell me if you change your mind and want to stop, okay?"

I nodded.

"Whenever," he emphasized.

"I want this," I reassured him.

He touched the lace of my bralette. Slowly, he peeled away the fabric, and I ran my fingers over my skin before he did. He stopped and looked at me the way he looked at classical paintings, like the chiaroscuro pieces he adored.

"Fuck," he swore under his breath.

My body was his canvas, and his lips were paintbrushes. He kissed me everywhere but my mouth. With his teeth, he yanked down a bra strap. I shivered, running my hands through his curls. His tongue drew a jagged line across my breasts.

"You're perfect," he exhaled harshly, and threw his shirt off over his head.

"Noah," I breathed, squirming and lifting my hips. The movement created ripples of friction.

"Don't tease me, Rain."

Tease him? I was a second away from begging for it.

"Kiss me," I demanded, but I needed more than just that to satisfy my ache. Smirking, he shook his head and helped me out of my pants.

In the silence, my nervousness doubled. I suddenly remembered I had put on a matching set of bra and panties. Riddled with anxiety, I gnawed the inside of my cheek as the past came back to haunt me.

Rob had never allowed me to wear revealing clothes, not wanting me to put what was his on display. But, even in our private moments, I was scrutinized.

Why do you care about what you wear? None of this matters to me when you're going to end up naked anyways. Are you thinking of me when you put this on, or other men?

I felt my skin burn under Noah's gaze. What must he think of me for wearing matching intimates? He probably thought I had lured him here just for sex.

I wrapped my arms around myself, shielding what I could.

"Stop," he said, pulling my arms away, as he had done at the coffee shop. "I want to look at you."

Pinned under his words and his hands, I looked up, silently searching his face for a hint of mockery or judgment.

There was none, because he wasn't Rob. He was nothing like him, and it was freeing.

I found his hand and guided it down. "Please."

"Let me take my time," he murmured, moving lower.

His touch ran over my hips, tortuously drawing out my need for him. The tension built, clawing its way up. My breathing became shallow. His hand finally found the thin fabric of my underwear. He pressed against it, reveling in the dampness.

"I want you," he growled, feeling the double-edged sword of his own teasing. "You're fucking beautiful, and the sounds you make…" He rubbed against me. My vision blurred. He pressed in a finger, and I expelled a moan, rolling my head to the side. "I want to hear you say my name just like that, alright?"

We had barely started, and I was a second away from losing control.

"Noah…"

"A little more desperate, Rain," he said, arrogance dripping from his tone. He kept pushing in and out. Kisses gilded my thighs. His tongue burnished the touch.

"Noah," I gasped.

He went rigid. "Fuck. Just like that."

A laugh tumbled out of me. "I'm not doing it for you. You feel that good."

"I'll make you feel even better."

Before I could say anything else, he moved my underwear to the side. I groaned as his tongue flicked up and down across me. My shoulders pressed into the pillow. My hips rocked against his grip. Effortlessly, he made a complete mess out of me.

He paused for a moment and looked up, and I whimpered at the loss of contact.

"I want to feel you pulse against my tongue, baby," he said.

"Don't stop," I begged, tangling my fingers in his hair. Whatever shyness I had felt in the beginning had dissipated.

"Don't hold back," he ordered. "I want you all over my face."

"Noah, if you keep talking like that—"

"I'll get what I want, won't I?"

He quickened his movements. I practically panted as his fingers took over.

"Baby?"

His voice was going to push me past the edge. When I didn't answer, he placed his tongue flat and started curling into me like that.

"Noah. I'm going to—"

"Good, baby," he groaned, fingering me as his mouth moved in tandem. "Do it."

Stars burst behind my closed eyelids. A shudder rolled out of my chest. He kept lapping me with his tongue and pressing into me until my hands released the bundle of sheets knotted around them.

He gently kissed my thighs once more, then came back up to me. I watched as he licked his fingers.

"You're incredible," he said.

Breathless, I ran a hand over my face. "That was—"

"—Perfect," he replied, with a smirk full of rotten pride and perverse affection.

I wrapped my legs around him, stupidly happy.

"Stop that or I'm never leaving this bed again."

I gave a lazy smile. "I'd be okay with that."

He nuzzled into my neck, inhaling deeply. "I want to feel you this close all the time. Kiss me, baby."

I traced the muscles on his abdomen as he brought our mouths together. He shivered, breaking away.

I bit my lip, knowing what should happen next. Reciprocation was only fair. I fidgeted with his waistband.

"I need to return the favor," I said as my hand dipped past his boxers.

He stopped me by grabbing my shoulders. "What?"

"I have to do something for you," I clarified, hoping to salvage what had been wrecked, but the demolition worsened. The disgusted look on his face was a wrecking ball, crushing me swiftly.

"You have to 'return the favor?'" he scoffed.

I sat up, wondering if I'd been blown to bits, because that's how it felt to be on the receiving end of a tone devoid of sensitivity.

"I don't understand," I whispered. "You don't want me to?"

"Do you know how fucked up you sound?" he asked.

I crossed my legs in front of my chest, suddenly embarrassed by my nakedness. "I didn't know how it sounded, okay? I'm sorry."

He sat up. "This was a bad idea."

Fear began to settle in. "I— I don't— I thought you— isn't it what everyone wants? Noah, I'm sorry if…" I trailed off, spewing excuses. "You did for me, so I just thought— I'm sorry I upset you."

"Stop!" he yelled. "What the hell, Rain? You don't have to suck my dick because I ate you out." Our gazes clashed like cymbals in a quiet room. For the first time, his eyes were clamorous, and I couldn't handle it. "I didn't do that hoping you would return the favor. I was fine just getting you off. Fucking thrilled until now."

"It's—" I swallowed roughly but couldn't continue.

He waited. "It's what?"

My mind went quiet. Even a whisper of what I was thinking was going to damn this moment to hell.

"Tell me," he demanded.

"It's not important."

"It's fucking crucial. Tell me."

"I had to return the favor. Always. He wouldn't if I didn't."

"Wait. What?"

"If he did it to me, I had to do it to him. If not, I'd be in trouble. There was no—" I paused, avoiding his gaze. "—no sex without it."

From the corner of my eye, I could see him grinding his teeth as he clenched his jaw. I didn't want to know what was going on in his head.

"I'm going to murder him," he said.

It wasn't what I expected. Without thinking, I took his hand. "It's not all his fault. Any cage he put me in didn't have a lock. I said it was okay. I thought it was."

His rage had morphed into something else, something sad. He cupped my face. "Baby, he shouldn't have wanted to put you in a cage."

I nodded against his hand.

"I don't want to think about things being like that for you," he said.

Slowly, I brought my eyes back to level with his. A beam of sunlight came from the window, catching one green eye in light and leaving the other in darkness.

"I shouldn't have said anything," I said.

"I'm glad you did. I would've have hated if you thought that's how it should be."

I faked a smile.

"Here's the way it works," he said, picking me up and putting me on his lap. "If you want to, then do it. If you never want to, I'm happy with that. I'm not going to live by that rule with you."

I looked away. "You must think I'm a trainwreck."

"I'll keep that rule to you, though," he said, as if I hadn't spoken. "I don't think I'll ever fuck you without going down on you first."

I curled into his neck. "How can you be so sweet and have such a foul mouth at the same time?"

"It's my specialty," he grinned, peppering my shoulder with kisses.

Knocking at the door interrupted us.

"Are you expecting anyone?" he asked.

"No, but I should check. It might be Lucia or Monica."

"Wait here," he said, hopping off the bed. I couldn't help gawking at him as he grabbed his shirt. His body was sculpted, and his tattoos were tantalizing accents.

He caught me staring and smirked.

"I hadn't really seen your tattoos. Not in the daylight anyways," I explained awkwardly. "You're so out of my league."

"Baby, I'm lucky you even glanced at me. I'll be back."

I dressed, feeling weightless. Everything with Rob seemed so muddled now. The way Noah reacted, how hurt he was by how things had been for me—it solidified what I suspected, what Mikayla had been trying to tell me. Our relationship hadn't been healthy. Neither was our sex life. I wasn't sure what to call it. 'Assault' sounded harsh, but 'normal' sounded even worse. True to form, Rob and I had danced in gray areas of what was good and what wasn't.

All I knew now was that this thing I had with Noah felt better. It felt safer. It felt good.

I heard the door to the dorm open, then Noah's voice. "Dawn. What the fuck are you doing here?"

Oh, shit.

I darted out of the room.

Dawn stood there, looking strung out. Her stone white hair spilled out of her bun. A squiggly vein in her forehead was as pronounced as the twitch in her eye. She punched Noah in the ribs.

"The hell!"

She hit him again. "What's wrong with your phone, huh? It must be broken to pieces for you to ignore me for hours. *Hours!*"

"Hey, bring it down a notch," he said. "Look, I'm sorry, we were studying, so I turned it off, and—"

"And what? The last time someone didn't answer their phone in this family—"

"Dawn, I get it. I don't even know what time it is."

"It's five, you idiot. You were supposed to be at my place at ten," she lectured, though her fiery glare weakened. "Ten!"

"I'm fine, okay? I'm sorry. I should've called. How did you know where I was?"

Dawn rolled her eyes, then focused them on me.

"Travis said you might be here with her."

"Is everything okay?" I asked.

"Yeah, I'm just a big fuck up who forgot his sister has issues with phone calls," Noah said.

"Seriously?" Dawn growled.

He shrugged. "Well, you do."

I glanced back and forth between them.

"You need to call or text before you take a break from the world," Dawn lectured.

"Okay, fine. Can we drop it now?"

Her exhale hissed between her teeth. "Oh, I'm not done. Get your shit. You owe me dinner since you bailed on breakfast."

"Dawn, if you think—"

"Noah, it's okay," I said, jumping in. "We just finished... studying, anyways. I'll see you tomorrow."

"I don't have to go," he told me despite Dawn's glare.

I smiled a little. "I have a paper to write. No worries."

He squeezed my wrist, and I noticed how his index finger and thumb met. Whatever sexual tension from before had died, but seeing his fingers make a ring around my arm—it did things to me. Things he somehow read on my face because his lips twitched. I pulled away.

"I'll call you," he said to me, then turned to Dawn. "You can be a real bitch, you know that?"

"Yeah, and you're not worth the headache," she said to him as they walked down the hall.

§

"Your sister hates me," I told Noah on Wednesday afternoon.

We were the last two at the shop again. It was day three of Dawn's silent treatment. In the middle of sanitizing his workstation, Noah threw me a dismissive smirk.

"She doesn't," he obtusely remarked. He was convinced it was all in my head.

As I packed my laptop in my bag, my eyes were drawn to my phone by a notification, like a flare in a moonless sky. Plastered to the screen was the profile image of a person I should've blocked. *Oh, no.* I clicked it and saw the three dots bubbling under Rob's icon.

Rain.

Can we talk?

The words singed my hands like coals from a forgotten fire.

"Rivas?"

My phone hit the counter, bounced like a rock. Quickly, I stuffed it in my bag, not even checking to see if I had cracked the screen.

"Y-yes?" I said, my voice struck with nerves.

Noah squinted his eyes at me in a childish guise. "What are you thinking about?"

I laughed, paranoid. "Nothing."

I couldn't tell him about Rob.

Rain. Can we talk?

Could we? Should we?

"Liar," Noah probed, painfully oblivious.

"I'm thinking about Dawn," I lied, finding my footing. "Lately, I get icy frostbityness from her, and I don't think you and I being whatever we are is helping."

Noah, easily amused, laughed. "Frostbityness? You're really earning that English degree."

I tossed a roll of paper towels at him. "It's with an emphasis on creative writing," I argued lamely. "Don't you see how weird she's being?"

The shop became intimate and eerie when Noah turned off the light. Almost nostalgically, I memorized the way his devilish smile widened the closer he came to me. I tried to capture the warm feeling of his arm going over my shoulder and the zesty, clean whiffs of his citrus cologne. My arm curled around his waist naturally. It was simply how we walked—arms comfortably around one another, with veiled hints of intimacy.

I wished I could preserve us and press us into a book, like a flower. We were fleeting, and I felt myself grasping at the petals. I leaned into Noah's chest. His heartbeat had become the steadiest rhythm of my life.

Rob's message was a threat to whatever we were, and I didn't know what to do. Rob and I had shared a relationship. But Noah and I were happening *now*.

But what Noah and I were building wasn't real. We were running away to each other. Pledged to nothing more than the corner of a small dorm room, no one knew about our growing catalogue of inside jokes, the beehive mug out of which we shared drinks, or our favorite sleeping positions. No one knew about the things we did when we played around in the gray area of our friendship.

Our bedroom experiences had been a strictly "him to me" ratio. It wasn't that I didn't want to do anything for him, but our conversation on Sunday had complicated things. I had panicked and hadn't gone past his waistline. I wasn't angry or upset, but I was hopelessly embarrassed. I hated learning from Noah that, at twenty-one years old, I still didn't know what healthy sex was.

Rob's way of thinking still made sense to me. If he went down on me, shouldn't I return the favor? If I wanted foreplay all the time, shouldn't he?

Shouldn't I love pleasing my boyfriend? Yet, I was relieved to know that Noah thought it was wrong. The promise of a blowjob shouldn't be a required ticket to sexual satisfaction. Deep down, I had always known that felt *off.*

Noah was physically present, but he wasn't there for me. We had a mutual understanding. But Rob and I had history.

I released a heavy breath. My brain was doing its worst—spinning like a possessed merry-go-round off its rails.

On the way to the dorms, I said, "Hey, why don't you stay over this weekend instead of tonight?"

Noah frowned. "We're almost at your place already. And you won't get to see me again until Saturday night. I'm helping Travis' parents move furniture to their lake house tomorrow, remember?"

"Maybe you'll miss me enough to show up at my door with Chinese food," I said, placing my head on his shoulder.

"I can get you some tonight if you let me stay."

"Noah, I need to study. Let's just wait 'til Saturday," I whined as we pulled up in front of my building.

He huffed. "Fine. But you're gonna miss me."

We kissed for a long time, and I walked away, wondering if we could ever be anything more. Hidden away, we made perfect sense, but out in the open, we didn't stand a chance. I was a basket case. He was no one's case.

13

It had been a day since I'd heard from Noah. I hadn't messaged Rob back, but I hadn't blocked him, either. Lanes of communication were open, and I didn't know if it was right or wrong. The single Instagram message had been his only attempt. When we had broken up in the past, one message was enough to call me back, like a lighthouse beckoning me to harbor. I was too far adrift now. I was out in open sea, hoping Noah would reel me in.

I lowered my music, anxiously rereading our old text messages.

Stop it, Rain. You two are fine. You're not crawling back to Rob. This is progress. It definitely didn't feel like it.

Mikayla was meeting me at a coffee shop by the grocery store. We were supposed to do our weekly shopping trip and walk back together. I arrived first and waited for my iced coffee at a table hidden in the back. I slumped in the chair, immediately opening all avenues of social media and switching between platforms every few minutes for maximum meme content. The past week had been hectic, and mindlessly scrolling through social media sounded like a treat.

The door near me chimed open. Jen walked through.

There was nearly no one in here, but the café lighting worked in my favor, leaving me in the shadows. If I were a table to the left, Jen would've stumbled right into me. She hadn't seen me, but my hand froze in place halfway through combing my hair, trying to avoid catching her attention.

Jen oozed confidence. She didn't care if people stared, and she didn't care what they thought. She wore jeans that looked too casual for her and a powder-white, silk blouse with one button fastened, revealing her flat stomach as she walked. Her skin was glazed like a doughnut, and she smelled exquisite as she walked by, like a sexy, spiced fragrance I could never afford. She carried a bouquet of daisies and baby's breath in front of her like a bride.

She ordered a lemon bar and sat by the counter. She looked bored as she sat, tapping her silhouetted, nude nails on the table, and not even bothering to eat the lemon bar she had ordered.

I realized I was staring like a stalker. I texted Mikayla to hurry.

The door chimed again, and this time, when I lifted my gaze, I thought I had stepped into an alternate universe. Dawn was heading towards Jen.

I bowed my head, stealing a glance through my curtain of hair. Jen clasped her hands on the table and sighed. Dawn's chair screeched as she scooted forward.

"You don't have to keep doing this, Jen," she said politely.

Without so much as a change in breath, Jen slid the white bouquet along the table. "I doubt he'll bring one. Just take it."

Silence stretched.

"He doesn't have feelings for you, Jen. I'm sorry."

"It's for her, not him."

"She wouldn't have kept accepting them. She'd tell you to move on, since he clearly has. Mom was blunt like that."

Ohhhh.

"I'm happy to do it," Jen stressed.

"I can't accept this," Dawn said.

"Order for Rain!" a barista yelled.

"Oh, fuck me," I cursed under my breath. Screw my mom for giving me this stupid, unique name.

They both scanned the room, finding me at the same time.

"Order for Rain!" the girl behind the counter repeated.

Reluctantly, I stood, mentally preparing myself to act like I hadn't heard their private conversation.

Avoiding eye contact, I went for my drink. At the counter, I received a text from Mikayla saying to meet her at the store instead.

That message would've been extremely helpful ten minutes ago.

I swung my backpack to my other shoulder to hide my face and bolted towards the door. I almost made it out too, but at my last step to freedom, Dawn's voice jumped out, lassoing me.

"Rain, wait."

So close.

I spun around. "Hi, Dawn," I said, awkwardly adding a wave, though she was hardly a foot away from me. Jen was gone.

Dawn crossed her arms. "You heard."

I felt like I had set off a tripwire behind enemy lines. I shook my drink, swishing the ice. "I wasn't trying to eavesdrop. I'm sorry."

"They've been broken up for weeks now," Dawn said.

"But she's bringing flowers to your mother's— Never mind," I interrupted myself. I prayed that my face didn't say what I was thinking because it was nothing nice.

Dawn scratched her forehead. "Jen thinks it'll change things between Noah and herself."

I fidgeted, uncomfortable. Jen did have a heart and it was plated in gold. In the hope of Noah returning her feelings, Jen brought flowers for his mother. Guilt churned in my stomach as I thought about me having Noah's attention while Jen starved for it. When he told me about his mother, I had made him sit with me because I was a mess. Jen brought flowers. I got him drunk from vodka in a beehive mug.

I wrung the strap of my backpack. "I should go. I'm meeting a friend."

"What do you know about our mom?"

"He said the accident took her when he was eight. He never talks about her more than that. And his resentment."

"Noah hasn't told anyone about our mother or our father. Ever."

"Oh," I replied, wondering what else I could have said. *Should I apologize again?*

"Jen brings the flowers, but you're the one he talks to you," Dawn said, spelling it out for me. "That's a big deal."

I blinked in surprise, feeling awkward from the revelation.

"I know it's not the same, but my Aunt Rosen died when I was younger. She raised me," I blurted out. "She was my mother for all intents and purposes. He probably thought I'd understand."

"How did she…?"

"Cancer," I muttered softly. That single word felt like a fatal stab wound in my chest. Having to explain further would just be unnecessary twisting and suffering.

"Rain, I'm so—"

"It's okay," I interrupted.

We stared at each other, not saying anything.

My phone chimed. Mikayla was asking where I was.

Dawn cleared her throat. "I'm going to the cemetery now. I usually go after Sunday breakfast, but Ana has a soccer game tomorrow."

I nodded.

"Do you want to come?" she asked. "I can bring you back later."

I guess Dawn doesn't hate me.

I hesitated. Noah and I were just friends. *Friends with benefits*, I reminded myself. I wasn't supposed to miss him while he was gone.

But I did.

"I don't want to overstep," I told her. I didn't want to freak out over this, but I couldn't help it—I loved that Noah trusted me in ways that he didn't even trust Jen.

Dawn smiled. "Please, I'd like the company."

§

A month before she had died, Aunt Rosen had told me not to visit her grave, and instead, to talk to her as if she were standing right next to me. She said she'd take a break from hassling all the famous dead people up in the sky and come visit me anytime I did so. Her words, not mine. So, that's what I had always done. I sparked random, one-sided conversations with her whenever and wherever I wanted.

I'd never been to a cemetery. It was weird driving into one now. I expected fog to disperse like a dark cloud or for shadows to lengthen and cover the ground, but there wasn't even a crow on a sparse branch. The sun was hopefully bright, the grass was evenly tended, and the headstones were freshly polished. Most of them had flowers. The unexpected mental image of Aunt Rosen's barren headstone suddenly made me sick to my stomach. *I'll bring you flowers next time I'm home*, I promised.

"I'll wait here," I said as Dawn parked under a tree.

She smiled, bemused. "Rain, I walk over there, wipe the headstone, and drop off flowers. I don't have some dramatic, talking, movie moment. I do say, 'I love you,' out of habit when I leave, but I swear it's not as depressing as it sounds."

"Okay," I conceded, following her out of the car.

I stayed a step behind, carrying the bouquet of flowers. Dawn walked four paces to the right and stopped. I saw the name Donna Michaels Colt on the headstone. It sounded like a beauty brand that had its own counter in a nice mall.

Donna was only forty when she died. I read the epitaph, gawking. "'Devoted mother, wife, and friend. Find me in the poems.' Oh, my God. Noah knows poetry because of her, right?"

"Yeah, he does," Dawn replied.

"Who were her favorites?"

"Anyone who sounded pretty," she smiled. "She would tell us that poetry was meant to be heard. She read to us a lot."

"Noah said she used to read Blake."

"That was one of them. I liked his poem about the tiger."

I smiled a little. "I sort of thought Noah was lying or exaggerating."

Dawn crouched on the ground, swapping two withered bouquets for the fresh one. "He kept all her books. You and Mom would've geeked out over poetry."

She spoke plainly, like the weight of what we were doing didn't affect her. However, when she turned to the headstone, her voice became soft and quiet. "Jen bought these for you, Mom. Hope that's okay."

She stood and showed me her phone. "This was her."

Donna Michaels Colt had blonde hair, like Dawn. Their green eyes came from her, as did Noah's straight nose. It was a photo of her mid-spin. Hair as wild as her smile, she looked at the person spinning her instead of at the camera.

Dawn answered the question I hadn't asked yet. "Our dad."

It was just his profile, but I could tell Noah was more his dad than his mom. They had matching wavy locks, though his dad kept his short. His brows and lashes were thick, like Noah's.

"They look so much alike," I stated.

Dawn put the phone in her purse. "I don't see him often, but I try to go a few times a year."

"He's not buried here?"

She snorted. "They only bury the dead here, Rain."

I must not have been able to hide my shock, because she looked at me like I was crazy.

"Who told you he was dead?"

My jaw hung open. "Y-you said— He, I—"

I couldn't say it. Noah had lied a whole parent away.

Dawn bit her lip. "I guess that's how Noah feels. Wow." She sighed. "Mom would be happy that I go to see Dad. He loves us. He's been sober for eight years now. The prison has a decent AA program."

"Dawn," I uttered, blinking too much, moving my hands too much, "you don't have to explain. I'm sorry. I think it's great," I said, mostly because I knew nothing else would sound right.

"I pretended he didn't exist for the first two years. Our grandparents would leave his letters on the table for us. After a while, I started opening them. It wasn't until I was pregnant with Ana that I actually replied and met with him."

"Does Ana go with you?"

"No. Maybe one day I'll see if she wants to see him, but I'm waiting until she's older. He'll get out when she's fourteen."

"Oh. Wow."

"It's hard as hell not blaming him, but I also blame my mom. She was in the passenger seat. She knew about his problems more than we did and got in the car anyways. It wasn't the first time."

I stood with my mouth clamped shut. Maybe Noah confided in me because Dawn's forgiveness was too specious. I couldn't understand how she came here without falling apart or visited the man who had killed their mom. I had no one to be angry at, but I felt like I was holding a terrible grudge with the whole universe for taking Aunt Rosen from me.

I reached down, removing a leaf. Noah's loss had resulted from a decision to get into a car—a mistake that had rippled through every piece of his and Dawn's lives. My mom had lost her parents and Aunt Rosen, and was slowly losing me.

Death was a guarantee, but loss was a birthright. No one lived without losing.

"Grief will destroy you if you refuse to move on," Dawn said.

"Has Noah moved on?" I asked, then felt I had overstepped. "I just—I don't know why I asked that. I'm sorry."

"I hope he will," she answered. She wiped the stone again. "Sorry for being a bitch this week."

"I knew you were pissed!" I exclaimed.

Dawn laughed, lightly swatting my arm. "Come on, let's get out of here." She turned to the headstone. "Love you, Mom."

I nodded but stalled. "Can I say something? Is that too weird?"

Her brows rose. "Go for it."

I had no clue what I wanted to say but leaving without saying a word felt wrong. *It's just like talking to Rosen,* I thought to myself.

Dawn stepped away, and I wasn't sure if she could hear me or not.

"Hi. I'm Rain. No, it's not some pretentious, moody nickname. Sorry. Okay. I know your son and Dawn," I said, feeling awkward. "They're great. They kind of adopted me into their little family, which I appreciate. I don't have a lot of family. I just want you to know that I'll be there for them. Noah means a lot to me. They all do."

Leaves crunched beneath my feet as I left.

When we got into her car, Dawn said, "You know, I thought Rain was a pretentious, moody nickname when we met."

I looked away, embarrassed.

"This is why I keep my visits short!" Dawn laughed. "The cemetery makes people weird."

I sank into the car seat, stifling my laughter.

§

Sunday mornings were my day to sleep in. I made a hole in the blankets and burrowed until I was convinced I had ruined the mattress springs. Eventually, my longing for Noah left me no choice but to leave my bed. The citrus hints of his cologne on the sheets had gone from a happy reminder to a lingering form of mockery.

He had gotten back too late the night before to do anything fun. We had texted back and forth, planning to meet later today, and I woke up desperately excited to see him. I wasn't about to tell him that, though. He was already arrogant enough, and I wasn't about to stroke his bulletproof ego. I didn't want to play games with him, but I needed him to be the first one to take action. Which was why I got up, restless, and spent my morning exhausting those feelings on a treadmill.

My legs were noodles on the walk back to my dorm. I lowered the music on my headphones, watching the world around me. Fall was beginning to set in. The green leaves of summer had tarnished into all the shades of autumn, and the walkways were littered with the fallen foliage. I wasn't ready for the weather to get colder, but I loved seeing the seasons changed. I didn't even notice summer vanishing until fall was already taking up too much space.

Change stays subtle until you can't ignore it, I thought to myself.

The front doors of my dorm swung open. I looked up, startled, at the sight of Noah in front of me.

The excitement I had tried to suppress came out of remission.

"You're back," I said breathlessly.

"Yeah," he replied hesitantly. He stuffed his hands in his pockets, and it just made me want him more.

We stood there, chess pieces waiting for the game to start, until the rush of happiness compelled me forward. He had been so eager to see me that he'd shown up before eight in the morning. My lips spread into a carefree smile. He held his arms apart and I ran forward, leaping onto him and wrapping my legs around his waist. My hair tossed around his neck like a scarf. We held each other tightly.

"See? You missed me," he said into my ear. He was already playing the game.

I gripped him harder, nodding into his shoulder. Then I remembered how sweaty I was and unhooked my legs. "Oh, I'm sorry, I'm gross," I cringed.

"Like I care," he muttered, but he still let my feet touch the ground. He cupped the back of my neck. We kissed, and my whole body seemed to sigh with relief that he was back.

"What are you doing here? I didn't think I'd get to see you 'til later." I led us around the lobby to the elevators, our hands entangled. "I really did miss you."

"I couldn't wait 'til later," he said. "How was you run?"

"Slow but nice. How was moving?"

The elevator doors closed. The look on his face made it clear that talking wasn't what he had on his mind. We were alone, and it was like a checkered flag being waved in the air, starting us. He pressed against me, immediately stirring up less-clothed memories. My nails ran up his arms. Our lips molded together. He tasted like mint, cool and refreshing, a simulating contradiction to my warm skin. He drank me in, slipping his tongue across mine, then dipped his head and dragged a messy kiss along my collarbone, leaving a trail of goosebumps on my skin. I sighed deeply, weaving my fingers through his hair.

The elevator doors slid open. Panicked, I shoved him away and smoothed my hair.

"You're lucky no one was waiting," I hissed, checking the empty hallway.

Noah's chest rose and fell as viciously as crashing waves. "Why?" he said. "I'm sure they'd enjoy seeing you blush."

My lips twitched. "Exhibitionist kink. That's new."

His laugh echoed behind me. "I'm too possessive for that."

"Possessive? I didn't think you were the type."

I pushed my key into the lock. He followed me to my room, plopping on the beanbag chair.

"I don't sleep with more than one person at a time," he said.

"Dang. Guess I have to cut some things off," I said, grabbing clothes from my closet. When I looked his way, his glare was murderous.

"I know you're kidding," he growled. "I know what we have, the messes you make. You wouldn't find that anywhere else."

I shook my head. "Are you—"

"—Dying to touch you?" he interrupted. "Yes."

"Not until I shower. I'll be back."

"I'll be here." He retrieved the sketchbook he had stashed behind my mini fridge and pouted dramatically as I left.

I showered quickly, wanting to get back to Noah as soon as possible. When I walked back in, he was still sketching. He glanced up and moved the sketchbook off to the side. Before going to him, I wrapped a gray cardigan around myself. My wet hair was wound up in a clip, and I was cold. I sat on his lap and put my hands on his neck. Immediate warmth sparked at my fingertips.

"Fucking hell, Rivas, you have icicles for fingers." He tried wrestling me away, to which I simply laughed and hooked my feet under one of his legs.

"I can't help it. My hands are always freezing after I shower."

"What a character flaw," he muttered playfully, taking my hands and breathing over them.

My eyes widened. "Oh, and what's yours?"

"Nothing," he grinned. "I'm perfect."

"My perfect, personal heater," I concluded. "What were you drawing this time?"

He stared at my dark blue nails. "You."

"What?" I exclaimed, jolting up. "I want to see! Can I?"

"No."

It felt like he had taken my picture then refused to show it to me. What if he had drawn me from a terrible angle?

"Come on!"

He smiled. "Not until I'm done."

"Fine," I huffed. I played with the buttons of his shirt. "So, I hung out with your sister yesterday."

"No," he exhaled, dropping my hands. He stood up and started pacing.

"Yeah, we did. It's funny, I was supposed to meet Mikayla—"

"Did you go to my mother's grave?" he interrupted.

I froze.

"*Did* you?" he demanded.

I could tell I was in trouble with him. I averted my gaze.

"Not the fucking eye contact bullshit. Look at me," he demanded.

My eyes went to his.

"*Stay* looking at me. Did you go to her grave?"

"Dawn invited me," I explained in a whisper. I was afraid to blink.

He scratched his jawline in disbelief. "You crossed a line."

"I didn't know we had lines."

"What do you think 'friends with benefits' is, Rain? There's lines all over us!"

"It was by chance that I saw Dawn. *She* invited *me*," I emphasized.

"Yeah, well, I didn't want you to go!" he shouted.

I flinched. "I didn't know."

"And you didn't think to ask."

"Noah, I'm sorry. I couldn't say no—"

"Yes, you could've."

Was knowing him off the table now that we'd been intimate? How had we taken a step forward while also going two steps backwards?

My breath shook. "We haven't talked about boundaries."

"Am I interrogating you about your family? Am I going to Rosen's grave?"

My voice strengthened. "You told me about your mom. I told you about my family. Why can't you open up to me?"

"Was I supposed to open up before or after you went behind my back?"

"You act like we're dating. You spend the night here whenever you can. You kiss me in public. You reach for me when we sleep. This isn't in my head."

"We're not what you think we are."

My chin wobbled, and I hated it. "We're not… friends? We're not… more? Which one?"

"I told you this wasn't anything serious, Rain," he said, grinding his teeth.

"I thought us doing… stuff would be—just that. But you're making everything blurry. I didn't know me going to the cemetery with Dawn would upset you—"

"Jen was right."

I stopped. The ceiling felt like it was crushing me. "You saw Jen?"

"Yes."

"When? What did she say?"

His jaw clenched. "Last night."

It was like he had slapped me. He didn't elaborate, so my imagination ran wild, and, since I thought the worst, I felt compelled to say the worst, too.

"So, you two hooked up."

He shook his head angrily. "I already told you—I only sleep with one person at a time, even casually."

"How long has she been buying flowers for your mom's grave?"

He stumbled back, finally feeling a blow from this fight. "Does it matter?"

"You pretend to be this nonchalant, sweet guy, but you're not. She's been doing it for months, and you've pushed her away because of it. You get scared by anyone caring about you, by someone liking you. And it's bull... ship."

"Just fucking cuss, Rain! Not every word is an attack!" Frustrated, he ran his hands through his hair. "You're criticizing me, but she wasn't my girlfriend. Neither are you. But you! You can't look me in the eyes when we argue. You can't handle a raise in voice or a tiny cuss word. You said you wanted easy. Do you think this is it? We're kidding ourselves."

I didn't know what we were fighting about anymore, but I hated us.

He must've seen that in my face.

"Fuck, Rain. I'm sorry," he apologized, stepping forward.

"N— no." My voice cracked. "Screw you, Noah. You know why I don't keep eye contact? Because my ex would start a fight if he thought my eyes were on anyone but him. I could be looking at someone's shirt, and to him, it was the first cannon strike in a war. I seriously couldn't look at people while walking down the sidewalk. I can't handle you cussing when you're mad at me because you sound like him when you do. I'm broken, okay? It's not a damn secret. Though you pretend not to notice because you can't handle getting too emotional. You're so bad at handling it that you lied to me about your dad. Him being dead is easier than him rotting in a jail cell, right? But you think you're handling everything fine as long as you have a drink in your hand.

"Look in the mirror, Noah. You're broken, too."

He was too stunned to speak. He might've thrown the first blows, but I still knew how to throw a knife.

He stormed past me. "We're over."

"Good," I whispered even though I didn't mean it.

"Riddance," he responded. He was even better than me at playing mean.

14

I was back in bed and in the same pajamas from yesterday. A parade of comfort movies shined out from the projector. I'd randomly check my phone, assuring myself that the ringer was on. I convinced myself a few times that I felt a phantom vibration or that my phone wasn't working.

My nose ran so much that I started to wonder if maybe I had a cold. I wanted to disappear within myself, melt like ice in a puddle on the street, pretend the last four years could be erased by a miraculous case of amnesia, or go back to the night I had arrived here and lock myself in my room instead. I'd also appreciate some type of fast-forwarding, especially to a future era where names like Rob and Noah were just names again. I wouldn't care that I'd be older and miss a gap of experience. I just wanted to be very far from today.

Rolling over, I grabbed my favorite book. *This will cheer me up.* I flipped a page and stared at the words. Then I remembered when I had caught Noah reading it. The way he had huddled over the pages, studying my annotations more than the actual book itself, his long hair falling over his forehead like a waterfall. He would toss his rogue locks back when he looked up, but I secretly loved when his hair was in his face. It softened his pensive smirk.

Vignettes of him like that were everywhere, like landmines. He had tattooed himself upon my life, vandalizing large swaths of it, and even reaching the small, hidden corners. Even my favorite book had Noah's indelible, invisible mark upon it. Ruined by him, I chucked the hardcover off my bed.

"At least Rob didn't do that to me," I muttered.

I rubbed my face. This couldn't be happening. Noah was perfect to have fun with because it was supposed to be just that—fun. I hadn't expected things to end so soon and so terribly. It was our first fight. Here I was thinking that it wasn't me—that Rob and I had fought because of *him*—but I had barely lasted any time with someone else.

I rolled over, shoving my face into the pillow.

"Raindrop, cha-ching!" Mikayla's voice rang through the dorm. "I got paid today which means I have snacks, baby!"

Maybe if I just forget I exist, so will Mikayla.

My bedroom door flew open. "I know you're not asleep. You're too much of a light sleeper for my lovely voice. What's wrong?"

"I forgot to lock my door, that's what's wrong," I answered, raising myself up on my side.

She halted her invasion midway up my bed's ladder. Through her frizzy bangs, she narrowed her gaze. "What's got you blue?"

I sighed. "I may or may not have begun doing more than friendly things with Noah."

I waited for her surprise. But Mikayla's passive, polite smile remained in place.

"You knew."

She threw a hand in an oh-shucks, cheesy kind of way. "Raindrop, you'd sneak him in then laugh all night. Plus, he made a habit of leaving his toothbrush with ours."

I deflated. "I thought I was getting away with it."

"Why hide it? You're both single."

"It doesn't matter now. He just ended it. In a shitty way, too." When her expression didn't change, I rolled my eyes. "You knew that, too."

"I only *look* like a fool. Remember that. Now, get up! Tell me what happened."

Despite wanting to burrow under the covers, I did want to tell her what was going on. I crawled out of my bed.

"Yay! I got us the hot Cheeto popcorn you like and those big cinnamon rolls."

I smiled weakly. "You have impeccable timing."

"I know. My crystals told me you needed it," she answered.

She had added crystals to her yoga. I didn't understand it one bit, but I couldn't mock her. After all, she wasn't the girl who holed herself away in her room and muffled her cries with the palm of her hand when she was sad. Mikayla was the scream-and-cry-as-needed type of girl who was good at recognizing her own emotions.

I followed her to our little living room as she spilled the snacks out onto our coffee table. I had just popped open a bag of chips when my phone rang. I lunged for it.

"Is it him?" Mikayla asked, craning to see the screen.

My heart sank. It was Mom.

"Oh, well, you should answer that anyway," Mikayla said. "I'll get a movie going."

"I can't. This is my mom. She doesn't call me. We text. Rarely."

"More reason to answer. Now, talk!" she said, moving quickly and tapping the screen.

She answered. My roommate just answered my call! I glared at her, wishing I could channel the power of Medusa for a second and turn her to stone. Mikayla just shrugged and raised her brows, daring me.

"Hi, Mom," I said unenthusiastically. "What's up? Are you okay?"

"I'm fine, Rain. I was calling to you let you know that I saw Robert."

"Robert? Oh. You mean Rob."

"Why didn't you tell me you weren't with him? I went up to him thinking you two were together and looked like a fool."

I cringed. With our strained relationship, I had left out that he and I had broken up a month and a half ago and that I was sort of with someone else.

And now, not with someone else.

"What did he say, Mom?"

"Well, I ran into him at the grocery store. I asked how you were. He humored me as if I were a confused, senile old woman and told me he hadn't seen you since you two broke up."

"Did he seem sad? Upset?"

"Not at all! He said he's seeing someone else. Why would he be upset, Rain? Breakups happen."

I couldn't find my voice for a second. "I don't want to talk about it," I replied.

"I would have liked to have known. How are you doing?"

Although I knew she dealt with her emotions in her own way, I couldn't take her pretending to care about me seriously. It hit like a bad joke.

"I'm fine," I said curtly. "I'm about to watch a movie with my roommate."

"Oh, really? Which movie?"

I stopped. *Which movie?* This was the part where the call was supposed to have ended.

"I don't know. It's Mikayla's turn to choose."

"Mikayla," she said, getting familiar with the name. I wasn't sure I had told her about my roommate before now.

"Yep."

"How is school? How are your grades? Aren't midterms happening soon?"

"Fine, A's, and at the end of this month," I said, thinking, *Maybe if I can answer all her questions quickly enough, she won't ask more.*

"Are you nervous?"

"Kind of. I want to do well."

"Rain, I wanted to ask if I could visit sometime soon."

"Why?" I asked bluntly.

"Do I need a reason to want to visit my daughter?"

"Mom, I'm pretty busy. I have work, exams. I have my bosses' wedding."

Silence.

I wondered if I had hurt her feelings, telling her not to come see me because I was going to a wedding. I thought of the invitation Dawn had handed me at the birthday brunch. I had been so excited. I would've been going with Noah, and we would've also been celebrating exams being over.

I chewed on my lip. Mom was trying. Did I appreciate her effort? Maybe. Did I want a better relationship with her? Honestly, I didn't know. But I wanted to feel like I had a family again. For a brief moment, I had felt at home with Noah and the life he had invited me into, but the sudden loss of him made me desperate.

"Maybe you can come that weekend," I said quickly, not giving myself time to start thinking in circles again. "I won't have to worry about work since the shop is closed for the wedding, and my midterms would be over."

"Are you sure?"

No, Mom, I'm not sure at all, I thought. But what I said was, "I wouldn't be offering if I wasn't."

"I'll let you know when I book the hotel."

Breathe, Rain. "Okay."

"I'll talk to you soon."

"Okay."

"Take care of yourself."

"Mmhmm," I replied, hanging up.

I stared off at a random corner of the room. "I just invited my mom to visit," I said. I wasn't sure if I was talking to Aunt Rosen or Mikayla.

"Oh, good!" Mikayla chirped. "I'd love to meet her."

My body collapsed on the couch, but my mind was hundreds of miles away, in a house that could never disguise itself as a home.

"We don't have a good relationship."

"Yeah, no shit."

My gaze struck her.

"What?" She plopped down next to me. "You didn't say I love you when you hung up."

We never do.

I took out my feelings on a bag of chips. Devouring the junk food must have been good for my brain because, five minutes and five hundred calories later, I finally caught up and processed the conversation.

"She saw Rob. She found out that my boyfriend and I broke up from my boyfriend," I mused. "She doesn't even know about Noah."

Mikayla snatched the chips. "That's because you didn't tell her about any of this," she quipped.

I ignored her. "A month and a half ago, I would've been upset over Rob. Two weeks ago, I would've been crying about the stupid fact that I let six months of happiness outweigh years of fighting. Now, I just hate that Noah and I are done. And then there's my temporary insanity that led me to invite my mother to visit! I would never in a million years have done that if it weren't for this other stuff."

"Silver lining, huh?" Mikayla said, lightening the mood. She scooted closer to me until our shoulders touched.

"I can't do this, Mikayla. I'm a disaster, and she will enjoy pointing out all my bad decisions to me. I cannot have her here."

She smiled dismissively. "Things with your mom will get better if you want them to. If she's trying and you want to try, I say it's great. If not, then uninvite her. It really is that simple.

"But! I saved the grand finale for last. Ready?" She jutted out jazz hands, wiggling her fingers. "Noah will come back."

"You really think so?" I breathed.

"He's into you, babe. Trust me. Buuuuuut," she drawled, "The question is, what should you do when he does?"

"Mikayla, do not talk in riddles right now. I can't take it."

"Hurt people hurt people."

"Why does nobody ever talk about healed people healing people?" I asked.

"Because it's not really your job to heal him. But it *is* his job to not hurt you. So, whatcha gonna do?"

I thought about Noah. He came from a glittered, snow-globe past. His early childhood was a shiny dream that others would've wished for. When the globe broke, the fake snow floated out, spilling out the magic. Even Dawn could see that Noah had never moved on from the crash, and now, he refused to let anyone in. All because the last real love he had felt was lost by the life-altering accident that had shattered his globe, destroyed his family, and torn him apart.

Losing Aunt Rosen hadn't killed me like I thought it would. Strangely, it had motivated me. I had worked hard to move away, chasing what I wanted and determined to find what I once had. Despite what had happened to me, I still let people in.

Noah didn't.

"Raindrop?"

"I'll have to figure it out when it happens," I muttered.

We ended up watching half a season of *One Tree Hill*. We sang an entire playlist of guilty pleasure songs. At midnight, I went to my room and poured my emotions out onto blank pages. I wrote about endings sparking new beginnings. I obsessed over my mercurial feelings, worrying that they weren't real or healthy because they changed too quickly. I fell asleep wishing I had written in pencil and could erase my confessions, but my notebook and pen bore silent witness to what I couldn't say aloud.

Later, I reblocked Rob.

At three in the morning, my phone rang.

"Hello?"

"Hi, Rain," Dawn said. "I'm sorry to do this, but I can't find Noah."

15

It was full-blown panic in my dorm room after that—me pulling on my sweatpants, sweatshirt, and Vans while juggling my phone from hand to hand, Dawn word vomiting a list of places she had checked and anywhere he might be. I grabbed my keys and was about to name off all the bars he talked about, but when I opened the door, I yelped.

"What?" Dawn shrieked.

"He's here. On the floor."

"Preshent!" he slurred, throwing an arm up in the air like he was in first grade and I was a teacher taking attendance.

Noah's bloodshot eyes could barely focus on me. Fresh scrapes decorated his knuckles. His jeans were dirtied and torn. If it hadn't been for the fact that his face was untouched, I would've bet he had been in a fight.

He began toppling over as I opened the door further.

"He's drunk," I grimaced.

"I'm heading over," Dawn said.

"It's okay. I got him."

"Rain, you don't have to do that."

"He just needs to sleep it off. I promise."

She sighed. "Okay, thank you. I'll talk to you guys in the morning."

"Okay. Bye."

I hung up and redirected my attention to him.

Ohhhh, Noah, what have you done?

I kneeled and attempted to wrap an arm around his waist. He clasped onto me like a drowning man, expelling sour breath into my face.

"Wait!" he pleaded, trying to blink the drunken haze from his glossy eyes. His face screwed up in distress. "I'm sorry. I'm sorry for what I said, for yelling at you."

I tilted my face away. "You're drunk."

"And an idiot."

At that, I smiled.

"I'm an idiotic son of a bitch, and I miss you."

My heart melted, then immediately froze again. "You shouldn't. I'm not what you want." When he couldn't disagree, I tried helping him up again, but he was dead weight. "Please don't make me drag you inside. We'll both end up getting hurt," I urged, standing and holding out my arm.

After a few seconds, my words registered with him, and he helped me help him up. I got us through my dorm as quickly as I could, listening to the television sitcom laughter coming from Mikayla's room and praying it wouldn't stop. Thankfully, we made it to my room without either of us falling.

"Did you tell Mikayla about us?" he asked.

My eyebrows practically hit my hairline. "We're 'us' again?" I didn't wait for a response. I went to my closet and retrieved some clothes he had left behind. "Put these on. I found them when I was doing laundry," I explained, averting my gaze.

"Fuck, are we back to you not looking at me?"

He was stupid if he thought I was going to rehash our fight while he couldn't stand without swaying. I tossed him a water from the minifridge.

"Drink it and go to sleep. Enjoy your stay at casa de beanbag."

Smirking, Noah yanked off his shirt.

Oh, hell no. I spun around so fast my hair whipped my cheek.

"You can watch," he teased.

"Just hurry up," I demanded softly. "I'm tired, and Dawn is picking you up in the morning."

The sound of my bed creaking was my response.

"What are you doing?" I asked, glancing at him.

"What you asked." He was shirtless, in my bed, and chugging the water.

I stepped up to him. "You've been demoted to the beanbag."

He blinked in disbelief. "Don't make me sleep on that pile of foam shit, Rivas."

"I didn't ask to take care of you tonight. I was asleep, and you're an annoying drunk. That pile of foam is more than fair."

His face fell. "Don't call me a drunk. That means I'm like *him.*"

It took everything in me not to crawl to him and try to coax that idea from his head. "Noah, you're not like your father."

He stared at the disheveled blankets. My fingers twitched, wanting to touch him, but I kept my distance.

"You don't know that. I drink whenever I can't handle life," he replied quietly.

"You didn't drive here—you walked. You don't drink every day. You're different."

He shook his head, retreating to an aberrant silence.

"You don't have to forgive him, Noah, but I wish you wouldn't carry this pain with you."

"Stop," he begged.

I couldn't, though. I had called him broken, but I knew the shattered pieces were also the spots where light found its way into his soul.

"I care about you."

"I know," he said.

"But you can't be showing up here."

"Yes, I can."

"You ended us."

"Do you want me to go?"

My eyes fell with a heavy sigh. "No, I don't want you to go, but I don't want this to be situational. I thought—"

He reached for me, and I dodged backwards. We were a bad game of cat and mouse.

"Go to bed. I'm sleeping in Mikayla's room."

"I'll leave."

"Noah, you reek of alcohol. You already got into my bed and reekafied it. Don't fight me, okay? I had a bad day. Not because of you. I got a call from my mom and I think I'm getting a cold. Do me a favor and just sleep it off."

"Are you alright?"

"I'll answer you in the morning. Goodnight."

I grabbed my phone and a spare pillow, feeling a strong tug to stay with him and trying my best to ignore it. But just before I closed the door, he had to push things further.

"I can take care of you," he said.

Tension rippled through my muscles. It wasn't because I didn't like it. I just couldn't handle hearing things like that, knowing I'd have to pretend he didn't mean more to me when the sun came up.

"You said you might be sick," he elaborated.

The light from the hallway illuminated him but cast a spectral glow on his features. He was so beautiful that it hurt.

But my laugh was desolate.

"You can't even take care of yourself, Noah. Goodnight."

I closed the door without another word.

§

I forgot that I had slept in Mikayla's bed until she woke me up by jumping on me. After restarting my heart, I rolled over, pinning her like an animal.

"Mikayla, I swear, you're lucky you're so cute."

With bright eyes and dramatically helpless squirming, she said, "Lover boy got us a surprise."

Confused, I released her wrists and sat up. "Lover boy?"

"Tattoo Dude." She cocked her head to the side, raising a brow. Following her gesture with my eyes, I saw two iced coffees and a lumpy, brown paper bag on her desk.

Mikayla rustled behind me as I crawled out of her bed, resting her chin on my shoulder. "He said to check your room and not to forget the donuts."

My eyes widened. "Donuts, too?"

She grabbed the paper bag and waved it in front of me. "Yeah, but next time tell him to get two bags. Who the heck gets only one whole freaking bag of donuts?" she trilled.

A sappy feeling sweetened the frustration from being woken up in the middle of the night and forced out of my own room. I had come into Mikayla's room fuming, waking her up, pacing, and saying things I'd never have the guts to say to Noah. Last night, I couldn't believe a word he was saying, not with the drunken gloss clouding his eyes and judgment, but now, staring at the stupidly kind gesture, it left me doubting what we had been and where I wanted us to be.

"Not gonna lie, it's hard to be mad with coffee and donuts," Mikayla said.

I sipped my coffee, leaving Mikayla to dig for a strawberry-filled donut, and went to my room. I immediately smelled the difference—fresh linen instead of acrid sweat. A folded piece of paper rested on my perfectly made bed. I reached up and opened it.

Several neatly folded scraps of paper fell out like delicate snowflakes and hit my feet. I opened one and nearly choked. Placing my coffee to the side, I plucked up the rest, unfolding them one by one, and surrounding myself with unfinished sketches of… my face.

I sat on the floor like a child, gazing at the pages as if they were jewels. "How many times did he draw me?"

The answer was six. The first was of my eyes and forehead. My brows were feathery, smudged with half-circles. Tiny ovals dripped from my lashes. I smiled at what he had done—clouds and raindrops. Another was a rough outline of me studying, but the book had mountains sprouting from the pages. I had lost half of my face to a castle in another. There were two minimalistic drawings where I wouldn't have known it was me if it weren't for my tattoos. The last was a finished picture of me. My hair grew a forest, and hummingbirds extended from my winged eyeliner.

"I'm sorry."

Noah's voice made me jump. I looked up. He stood at the doorway with a helpless grimace. His eyes were fixed on me. He approached with gentle steps, like I was a deer in the meadow, and he was desperate not to scare me off.

"I was drunk out of my mind last night, and all I remembered was that I missed you," he said.

Was I still a sucker for the big apology? I stayed exactly where I was, not able to blink.

"I've never liked anyone the way I like you," he added, the sincerity in his voice enough to break me. "You're like charcoal, Rain. One touch, and you make my hands, my life, messy. I read your journal—"

"What?"

"—and I thought it was beautiful! Your mind is beautiful. I love looking at what you highlight and underline in books. I'm amazed when you explain it to me, or when you show me a new song. I didn't even realize 'til last night how well you get me."

"Noah—" I whispered.

"I'm fucking terrified that this is starting something I won't be able to stop. You might end up hating me, and what am I going to do then?"

I shook my head.

"You might," he said softly, crouching down to where I sat. Fear vandalized his face.

My heart hammered against my ribs. The sketches, the words, the genuine emotion underlying both—I moved slowly, making sense of what had happened and what he was saying. Noah wanted me. Noah wanted *us*. Confetti cannons should be going off, yet I hesitated, wary.

"Say something, Rain."

A beat passed.

"Which was the first?" I asked, scanning the sketches of how he saw me.

Long waves of hair curtained his face. He released a full breath and pointed to the one where the clouds dotted my eyes.

"When?" I asked, my eyes glued to it.

"Your first day working at the shop," he answered, and our gazes collided.

"You've felt this way… since then?"

He stared at me, hesitant to speak but itching to add more. Endearingly, he lacked his usual confidence. "Since I first saw you."

"I didn't think you'd want me."

"Rain—"

"I've been proven to be romantically challenged in the past," I said, running my index finger along the papers.

"I don't care about that. You know about my dad. If we're trying to see who's worse, I'll win."

"I don't want to be the added weight that splinters a fracture."

"Fuck, Rain. Don't you get it?" He cupped my face. "Baby, let me be direct—I like you, and I don't give a shit about anything else because you're making me feel more than I've felt in years. I'm sick of running away. I can't, not when it's from you."

"Baby?" I whispered.

He smiled, running his thumb across my cheek. "Do you have something against me calling you baby?"

I paused. It sounded right from him. Shaking my head, I replied, "You've only said that when were tangled up in each other."

He smirked. "If you let me be yours, I'll be saying it a lot more, Rivas."

"Holy shit," I blurted out.

Noah laughed loudly before bringing me close. Our noses almost touched.

Despite the paralyzing fear, I nodded, my eyes wet with tears, then crashed my lips against his. "Officially."

I had about one second of peaceful bliss before Noah tackled me. My legs slid out from under me, and my head bounced off the floor. My, "Ow!" clashed with his warm laugh.

"Less than a minute into dating and you're already hurting me," I grumbled.

"Sorry, baby. You okay?" he asked, crowning my forehead with kisses.

"You're lucky you sound nice saying that."

He smoothed my hair from my face with a lucent grin, settling his weight on my stomach. I heard a rustle beneath our melding bodies.

"No! You can't ruin my drawings!" I panicked, throwing jabs at his side until he climbed off me. Eyeing him a warning, I picked up the papers and smoothed out the wrinkles.

"Hey, those aren't yours," Noah said, watching me.

"Um, yes, they are. They're of me, were left for me, and presented to me. They're a gift. To me! Plus, this is retribution for reading my journal. I can't believe you did that!"

He shrugged, defeated. "Fine," he muttered.

I leaned in, pressing my lips to his. "It's the first thing my boyfriend gave me," I said.

There was an abrupt transformation of his expression. His scowl became a dopey smile. "Boyfriend? That's a first for me. I like it."

I stepped around him to my desk and carefully placed the drawings in my literature book. He stood and walked closer to me. We were both as hesitant as we were reactive, watching what the other did. When I couldn't stand the space between us any longer, I placed my hands flat on his chest and let him wrap his arms around my waist. His heart raced beneath his shirt.

"I really fucked up," he mumbled.

I looked up into his eyes. Remorse crystalized.

"I'm too quick to give up," I said.

"I yelled at you," he remarked harshly. "Because you did something you didn't know I wouldn't like."

"I yelled back and threw your father in your face."

His arms tightened. "Maybe I needed you to. I shouldn't be saying he's dead." He placed his chin on my head. "Rain, I will never be like Rob again. I promise you."

We had stumbled into emotional graveyards with restless ghosts. I wanted to walk through his—ask him what arguments buried people; wonder if years were lost in unmarked plots. I wanted to know everything. It didn't matter how lighthearted or melancholy the bits he shared with me were. I wanted the summers and the winters of him. The good and the bad. The happiness and the regrets.

Softly, I ran the back of my hand against his jaw. His eyes closed. In that moment, he was so beautiful—the boy who was scared to feel.

"I called you broken."

"You weren't wrong," he replied, his breath a wisp against my fingers.

"My broken pieces fit with yours."

He brought me closer, placing his forehead on mine. "Who sent you? I swear, you're perfect."

A lightness was restored when he squeezed my waist. I laughed softly. "I feel anything but."

"Travis and Lorie went to visit her parents. Come to my place tonight?" he asked impetuously.

My heart skipped. I hadn't been there yet and was tired of imagining him sleeping in a tattoo chair. I smiled.

"Is that a yes?" he asked, squeezing me.

"That's a maybe."

Squeezing turned to tickling. "Okay, yes!"

"Yes what?"

"Yes, I'll go over!" I twisted, feeling laughter mixed with spasms of pain.

"Go over and what? Sleep? Leave me?"

Gasping, I yelled, "I'll go over and sleep with you!"

Relinquishing his grip, Noah threw his head back and yelled, "Did you hear that, Mikayla? She's going to sleep with me!"

"Ew! Ew! Ewwww!" she hollered from the living room. Steps sounded, and she appeared at the doorway. "Look, I am over the moon. I mean, I am the literal cow jumping over it, perfectly ecstatic that you two have a rollicking sex life—"

"Mikayla!" I screeched, utterly mortified.

"—but I do not need to hear any of it. Tattoo Dude," she exhaled, "it's great knowing you'll be a permanent attendee at our comfort show binges. I'm thrilled. But hey, no sex noises?"

Noah grinned. "Just had to let you know."

"I want to die." My cheeks were burning like coals from embarrassment.

"Ah, can't do that," he said pointedly. "You already promised you'd sleep—"

"Okay! I get it!" I cringed.

§

I packed pajamas and an extra set of clothes. Oh, and a toothbrush. Noah carried my duffel bag to our Uber. He made small talk with the driver until we stopped in front of a one-story, gray brick house with a yellow door. Noah's truck was in the gravel driveway behind a white car. Wildflowers were planted beneath two large windows.

My first thought was that it looked homey.

"Ladies first," he said, opening the door for me. I smiled to disguise my nerves.

Noah moved behind me, flicking on the kitchen light. I bit my lip, stressed, and happy I wasn't facing him. I breathed in deeply. *Okay, Rain. When you breathe out, you're going to be fine.*

"I'll put your stuff in my room," he said, and I spun on my heels, following him. His lips twitched as he passed me and lightly kicked open the door on the left.

Noah's room was underwhelmingly normal. The mattress was on the floor. He had a black comforter and a black rug. His cherry-stained dresser had a few framed photos. One was of him and his mom. Noah must have been five or six years old in the picture, and his mother was hugging him. Another was of Dawn and Ana sitting on their porch steps.

"Rain," he called.

I had zoned out on the pictures. "Sorry."

Noah had put my bag on the bed. I felt cornered by the thought of being alone with him. We had spent the night together several times, but there was an awkwardness now that felt like it was our first time. In more ways than one, it was.

"Relax," he sighed. "Make yourself at home."

My laugh wheezed. "I don't even know what home is."

Noah's brows lifted, but he said nothing.

"Oversharing. That's what happens when I feel out of place. I'm sorry."

He slipped his hand in mine and pulled me in, bringing his lips to mine. "I'll kiss you every time you apologize."

"Does it annoy you?"

"Nope, but it's better than telling you not to every time."

A kiss for an apology. I smiled weakly. I could work with that.

"What do you want to do?" he asked, playing with a lock of my hair. "We could go downtown?"

"I don't know." I hadn't expected us to be here. My heart didn't need to process us being together, but the rest of me did.

"You're overthinking. I can tell."

"Are you sure about this? I thought you didn't date or that I was too much to even consider—"

"Rivas, shut up," he interrupted, brushing his lips over mine. "You're impossible. I've been into you since we met, since you came in with the rain, Rain," he said, and my stomach did somersaults. "I'm good at lying to myself. I thought we'd be better off as friends, and who knows, maybe that's what we'll feel later, but right now, I want to try this with you."

"Noah," I warned. What I didn't say was, *You're going to make me fall in love without trying.*

"I've tried not wanting you. I've tried looking at other people, seeing other people, and I've been wasting my time," he stressed, gripping my waist. God, I loved how he emphasized certain words in the ways he held me. "It's fucking pointless because, no matter what I do, I'm wanting you."

Noah turned to his bed, bringing me with him onto the mattress. He smiled as I lay on top of him.

"I've never had anyone in this bed besides you," he murmured. "What else do you need?" He was expectant and caring, and the empathy of his gaze dissolved my skepticism.

"Honesty," I said, "and nothing more. If you want me, then I'll be here until you don't."

He frowned. "Don't look for an expiration date. We'll just ruin whatever this is faster."

My mouth twisted. "You're contradicting yourself."

"Yeah, well, you're holding back when I've already cut my ties. Catch up, Rivas," he replied.

I kissed him, figuring this was the best way to cut my reservations. I ran my tongue across his. His touch sparked fires up and down my back. I brushed my fingers through the tangles of his hair. When my hands hit his neck, I dragged my nails. He swayed to the side. My smile got lost in the kiss like a whispered secret.

For a second, our eyes, glazed with desire, shined at each other as we took a breath.

Letting adrenaline take over, I planted my hand on his chest and used his body to push myself up. He exaggerated a groan, but it was cut short when he saw what I was doing. I straddled him and pulled my sweater over my head. My hair tumbled around my neck. He had made it a point to bring up my lack of eye contact. I was adamant about maintaining it now.

"Rain," he breathed, dropping his eyes to my chest. "What the fuck are you wearing?"

It was a green bra and matching thong that I had never worn before. After Noah had made the joke about us sleeping together, I had to be prepared, but now, as his gaze burned me, I wasn't sure he liked the effort. The prolonged silence and my own memory made a mockery of me.

You don't have to dress like that. I already want you.

I don't care for it.
You're better naked.
You don't need any of it.

The set I had picked out to match Noah's eyes felt like a joke, a costume. The intensity of his gaze started to look like disdain. I couldn't be what he wanted. I couldn't even be what Rob wanted, and I had been with him for years. If I managed to be acceptable for a night, it was only because I did what I was told.

You don't need any of it. You're being ridiculous. I didn't say you looked bad. I just don't like it.

"Do you hate it?" I asked, hating the tremor in my voice.

"Fuck, I was kidding about us sleeping together, baby."

I shuddered. "What?"

"No! Not like that," Noah insisted, recognizing his mistake. "I mean, I didn't want to pressure you. I was being stupid, trying to mess with Mikayla."

"Oh. So, you don't want this?"

"I didn't say that," he answered. He stretched his hands across my stomach.

"Oh," I repeated, not able to say much.

"I'm not expecting anything," he clarified, and I nodded.

"That's okay," I said, moving to get off him.

"No," he replied immediately. He grabbed my hips. The hands that were once velvet gripped me like a vise. He pulled me lower, and I felt him hard through his jeans. "I want you right here."

"Okay," I whispered.

His thumb ran over my bra. I closed my eyes, getting lost in the effect of him.

"Rain."

"Hmm?" I couldn't concentrate, but I opened my eyes when he stopped touching me.

He looked cautious. "What do you want?"

What *didn't* I want? I grabbed the collar of his shirt, leaning forward. "You're not pressuring me."

"Okay." He breathed unevenly, and it was the first sign of his control slipping. He dipped a finger in the waistband of my sweats. He skimmed over my underwear, eyes sparkling when he realized it was a matching set. "You did this for me, baby?"

"Do you want to see it completely?"

"Fuck, yes," he said immediately. He hooked his hands behind his head. "Put on a show for me, baby."

Noah's confidence was unmatched, radiating off him, and onto me, apparently, because I brazenly stood, sliding the fabric down my thighs. Once the pants were off entirely, I spun to toss them aside.

"You're a dream, Rain."

I stepped between his knees. "Let's make it a reality."

He sat up, his face in front of my hips. "I'm at your mercy." His hands skated up my thighs until he grabbed my ass. "Tell me if you change your mind or if something's too much."

"Do I tell you if I like something?"

"Yes." He looked at my underwear, moving his hands along the thin line of fabric on my hips. "But you don't have to tell me in words." He kissed my stomach. "You could moan my name." I gripped his shoulders, feeling drugged. "You could bite me." He parted my legs. "You could choke me. Hit me." He touched me through the silk fabric, and I thought my knees would give out.

"Noah," I hummed.

He gazed up. "Hm?"

I tucked a piece of hair behind my ears. "I'm not a—"

"I know." He shook his head as soon as the words left his mouth. "Fuck. I didn't mean—" But he didn't continue.

Feeling our entangled bodies, I was hit with a sudden reality check. His body count was numberless, but he was only my second.

He wrapped his arm around me while his other hand stretched across my jaw. "I don't want to be your rebound, Rain."

We were both scared. Me, of being just another person he killed time with. Him, of being nothing but a painkiller for me.

"You're not."

He looked at me, his eyes probing me for any hidden hesitations. On the verge of begging, I leaned forward, but he suddenly kissed me. A rush of energy transmitted between our meshing lips, and my whole body throbbed.

Rolling me underneath him, he let me catch his weight. My nerves, my heart, even my mind, everything vibrated in anticipation. The grip he had on my hip went from sweet to fierce.

Despite his intensity, I held a rein on him. Pulling his hand to my navel, I gauged his reaction as I pushed his fingers lower. He parted from our kiss, watching me closely as he finally touched me below my clothing. Instantly, my body became slack with relief. *More*, I wanted to plead. Desire edged as he touched me slowly. My eyes shut in pleasure and frustration. I reached for him under his jeans.

"I can't wait," I panted. "I need you."

"What if I want to take my time?" he asked, the words slow and sensual.

I could've cried out.

His eyes bored into mine. He held himself, knowing he'd take me any second. The intimacy was like humidity in the air—a delicious blanket of heat glittering on my skin. My back arched, giving in to the feel of him. My breath came quick and uneven. He kissed my chest, teeth grazing my skin.

"You're incredible, baby," he murmured into my neck, yanking my underwear off. "I just want to watch you come."

He finished undressing and brought me close. Our foreheads pressed against each other. His thumb smoothed over my mouth, parting my lips. That one gesture elicited a moan from me.

"Noah," I exhaled.

He smiled, staring at my mouth. "Don't stop saying my name."

He pressed into me, and I moaned. My eyes rolled back when he pushed in further. He stopped, sliding out slowly.

"Are you okay?" he exhaled.

"Noah," I said, gripping his neck, "stop being gentle."

"Fuck, Rain," he muttered.

Pain swirled with pleasure, and the feel of him thrusting in and out made me hungry for more. My hips reflexively shifted with him, and my legs tightened. Almost instantly, he noticed the change, getting harder. My head pushed back deeper into the pillow while he placed one hand on my neck and the other on my hip.

We lost ourselves, running high off each other. I gasped out sounds into his neck. He left utterances of praise in my hair.

"You're taking it so good, baby."

I moaned to the sound of his words the instant he said them.

"I'll never get tired of being inside you."

"Oh, Noah…" I couldn't stop saying his name.

His movements quickened. "Fucking moan all you want, baby."

"Noah. God. Fuck." And then, all I could do was moan.

When we finished, we cuddled beneath the blankets. "You're going to be the death of me, Rain."

My laugh peppered his shoulders. "Then I'll die with you."

Part 3

Pushed out of your arms & into someone
else's. Your biggest fear My biggest affliction.

In the cracks of us,
I started planning my getaway
The roads unpaved
The tall grass & wild tree branches irritate
me
Fear & loneliness beg me to turn back
But the air feels so good here
My hands run so free
Looking back, it was wrong to love you
While not loving me.

There are pieces he thinks are too much
A fortress holds his touch
I'm happy outside
admiring the strength, tripping over jaded
tricks.

Sh' Don't tell a soul!
He makes me leave my mind.

I can't fight it — he has consumed my might
It's new and different
the reassurance he gives not being mine
We aren't anything to say
and we are less to claim.
And as much as he tries to run away,
He finds me every time.
We run in circles, dancing blind
until our backs hit & our hands grip.

Sh' Don't tell a soul!
Liking him feels better than loving you.

16

"Tell me about your mom," Noah said.

We were three weeks into this new, official relationship and had barely spent a night apart. It felt like we had taken the next step into something which had always existed. Now midterms were over, and D-Day was upon us.

Diana Day.

I wondered if I would've allowed my mother to visit if Noah and I hadn't had a fight that Sunday morning, almost a month ago now. Not that I could do anything about Mom. She was flying in today and I had offered to pick her up from the airport because I knew that's what I should do as her daughter. Noah had offered his truck because that's what he thought he should do as my boyfriend. We drove out of our little college town and into the city, smiling and laughing, but on the inside, I was losing it.

"Don't you want to listen to some music?" I asked instead of answering him. "I found this really cool band..."

He gave me a sidelong glance. "Tell me about her."

"We don't have a good relationship," I poorly summed up.

"Yeah, I got that much, Rain, but what else? What's she like?"

I stared down at my black dress. It was simple with a white lace collar. I was two braids away from being Wednesday Addams. My makeup was light and minimal. My jewelry was reduced to a single pair of conservative gold hoops.

"Do I ever look like this?"

"What?"

"Do. I. Ever. Look like this?" I said, emphasizing each word.

Noah quickly scrutinized what I wore. "You look beautiful."

I rolled my eyes.

He reached over, squeezing my knee. "I miss your flare, but this is nice, too. Does your mom care about this stuff?"

"'Care' is an understatement. With her, everything has to be just so. Everything that doesn't matter, at least." I let out a breath, feeling years pile up on my chest. "I'm scared, sad, and apprehensive. And strangely hopeful."

"That's good. Right?"

"Misplaced hope is how disappointment is created."

"Why are you stressed about it, baby? This might be good for you two."

"Because there's all this pressure!" I exclaimed. "We're playing the roles of mother and daughter, but there isn't a director yelling 'cut!' So, we're stuck improvising. Plus, we have this emotional sludge to navigate. When we hit it, we fight, and then we sink. We sort of suck, Noah. Growing up Hispanic, there's this importance of family embedded in the culture. I experienced it with my friends' families but not my own. We also ignore anything pertaining to our feelings, so at least that's one stereotype my family pumps truth into."

"Who gives a shit? There's family you're born into, and then there's family you choose."

Yeah, well, I have neither.

I massaged the knots in my neck. "Promise me you'll still want me after this weekend?"

"Trust me, I'll want you."

"Promise me your family won't hate me after they meet my mother?"

"I doubt she's evil enough to fuck up Dawn's wedding," he grinned.

Just then, my phone vibrated.

"She's landed," I said.

"She's landed? Baby, we're still pretty far away."

"Then I'm sure she's getting some much needed sunshine," I grumbled.

Noah laughed. "I know it's complicated, but I'm still happy to be meeting your family."

"You're meeting my mom, not my family," I said coldly.

"Rosen loved your mom," he tried. "She can't be all bad."

I looked out the window. "My aunt had to love her sister."

Noah squeezed my hand in unspoken solidarity. I turned up the music, hoping to relax before my mother was in front of me.

The city wasn't New York level compact. Being true to Texas, everything was relatively spaced out, and the traffic to the airport wasn't as bad as I had hoped. Within seven minutes, we were pulling up to the arrivals gate. Noah parked under the sign for her airline, putting on his hazards. My gaze slid across people and luggage until it landed on her.

"There she is," I announced.

She stood by a tree, frowning at the shade she had picked. Half of her face was covered by oversized sunglasses that made her look like a large insect. Draped in a plaid trench coat, standing in pointy heels, she looked like a villain in a kids' cartoon.

"Come on, then," Noah said.

I groaned as I got out of the truck. His hand went to the small of my back as we walked toward her.

"Hi, Mom," I said, forcing myself to go in for a hug.

She embraced me quickly, then let go like I had zapped her. *Okay, then. Nice to see you, too.*

"Mom, this is Noah Colt."

She grimaced.

Noah smiled. "Nice to meet you, Mrs.—"

Instantly, my mom's ever-present frown deepened. "Diana."

He extended his hand. She hesitated, then accepted it, barely touching him. Almost immediately, she reached for her hand sanitizer.

"Mom!" I hissed.

"Diana," Noah said, overpowering me. "It's nice to meet you."

"Please thank your family for extending an invitation to their wedding."

"My sister, Dawn, is excited for you to come. The more the merrier. Here, let me get your bags into the truck."

My mom looked at it like it was a cardboard box on wheels.

"It was nice of him to want to pick you up," I said through gritted teeth and a pained smile.

With her sunglasses digging into the bridge of her nose, she turned to me. "I didn't say a word, Rain. But is there enough space for all of us?"

"Yeah," Noah said, carrying her bags. "It's a bench seat."

"A what?"

"We can fit," I assured her.

When Noah chucked the bags into the bed of the truck, my mom clutched her coat as if she were on the verge of a heart attack.

"It's just luggage," I snapped.

"I'm not saying anything, Rain," she chided.

"Of course you're not."

We squeezed into the truck and began driving, shoulder to shoulder.

Noah lowered the music, flashing me the widest grin. I sighed. That was my cue for us to talk.

"My roommate, Mikayla, is in class right now, but she'll join us for dinner later, if that's alright with you," I said.

"Of course it's fine. She's your *friend*," Mom replied, emphasizing the word and regarding Noah pointedly.

The drive was purgatory. I pointed out random landmarks, talked about my midterms, and went into extreme detail over my degree plan. Then I tried not to panic wondering what else I'd have to talk with her about for the rest of the weekend.

"Noah, what is it that you do?" my mom asked as we pulled into the dorm parking lot.

I had overtalked most of the way, and now she only had a few moments to ask her judgmental questions. In my head, I patted myself on the back.

"He's an artist and is also studying business," I answered for him.

"You work as an artist?" she asked Noah.

"Tattoo artist, yeah," he said with a small grin.

Realizing how that would sound to her, I said, "He's really talented," then turned to see if she would have a retort.

"I didn't say a thing, Rain."

I exhaled loudly.

"Can I ask why you named her Rain? My niece met her and told her, very ardently, 'Rain is a weather, not a name.'"

My mother's stony expression cracked slightly, and she offered a weak laugh.

"I thought the name was beautiful," she said. "Your niece sounds practical. Rain was like that as well. She used to be obsessed with Emily Dickinson when she was seven. I went up to her, asking, 'Why do you like her so much? Her poems are morbid.' Do you know what she said?"

He shook his head, visibly amused.

"'Mom,'" she began, mimicking me as a child and raising her voice high enough to strain the vein in her neck, "'Death is death. The worst part about it is that people spend their lives in fear of it. You can't ignore it.'"

I crumpled in on myself. My mother was all about appearances. If she had a fact that shined like a cubic zirconia, it didn't stop her from saying it was a diamond. She pretended like she knew me, and I'll admit it, sometimes she could even fool me.

"I don't remember that."

My comment didn't slow her down. "And I was angry because your Aunt Rosen kept letting you read that stuff."

"Because she was my favorite."

"What's her favorite now?" Mom asked Noah directly.

Cute. She should be testing herself, not him.

"*The Prophet.* She carries it in her bag. She has to explain the meanings to me, though."

"He likes hearing my interpretations," I interjected, but Mom kept the interrogation lamp on him.

"You do not like literature?"

"Unfortunately, I wasn't kidding. I need a dictionary or footnotes to get through most of the work she shows me."

"He's not stupid," I jumped in.

She aimed a stern look at me. "Did I say he was?"

Eyes narrowed on both sides.

"I don't want you thinking it."

"You're not a mind reader, Rain."

"I—" But, feeling like she had scored a point, I didn't say anything else. We parked. My mom and I got out and Noah got her bags.

"I wanted to ask you," Noah began, obviously stalling to keep us here for a second longer. "How did you get to be a dentist?"

"What?" my mom and I said in unison.

He glanced at me, shrugging. "You said she was a dentist."

"Are you thinking of trading tattoo guns for probes and forceps?" my mother asked, and I was shocked to realize she was giving friendliness a chance.

"Possibly," he laughed. "Though we call them tattoo *machines*. We do live in America, after all. Let's not say the 'G' word."

As soon as he said it, I slapped my hand on my forehead.

Mom stared at him for a beat. Then, she cackled like a witch. I peeked through my fingers, aghast at the noise, to discover that, yes, my mom was genuinely laughing. I wasn't sure I had ever heard the noise.

Meanwhile, Noah was beaming with pride for making the ice queen laugh.

"You're as morbid as *she* is," Mom beamed.

"Ah, so you approve of me?"

She waved him off. "Rain doesn't care for my approval, but I will admit, I might like you better than the last one."

"Oof," he replied, clutching his chest against the illusory blade that had pierced him. "You must hate me to compare me to the other guy."

What the hell was happening? They were getting along.

"Um, Mom, Noah has to go. Downside of a family business and all."

He raised an eyebrow at me, but there was only so much of *The Twilight Zone* I could handle. I shook my head. I couldn't believe it. He had charmed her.

"I wish I had more time," he said, offering his hand. "Again, it was nice meeting you."

"Likewise," she replied, returning the handshake, but this time, without the hand sanitizer retrieval.

Noah strutted away like a champion. I writhed inside my own skin.

"Mom, I'm going to say bye really fast," I said, not waiting for her response.

I skipped up so I could grab Noah's hand.

"I'm great, aren't I?" he gloated.

I arched up on my toes and kissed him. He reacted instantly, lifting me up.

"Thanks," I whispered.

"For?"

I threw my arms around him. "Making it easy to like you."

He squeezed me again before setting me back down. "You make it easy also."

I was pretty sure I was dangerously toeing the line of love, but it was weird—I was worried about my feelings, but I wasn't exactly scared. He made falling feel safe.

I wanted to kiss him again, but his phone started ringing.

"Go," I ushered. "I'll see you tomorrow."

He looked bummed but agreed.

"Tomorrow. Bye, baby."

17

At dinner, Mikayla was the perfect buffer. She droned on about her classes, her family, and her adrenaline junkie adventures. My mom was entertained, and I wasn't as nervous. I'd be thanking my roommate for the rest of the year.

I showed my appreciation by not waking her up the next morning, even though I itched to play music while showering. I had four hours until Mom arrived from the hotel so we could drive to the wedding. Getting ready together wasn't our thing. Honestly, it wasn't mine and Aunt Rosen's, either. Out of the three of us, I was the only one who liked taking the time to get ready. Aunt Rosen would've put on a pantsuit, pinned her hair back, and been done. Her style centered around simplicity and not listening to anyone. She was feminine some of the time and androgynous the rest. She wore what she wanted regardless of which section of the department store it was from. She would've been ready in less than an hour and still earning second glances from everyone, because confidence that radiant didn't seek out attention—it just happened.

Meanwhile, my mom would probably wear stuffy clothes that left her looking ten years older than she was.

I sighed, grabbing my razor. Meticulously, I smoothed the blade over my legs. And other places. Then, I focused on double shampooing and leaving a conditioning mask because my hair was about to go through a whole lot of heat damage.

Afterward, I stepped out and applied a face mask while drying my hair with a towel. I decided on giving myself the best at-home blowout a girl could manage and did a quick manicure and pedicure.

Mikayla walked in while I was going insane waiting for the topcoat to dry. Her hair was a tangle away from being classified as a tumbleweed.

"I love makeover montages," she said, not batting an eye in my direction as she retrieved her illegal coffee maker hidden under a towel beneath the sink. The dorms had the stupidest rules. "Single or double?"

"Double."

She worked with half-closed eyelids. "I look like your before picture."

"I thought the same thing."

We both laughed, and she playfully mumbled, "What a bitch," under her breath.

"What did you do last night?" I asked. "I doubt that dinner caused—" I stopped and gestured to her slovenly appearance, "—all of this."

Randomly, she turned and threw her head down to her knees and flipped her hair back aggressively as if she were auditioning for a hair commercial. "I," she huffed, "met Lucia for a drink."

My lips tugged in that not-so-secret, knowing grin. "What happened?"

"What didn't?" she almost yelled, slapping her arms against her body.

My eyes widened. "Oh! That's great!"

"We're supposed to meet up and talk tonight."

"Okay. Do you want to go over what you want to say?"

"No, I want to drink our coffee and disassociate for a minute."

She was definitely paying attention in her psych class. I glanced at her, waiting to see if she meant it or if she'd explode, because not talking about something usually meant thoughts were running wild through her mind. She brushed through her bangs. She seemed stressed, but I decided not to press her. She'd tell me what had happened whenever she felt ready.

"Hey, I wanted to say thank you again for coming to dinner. My mom had fun."

"I like Diana! I don't why it's so hard for you two to talk, but I wasn't raised by her."

Yes, Diana, the mother of the year, who opened up long enough to tell stories of the sister for whom she had put her life on hold when she got sick, who got along with everyone but me. She was calculative and selective, using only certain colors to paint that version of herself. She seemed wonderful, a truly devoted sister and mother.

We wouldn't last five minutes if it were just us, because she wasn't a mom until she was forced to be. Before Aunt Rosen got sick, Mom was never there. She wasn't abusive. She didn't hit me. She just never spoke to me or comforted me. She gave me anything I needed, as long as a price tag was attached. How was I supposed to let years of being pushed to the side go? How was I supposed to think she loved me?

"Years of resentment make conversation difficult," I muttered. Mikayla's eyes were hooks in my back as I leaned forward, pretending to fix a nail.

"Give her a chance. People change."

My walls grew another foot taller, and I pretended I didn't hear her.

"Here," she said, waving a coffee in front of my face. "Forget what I said."

"Thank you," I replied stiffly, and it wasn't for the coffee.

"I gotta run something by you, Raindrop."

I sipped. "Go."

Her gaze slid to the side. "You know how you're spending the night with your mom?"

"Ugh, yes."

Mom had invited me before last night came to an end. *Will you come stay at the hotel after the wedding? We can catch up.* I had hesitated, then said yes. Maybe it was to avoid the stricken look of disappointment across her face, or because Aunt Rosen would've wanted me to. Maybe it was because my inner child, who watched mothers and daughters on TV having chick flick moments, thought we could be like those paid actors for a night. I didn't know what caused my mouth to form the word "yes," but it's what happened.

"Do you think it'd be a terrible idea if I invite Lucia to spend the night?" Mikayla continued.

"Invite her!" I squealed.

"You don't mind?"

"Of course not! Noah is always here. Ooh, can we double date sometime? I've never done that."

"Not even with Travis and his girlfriend?"

"I don't think eating dinner and breakfast at their place counts."

She smiled. "If tonight goes well, then duh."

I nearly combusted. The rest of the afternoon, Mikayla handed over every big and miniscule detail about the two of them. We moved to my room, and she told me about the signs as I did makeup. Pure and good, my stomach fluttered for her.

As we talked, my body relaxed. I had so many things I used to wish for. I had a best friend in Mikayla and this shoebox of a room as our domain. I had a steady boyfriend in Noah. I had his family as mine. Most importantly, I had me. I could finally *be* me. If the relationship with my mother was a thorn to this bouquet of roses, then maybe its sting wasn't so painful.

I stepped into my dress, feeling levelheaded again. The forest green, satin dress flowed at floor length. Mikayla helped with the delicate, laced back.

"You could be a Disney Princess, Raindrop," she said in awe.

"You're funny."

"I'm not kidding. You look amazing. Heels?"

I searched my closet. "Here."

I opted for citrine stones for my earrings, and matched them with a gold horseshoe necklace Aunt Rosen had given me on my sixteenth birthday. *For luck.*

It seemed my necklace was already working. Exactly at that moment, Mom called to let me know she was pulling into the parking lot.

Mikayla clasped her hands together and grinned widely.

"What?" I asked, stuffing my lipstick and wallet in my clutch.

"Noah's going to cream his pants."

I threw my head back, laughing.

§

The ceremony was outside the reception hall, right at sunset. Ana was both the flower girl and maid of honor. She walked down the aisle casting flowers in her wake, looking adorable in her pink, puffy dress. The ladybug bows in her hair were the best part.

Dawn was the perfect bride. She wore an elegant white dress with long, lace sleeves. When she and Chris met eyes at the altar, I cried. They had that we-made-it look, and not even Noah in a tux could divert my eyes from their happiness.

I had never been to a wedding before, and innately, I loved the celebration of love. It reminded me that happy endings could happen, and life could be beautiful. I soaked it all in.

Afterwards, Mom and I entered the reception hall. The theme was autumn with a sprinkle of Halloween. Rich amber and gold accents were sprinkled everywhere. Shimmering leaves decorated the long rectangular tables. Orange floral arrangements hung from the ceilings. With the smattering of black candles and pumpkins, it was a witch's dream. A classy witch who had a crystal cauldron.

"It's beautiful, isn't it?" I said as we sipped on our first glasses of champagne.

"Yes," she agreed.

Just as reticent as ever. I sighed.

My mom wore a simple blue dress with jewels embedded throughout. She placed her hands in her lap, careful not to ruin the fragile seams.

I tried again. "You look great, Mom."

She eyed me.

"I mean it," I replied lightly.

"You look beautiful, Rain. I'm happy to see you still have that necklace."

My hand instinctively covered it. "Aunt Rosen gave it to me."

"I know," she said.

"Is something wrong?" I asked.

But before she could answer, Travis and Lorie found us. Introductions were exchanged. Mom, with a wrinkled frown, listened politely as Lorie hijacked our conversation, asking her about dentistry. I took the opportunity to escape and find Noah.

People were trickling in, and in the sea of black tuxes, I couldn't find the one I was looking for. After a few minutes of hopeless searching, the music crescendoed, and Dawn and Chris were announced. The door behind me opened, introducing the happy couple, but my attention had been caught by a figure holding a champagne flute in the corner.

Noah.

My eyes alighted on him, and I noted all the details I had missed during the ceremony. His hair was shorter. Instead of an unruly mess hitting his shoulders, the curly locks had been tamed near his jaw, intact but refined. He was alluring in a tux. Beautiful. His pale skin was creamy against the dark fabric, and his eyes were like lucent moss in the candlelight. The only less-than-perfect detail was his lopsided bowtie.

The scene, the man, the formal attire—it was a page from the sweetest book of poetry. It was the stanza I'd underline three times so I wouldn't forget it.

Noah stared at me without lifting his face fully as I approached.

"Aren't the groomsmen obliged to watch the first dance?" I asked, meeting him.

He leaned in, blatantly checking me out. "What are you wearing?"

My first response was panic. *Does he hate it?*

"You're stunning," he said. "I can't take my eyes off you."

He reached out an arm and opened his hand toward me, not saying a word. I walked my fingers along his palm. The playful touch sparked his trademark smirk. He seized my hand and pulled me forward.

"What are you doing?" I said, laughing.

In answer, he slid his hand above my collarbone and down my arm.

I couldn't stop smiling. "Better than my matching sets?"

He kissed me gently, skimming his tongue over my bottom lip.

"Don't make me choose," he growled, lingering closely.

"You don't need to," I whispered into his ear. "I'm wearing them underneath this."

The resulting passion in his eyes was worth it. But when he reached for me again, I teasingly pulled away.

"My mother is waiting for me."

His expression shifted instantly. "How has it been?"

"I'm managing."

He squinted at me skeptically. "Really?"

"Have I wanted to reply with a snarky comment which would inevitably lead to a fight? Yes, several times."

"Self-control. Go you. I could use some of that."

"What do you mean?"

"You look incredible, and I have to sit all the way over there," he grumbled, nodding in the direction of the wedding party table, "and pretend I don't want to drag you out of here."

The thrill his words gave me left me breathless and reckless. Reaching up to adjust his bowtie, I made sure my body grazed his.

"Where would we go?" I asked innocently.

"I doubt 'my room' would be a good answer," he replied lightly.

"It's the perfect answer, Mr. Colt."

He lunged for my waist, but I danced backwards, laughing.

"The faster we get through the night, the quicker you'll have me tomorrow."

"Lead the way, Rivas," he sighed.

I smiled, triumphant and miserable at the same time.

Back at the table, Lorie and my mom were engrossed in a conversation about the decorations. Noah paid his respects in time to return to Dawn's side for a brother-sister dance.

My mom tapped me on the shoulder as they swayed. "No father?"

I grimaced. "No. Their family is as fractured as ours."

I said it without caution. I didn't realize how hurtful it was until I saw her reaction. As her face crumbled, I realized how many of the lines on her face were from sadness, depression… and maybe even regret.

I averted my gaze. She didn't utter another word.

Travis turned to me, signing, «That bastard. Look at him! I didn't know he could dance.»

Noah glided across the floor like a professional ballroom dancer.

«I swear, he's good at everything,» I said.

Once I found the open bar, the night fast-forwarded. I had downed three glasses of red wine by the time the DJ started playing the fun music. Surrounded by the flailing bodies, Noah found me on the dance floor and spun me around.

"Missed you," he said, his voice blending into the music. He wrapped himself around me possessively. I shook off the butterflies fanning my stomach, wondering if their wings showed on my face.

I think I love him.

Enveloped by the twirling silk of my dress, I was stopped abruptly by Noah's lips pressing on mine. He tilted my chin up, deepening our kiss. My epiphany remained a secret, but I couldn't unfeel it. I had fallen in love while falling out of it.

"Ew! Enough," Dawn interrupted, suddenly appearing at our side. "I haven't said hi to Rain yet. Thanks so much for coming! Where's your mom?"

"Congratulations, Dawn," I said, bringing her into a hug. Seeing Chris over her shoulder, I congratulated him also. "She finally made an honest man of you."

"We're no longer living in sin!" he cheered.

Dawn ignored our antics, tugging Chris to my table. "Let's go say hi."

Reluctantly, I followed. As soon as I had Noah alone, I could confess my feelings to him, but until then, I had to babysit my mother.

"Mom, these are the newlyweds, Chris and Dawn Carson."

"I love the sound of that!" Dawn gushed to me, then said to her, "We're so happy you could make it! We love Rain."

"Thank you for extending the invitation. The whole event has been beautiful." She forced a smile, and the wrinkles around her eyes deepened.

"Thanks! Hope you're having a good time, Mrs. Rivas," Chris said.

I cringed. We didn't share a last name, and Mom wasn't married. I wanted to correct them or apologize to Mom, but nothing came out. As the newlyweds walked away, Noah and I sat. I grabbed my drink, plotting how to steal him away from the reception.

"It's strange seeing you drink," Mom said after a minute.

"Really?"

"It makes me feel old," she confessed, and I genuinely laughed.

She reached out for my hand. "I'm happy to see you happy."

And I should have let her say one nice thing to me. We had shared a laugh. I should have replied with another nice thing just so we could break a record, but with the constant strain on her face and the forced trying, I couldn't.

I set my glass down with a clank. "Do you even know what happiness on me looks like?"

My voice came out louder than I expected it to. Noah coughed into his drink. Lorie bowed her head as if she wished she could disappear. Travis stared at my lips, wondering if he had read them correctly.

"Rain," Noah said warningly.

I felt their judgement upon me. None of them had lived with her for twenty years, yet somehow, I was the bad guy in all of their minds.

"I need some air," I grumbled.

I pretended not to hear Noah's call for me to stay. I got up and left, pushing through the doors and into the night, wondering if my tipsy flounce in heels made me look like a t-rex on a rampage.

I hated my impulsive need to hurt her, but my reaction was as instinctive as holding out my hands before a fall. Mom and I didn't know how to be around each other, and it wouldn't change for trying.

That didn't stop me from wanting to cry.

"Why does this have to be so hard?" I croaked.

The wind blew and the crisp, fall air made goosebumps prickle on my skin. Lights hanging from the patio ceiling twinkled. The table for smoking was vacant and looked like an oasis to me. I leaned against the metal frame, shutting my eyes.

A battle waged in my head. Was my mother being sincere? She could be pretending. Her track record supported my doubt. But finally, empathy kicked in, and my guilt trumped my pride. My mother might not know how to love, but she was trying.

I should be happy. I love Noah.

But what if he couldn't love me? He had never loved anyone other than family before.

The door squeaked open. The scuffle of dress shoes clunked with the sound of heels hitting the concrete. My gaze rose to the surprise duo of the century: Noah and my mother.

"What?" I demanded.

"We're simply checking on you," my mom replied.

I stared at her, dumbfounded. Checking on me? What act was she pulling? This was the woman who had spent years of my childhood shooing me away. Why would she think I'd confide in her now?

"Rain?" Noah's horribly hopeful voice echoed around the patio.

"I'm fine," I said through gritted teeth.

My mom's forehead furrowed. "Are you sure?"

Her face, wrongfully worried, infuriated me. As a child, you learn that your parents are supposed to love and protect you. As an adult, you realize that people can have dramatically different definitions of the words 'love' and 'protect.' Mom thought she had done her best. I thought she couldn't have done a worse job.

"I'm going inside. It's too crowded out here now," I said harshly.

I stalked past them. Alcohol and emotions clouded my head, so I focused on my breathing. *I'm fine. I'm fine. I'm fine...*

Out of the corner of my eye, I saw Noah turning to follow me. I quickened my pace.

"Rain?" a man's voice called, right before I walked into him.

"I'm so sorry," I began. "I wasn't paying attention to—"

I would've recognized those brown eyes anywhere. The woodsy smell of his cologne lingered around him. There, in plain sight, my sweetest nightmare invaded my reality.

Rob.

His arms held me upright. His eyes were wide with surprise. My heart flopped like a fish out of water.

Frantically, I blinked. This couldn't be real. Could it? Suddenly, my dress felt like a dishcloth. My chest burned under the wrong branding. My face was too caked. My guilt almost had me on my knees.

Footsteps settled beside me. I turned, aware of Noah's presence.

"What are you doing here?" But it was Noah's voice, not mine.

My gaze darted between the two of them.

"I was her plus one," Rob mumbled, gently releasing me.

"Whose plus one?" Noah demanded.

"I'm confused," I said.

Time moved at a fickle speed. My gaze picked up every random glance and stifled breath. Rob shifted to the side, revealing another ghost from the past.

"Jen?" I squeaked.

In a low-cut, black velvet dress, she sauntered forward like a winning chess piece and squeezed her arm through Rob's.

I had to be dreaming. Seeing him with her, here? I must have hit my head. Maybe I was in a hospital room somewhere across town.

"What's happening?" I whispered.

Jen's steel eyes centered on me. I stifled a shudder.

"Rain, it's great to see you," Jen said with a smirk.

"Let's go," Noah ordered, wrapping his fingers around my upper arm. I ignored him.

"Why are you here?" I asked Rob. "Do you know her?"

"Rain," Noah urged.

"No!" I snapped without taking my gaze off of them. "Rob?"

He looked away for a moment. The inability to read him settled in my body like a poison, killing me slowly.

"I tried calling you," Rob said.

"When?" I breathed, then realized he wasn't talking to me. His eyes had slid past me to Noah. "You— you tried calling *him*?"

My heart beat faster than my veins could handle.

My teeth ground together.

My hope thinned.

"You *know* him?" I choked out.

"Of *course* they know each other. They've known each other for years," Jen laughed.

"No, they haven't," I insisted. My head shook like a robot malfunctioning. "They barely even saw each other at the Tipsy Squeeze."

"Newsflash, Rain—we've *all* known each other for years. Rob was there to see *me* that night, not you."

"Jen, shut the fuck up," Noah hissed.

I stepped away from Noah. From the stranger I thought I knew. Whom I loved.

"Rain," Rob pleaded, "I thought you knew."

Noah's grip tightened on my arm. "Let me explain."

I tore myself from his grasp, refocusing my attention on Rob. For every horrible thing he had ever done, he had never lied to me before. If anything, *I* was the liar, pretending I was happy and fine with him.

"Rob, the night you saw me with him at the Tipsy Squeeze—that's why you were mad? Because you knew him?"

His jaw ticked. "I didn't expect him to steal my second girlfriend, too."

My eyes flicked over to Jen in dawning understanding. "The girl next door. The one who broke your heart when you were fifteen."

Jen shrugged, and her perfectly styled hair settled around her like a silk scarf. "Mistakes were made."

It took a moment for the words to sink in. Then I rounded on Noah.

"You— you lied to me," I said in shuddering breaths.

"Baby—"

"Do not call me that!"

He ran a hand across his face. "Yeah, okay? I know him. We used to hang out—"

"He's one of the friends I spent time with, back when my parents used to ship me off to my aunt and uncle's place," Rob said, his painfully confident voice overpowering Noah's. "Well, he *was* a friend. Until he stole my first love."

Memories of Rob talking to me about his friends in Austin echoed through my head. There was the deaf one who inspired him to learn ASL. And the other one, the one who stole his first love from him and left him the emotionally broken boy I had met.

Rob. Travis. Noah. Jen. Friends, lovers, enemies for years. All of them duping me.

"Fuck you all," I said, storming off.

"Rain."

"Rain."

The two male voices melded together like a choir.

My steps quickened, racing against the tears simmering from the betrayal. Any healed parts of me ripped to shreds. I pushed through the door and the dam of my composure broke. Everything came out in a wretched sob. The high tide of emotions felt like a tsunami, and when it drained, I felt like I was being scraped from the inside out.

I thought about the moment Noah and I had met. He had kept staring at me like he knew me. I thought it had meant something. I thought it was a sign that this was bigger than mere chance.

It wasn't fate—he simply knew *of* me. I was just a girl his friend had abused. Another prize for him to take.

I laughed.

"Rain, please," I heard from behind me. I didn't have to turn around to know it was my mother.

"What do you want?" I cried.

"What happened, Rain?"

It was hilarious to hear concern in her voice. No, it was an aberration. A cruel deviation.

"Rain," she said, now at my side.

Breathe in. Breathe out.

She touched my shoulder. "Did you and Noah get into a fight? I'm sure you two will be able to work it out. He seems to care about you a lot, and I know you—"

I shoved off her light grip. "You don't know shit."

Her eyes widened. "Wh-what?"

"You know we'll work out? You know nothing about me or my life! You never have. Fuck!" I exclaimed, completely losing it. "Did you know why things didn't work out with Rob? Mom, he was emotionally abusive. Did you notice when I stopped wearing colors because they were too flashy? When I stopped wearing v-necks because they were too revealing? When I distanced myself from my friends? When I use to cry every week? Noah saw him push me the night we broke up. He pushed me. Oh, and let's not paint Noah like an angel. Trust me, the halo was just a ploy because he knew Rob the entire time and kept it a secret. So, no, we won't 'work it out.' He doesn't care about me, just like Rob didn't care about me. Just like how you haven't cared about me for the past decade."

I breathed heavily, not regretting what I had said. Not even when her eyes watered and her hands shook.

"Rain, I am sorry. I didn't know."

Of course she didn't.

"Apologies don't fix how I feel. I needed you. I needed my mom. I could've turned to you when he started giving me rules, but you were never there! God, I couldn't even look at people walking by without getting in trouble. You could've seen how badly he treated me if you just paid attention. If you looked at me long enough."

"I didn't know," she repeated. Her voice withered in the wind.

My mouth twisted into a grimace.

"I came home one night after fighting with him. Aunt Rosen was in the hospital. My eyes were bloodshot. You asked me if I was alright. I told you we had gotten into a fight, and I saw your attention just slip away. You just talked about another round of chemo. I was nothing to you."

"Rain. Let's go to the hotel and talk."

She extended her arm, and I was repulsed. "The attention left your face because it was nothing more than a stupid fight with my boyfriend."

"Please."

"He said he hated me that night. Apparently, I was too naïve, and he was tired of looking out for me. We went to a party, and I danced. Some guys looked at me. Do you know how much I hated myself because I couldn't go a night without messing up? I thought dancing was *my* fault! I didn't know what was right or wrong. He hated me because I danced, and it wasn't enough to get your attention."

I shook my head, scattering the tears across my cheeks.

"Let's talk," she pleaded.

"Ugh! And I carry this fucking emptiness because I've been so unloved by you. Everyone tells me to forgive you, but I can't!"

She took a step, and I threw my arm out.

"No! Where was your love then? Where was it?"

"Rain, she was sick. I thought you'd understand."

My eyes widened. "You thought I'd understand you not caring about me? Just admit that's what it was. Why, Mom? Why is it so hard to care about me?"

"Rain, I'm your mother. I care about you."

I stood there, feeling nothing but exhaustion. The truth was that nothing could make me feel better. Years had gone by, but I was still that sixteen-year-old girl who felt like something was wrong with herself because her mom didn't love her.

18

"Mikayla?" I cried into my phone.

"Hi, roomie. Forgot your key?" she mumbled.

"I really need you to turn on your crazy energy batteries and use that car of yours, because I'm walking on the side of the road, and... I'm sorry," I sobbed, wiping my face, ruining my makeup. Then I remembered, "Crap. Lucia's there, isn't she."

"Whoa, whoa. Lucia doesn't care. You're important. I'm on my way, okay? Send me your location. Hold on."

"I'm so sorry," I said, not able to stop. "I don't get paid until next Friday and these stupid fifty bucks are supposed to stretch until then because I had to buy this ugly dress for this horrible night."

I heard shuffling. "Alright, I'm on my way. Start at the beginning."

So, I did. I walked along the road, ignoring the cars passing me. She let me ramble until she found me by the side of the road.

"Do we hate him?" she asked as we drove.

I stared out the window. "No," I replied bleakly.

"Fair. Do we forgive him?"

"Hang on a second, I need to call someone."

"Uh, sure..." she said hesitantly.

I sucked in a big breath and dialed the number. He picked up on the first ring.

"Rain? Is that really you?"

"Rob, I need you to be honest with me."

Mikayla practically sprained her neck. "Whaaaaaat?"

"I didn't know it would go down like that," he said, and I took in the information.

"You knew I'd be at the wedding," I concluded.

"Is there any chance of you not hating me?"

My throat tightened. I wasn't in on the joke. I *was* the joke.

"So, you wanted to get back at him for seeing me? Or was I your target?" I gave him his moment of silence because I knew he wouldn't lie to me.

"I thought you knew he and I had been friends. I just wanted to— I wanted both of you to see Jen and me together. I didn't know you'd be caught off-guard like that. Noah was playing you."

We had already broken up. He had already pushed me. Yet, he wasn't done. He just had to hurt me one last time.

I laughed and cried at the same time. "Goodbye, Rob."

"I'm fucking sorry, okay?"

I hung up the phone.

"That was something," Mikayla commented cautiously. "You'd better block the number."

"Done."

The car felt so painfully small, so insignificant, compared to the crumbing in my chest. I glanced out the window. We passed fields of nothing.

"Mikayla, pull over."

"What?"

"Pull over," I demanded. I couldn't explain it, but I needed to be in a space vast enough to absorb this heartache. I needed the ocean, but the fields would do.

The car slowed to a stop. She put on her hazard lights.

My bottom lip shook as I got out of the car. The fields of wheat lost their color under the night sky and looked like a block of shadows. Soft rustles carried through the wind. I threw my head back, looking up at the stars. Underneath the tiny specks of light, I let my shoulders sag.

"What is so unbelievably wrong with me, Aunt Rosen? I just want a family, someone to love me. What am I doing wrong?"

"Rain," Mikayla called, opening her door and meeting me by the side of the road, "what are we doing?"

"You were stolen from me," I shouted at the night sky. "Mom was never there for me. Rob was bad for me. Is that why this happened to me again? I'm terrible at love and needed to be taught another lesson?"

I had been looking for the love I so desperately needed from others, and where had that gotten me? Lonely on the side of the road.

"Raindrop?" Mikayla tried again.

I looked at her with tears in my eyes, and then I screamed.

I screamed so hard, for minutes.

I screamed until my voice cracked, and light seeped its way back into my heart.

"Fuck it. If that's what we're doing," Mikayla said, then started screaming with me.

A car slowed down.

Mikayla turned, saying, "Move it along. We're heartbroken." When they didn't leave, she yelled, "Move it, asswipe!"

After the tears came uncontrollable laughter.

Mikayla put her hand in mine. "Feel better?"

I stared at her, wondering what I did right to deserve her. I looked back up at the sky, feeling the weight lift. "Surprisingly, yes."

She looked up at the stars and kissed the back of my hand. "I know it doesn't feel like it, but I promise it's going to be okay."

Another tear fell, joining the rest coating my neck. "I know."

§

When the sun started to peak over the horizon, we drove back to the dorms. I carried my heels in my hand and walked with Mikayla on my arm.

She leaned over. "So, how screwed are we?"

"What do you mean?"

"Love and friendship aside, how good was he?"

I stared at her, confused. "Mikayla, what do you mean?"

She fixed my hair. "I need to know what size dildo to get you."

Laughter rang out of me.

She shimmied her shoulders. "Hey, whatever makes you feel better is worth every dollar."

I couldn't tell if she was being serious or not, but I couldn't stop laughing as we walked in.

Our lobby was nothing special. It was just an open space with a few tables and chairs and usually only had my RA behind the desk, chewing her gum.

In the middle of leading me forward, Mikayla stopped and squeezed my arm.

I turned.

My mom and Noah were sitting there.

Noah's eyes struck me, squelching my laughter. I gasped. His curls were gone. His scarred brow now had a twin injury. Along his hairline, eight stitches pieced him together. Aside from the bruising rippling across his cheek, his skin looked translucent and pallid.

I remembered that I shouldn't care anymore and fixed my face, fortifying it in indifference.

"What happened to you, Tattoo Dude?" Mikayla asked. "Hi, Ms. Diana."

Just keep walking, Rain.

"Rain, I'm sorry," Noah blurted out.

We looked at each other. We were steps away from touching, yet miles from the truth.

"Mom," I said, averting my gaze. "You can come up if you want." Out of the corner of my eye, I saw her rise to her feet.

I resumed my steps, slower this time, while clutching Mikayla's arm. It felt like I was walking on a frozen lake, and I was praying to make it without falling through.

You're almost there.

When I passed Noah, cracks broke out on the surface.

"I love you, Rain."

Everything froze. Even the RA stopped chewing her gum.

I placed a hand on my own chest, blinking away the stabbing pain of his words.

"Hey, Diana, let's head on up with our girl," Mikayla said.

I turned toward him. "You're cruel to say that."

He sighed and nodded. "I guess I deserve that."

Anger snuck into the sadness. "I deserve to not be harassed by you. What are you doing here?"

"Hear me out, baby, please."

I wrapped my arms around myself. "Rob told me everything."

He already looked defeated, but the shock on his face was just as intense.

"Rob?" He stepped back. "You've got to be kidding me. You ran back to *him*?"

"Who was I supposed to turn to for the truth?"

"Not to your ex who took a fucking plate to my head!"

My eyes widened. "He did this to you?"

"It doesn't matter. I'm used to fighting for you."

"I didn't ask you to."

"I'm in love with you, Rain. I'd do anything for you."

A betrayed heart has two emotions—anger and agony. I had pivoted between the two so many times that my stomach felt queasy, but it wasn't enough to stop it from happening again.

I swung back to rage.

"You'd do anything but tell me the truth. You lied to me the whole time. You were his friend. You knew who I was and pretended you didn't. God," I exclaimed, falling apart, "the worst part is that you knew how badly I needed to trust you. You knew and chose not to say anything. I should thank Rob. I should thank Jen! Send her some flowers as repayment. You should've told me!" I crossed my arms. "I can't do this. I can't be with you."

His fingers pressed into my skin. Tears welled in my eyes.

"Don't make me lose you, Rain."

I looked down at his fierce, desperate hold upon me.

"Get your hands off me."

For once, he did as he was told.

"Please leave."

"I'll come back," he vowed. The crackle in his voice burned like embers, stubbornly lit but fading. As tempting as it was to fold, my anger wouldn't let me.

"If you love me, you won't."

§

My mother planned to leave today. I had said yes to lunch. We sat at a booth with a fake sunflower in a cheap, plastic vase. I sipped my water several times and picked at the basket of bread. She ordered a salad. I needed comfort food and got the dinner-sized fettucine alfredo.

After a silent mouthful, I asked, "Did Noah say anything while you were waiting?"

Surprised, my mom's forkful of lettuce froze in the air. "She speaks."

I narrowed my gaze, waiting impatiently as she chewed.

"We have other things to talk about first," she said.

"I'm sorry," I replied, quick and rehearsed. "It was…"

"A lot," she finished for me, with a sympathetic grimace.

I looked down at my food, moving noodles around. "I shouldn't have told you—not like that—"

"I'm seeing someone, Rain," she interrupted.

My jaw went slack. "Mom, what the absolute fuck?"

Of course, the waiter picked just that moment to appear and refill my water.

"Rain!" my mom hissed.

"Sorry," I mumbled. "Thanks."

Once alone, I said, "You have a boyfriend?"

She smiled and shook her head. "I'm seeing a therapist."

"A therapist?" The word sat on my tongue like metal, tasting strange.

She nodded, squeezing lemon into her iced tea. "I have major depression disorder and generalized anxiety."

I put my fork down, gawking at her. She continued prepping her drink, adding a packet of sweetener. Her mundane movements looked bizarre after dropping that bomb on me.

"My family didn't believe in these sorts of things. If you were sad, it was because you were unmotivated and lazy. When I lost your grandparents and when your father left, I wasn't just depressed. I was barely a person."

"Mom—" I'd wake up any second.

"The only other person I could talk to was Rosen. But she was sick, so there was only so much she could do."

"Are you trying to suggest Rosen didn't try hard enough to help you?"

"What? No. Never," she assured me immediately. "What I meant was that if I was depressed in bed, she couldn't help me out of it, but she got you out of yours. We didn't know why I couldn't do it myself."

"What made you realize you needed help?" I managed to ask.

"Her dying and you leaving home. I had given you no reason to return. I had done the one thing I swore I wouldn't do as a mother."

I blinked at her, unsure of what I was hearing.

"I wanted to be there for you. I used to go to my room crying about how my parents were too busy with work for me and swore I would never do that to my own child. I thought I was building a real family for you, Rain. It was supposed to be better, so when it didn't happen—I didn't know what was wrong with me. I just knew I didn't want my sadness to touch you."

"So, you ignored me? That was your perfect solution?"

She sighed. "I was trying to get through the day, hoping the next day would be better, but then the days turned into years. I said the wrong thing constantly. I bought the wrong toys. I sang the wrong lullabies. I lost my temper when I shouldn't have. With Rosen... it was like she instinctively knew what you needed all the time. I thought you'd be better off loving her than hating me."

"You don't get it. You could've been terrible and I still would've loved you, but you didn't even try."

"I want to start trying now, Rain."

I twisted my fork and stuffed a strategically large bundle of noodles into my mouth. This was what I wanted, right? What I used to wish on shooting stars for? I needed my mom to change. I'd been secretly hoping for it for years. Yet now, with forgiveness on the horizon, it was easier to hold onto resentment than try to understand the person who had hurt me.

"Do you know why I named you Rain?"

I looked up. "You told Noah you thought the name was beautiful."

She smiled. "The night you were born, your father was asleep and I was holding you. I had a panic attack. I couldn't stop crying. Rosen came in and asked me what was wrong, and I said, 'I'm going to mess her up. I don't want my rain to touch her.' Rosen looked at me and said, 'Rain is beautiful, Diana. Where would we be without it?' I wanted you to have the best parts of me. I didn't mean to ever show you my worst."

"Oh, Mom..." I whispered.

I sat there, trying to convince myself that broken hearts could be mended. No, I couldn't forgive her yet, but I finally felt like I wanted to. I wasn't on the fence, wrestling with what I should do out of guilt. I had swayed to her side.

"Noah," she began, pausing to clear her throat, "shares your bluntness."

"He's not really my favorite person right now. What happened after I left?"

"Rob did the—" She motioned her manicured nail to her temple.

I drank a sip of water to force the food down.

"What exactly did Noah say?"

"Apparently, they fought after you left. You should've told me that you were safe. You disappeared."

I rolled my eyes at her lecture. Her mothering still felt like she was trying on a hat, trying to decide if she'd stick with it and take it home or put it back on the shelf.

"Can't you just tell me what he said?"

"He's decent, Rain. Rosen would approve."

The mention of Aunt Rosen again liquified the tension, crumbling my façade in a single blow. I glanced out the window. I felt like she was up in the sky moving us around like dolls in a house.

My mother continued. "Before she passed, she told me to keep an eye on you. She said you'd need someone patient. 'Diana, she needs someone to wait outside her door. A real Romeo.'"

My brows clashed. Aunt Rosen's response to cancer was to try and give us advice for all possible scenarios. Sometimes, she'd say trivial things, like I should quit trying to bleach my hair blonde, never mix alcoholic drinks, and steer clear from turtleneck sweaters because they would make me look shorter. Her tips and tricks were surface-level quotes that sounded like *Seventeen* magazine articles. Other times, she gave me the important, life-altering stuff. I had no idea Aunt Rosen had ever shared the important stuff with my mom or that Mom had listened so carefully.

"Technically, he waited in the lobby of my dorm," I grumbled.

To my surprise, my mother laughed, and not the lighthearted, polite sound I had memorized. This laugh started in her throat and fell out of her stomach.

Widening my eyes, I looked at her anew. We looked so much alike that I knew I was seeing my future reflection when I looked at her, and we had more in common than I had ever given us credit for. Our hearts were both damaged. We both felt too much. We both got lost in our laughs.

We became an obnoxious clash of sound.

"You are so stubborn!" she guffawed.

"Says the woman who took fifty years to go to therapy."

Somehow, she kept laughing, and I did too.

In the middle of our collective breakdown, my mom slid over to my side of the booth.

"This trip was supposed to be my grand gesture to convince you to forgive me," she said lightly, despite our heavy issues. "I am sorry." She pushed a lock of hair behind my ear. "I am so sorry, Rain. I'd go back and change everything if I could."

My bottom lip wobbled as I uttered a soft, "Me, too."

§

As I walked her out, we made plans for my visit home during Thanksgiving break. Going back to my hometown didn't seem like such a death march after our talk.

"Mom?" I mumbled before she climbed into her car.

"Hmm?"

"You can always call me and tell me about therapy or whatever else is going on," I said in a rush.

"Sure, Rain. I can do that. You call me too, okay?"

"Yeah." I twisted my fingers. "Can do."

I stared after her car and turned on my phone. As her car got smaller and smaller, the notifications on my phone got louder and louder. My anxieties swelled as the messages blasted onto the screen.

Unknown: I'm lost without you. You're all I wanted. How am I supposed to let you go?

Unknown: You looked beautiful.

Unknown: I can't stop.

Unknown: Call me, please.

And then Noah's voice, in a voicemail.

"I know you hate me. Trust me, I hate myself more. I should have told you, but you wouldn't have let me get close to you if you knew. I know what I did was messed up, but don't go back to him. You're better than that. He tries to mute you, baby. He tries to snuff out your flame. I guess I sort of it get it because I was half-dead when I met you. You're so bright. He was scared of you, but fuck, I'm not. I'm enamored. It's like my soul welcomed everything you are. I think my mom sent you. You know, that's what I thought when I met you. Your tattoo—God, Rain, I recognized it because of her. Maybe she and Rosen made a deal and conspired to bring us together. Please, Rivas, I love you. Directly. Intensely. I love you. I'm sorry."

The text message I sent back was brief.

Me: I can't do this.

19

The sun was out, but my life had gone dark again. Even my nights were starless. Light was rare, and I tried to remember how I had conjured it up the last time someone left my life.

My mind played mean tricks and stirred up the memory for me. *Oh, holy green eyes...*

Mikayla clung to my side because her worry was as persistent as my lies that I was fine. I spoke more to my journal than I did out loud. My lips were useless things that I no longer wanted to paint in berry colors.

When Rob and I had ended, the empty space had been absolute. I was starting completely over. In some ways, I wish Noah had taken up more space, so I could've been starting over at rock bottom. But he had left traces of himself behind. The memories of what we had left me haunted and defenseless to illusions of what we were.

For the first time in the past few days, Mikayla had left me alone to go get us coffee. I pushed my journal underneath my pillow and picked up my phone. I'd been putting off one task that I couldn't ignore any longer. I inhaled deeply and dialed Dawn's number. It'd been days since her wedding, and I needed to call her before she went on her honeymoon next week.

"Hey, I'm glad you called," she said immediately.

"Hi Dawn. Um, I'm calling because—"

She sighed into the speaker. "If you're quitting, you have to do it in person."

"What?" I gaped.

"Yep. It's store policy."

"Uhhh..." I stalled. No way that was a policy for a tattoo shop, but I didn't necessarily want to burn a bridge if I didn't have to.

After a beat of silence, she said, "Noah's still recovering from his concussion, so he won't be here. Does that help?"

I gulped. "Concussion?"

"Are you coming in or not?" she asked, her tone short and blunt.

Times when she had been mad at Noah flashed through my mind. I really didn't want that negative energy directed towards me.

"Dawn, this call should be enough of a notice."

"If you want your last paycheck, you'll come."

"Are you joking?"

"Rain, I get it. You dated my brother, but he wasn't the only one who fell in love with you. We all did. Have the decency to say bye."

Click.

I blinked in surprise. *She hung up on me?*

I kicked my mattress in a mini tantrum. *Fine.* Groaning, I crawled off my bed and slipped on my shoes. *Fine! If that's how she wants to be, fine.*

I opted to walk to Dawn's instead of catching the bus. I figured the fresh air would help, but when I opened the door of the tattoo shop, I realized the walk had done nothing for me. As soon as I saw the same shade of green of Dawn's eyes, I wanted to scream like I had by the side of the road.

"Hey, come in," Dawn said, her demeanor neutral and unpredictable.

I scanned the shop. Empty. Not even music was playing.

Dawn sat at the counter with a few binders open. "I'm just checking statements before I leave next week."

I looked away. "Oh."

She exhaled. "I have your check ready for you."

"Great!" I replied, too enthusiastically, and it caused her to stop whatever she was scribbling in the binder and turn her attention to me completely. "I'm sorry. I know this isn't ideal."

"Yeah, breaking my brother's heart does throw a wrench into my happiness. Oh, but wait. That's not what you're talking about, right? Don't worry, I'm sure I'll find last-minute help to cover the shop so I can still take my honeymoon."

My jaw sprang open. *Ouch.* Okay, I liked it a lot better when she was on my side and Noah was her punching bag.

She handed me the check, but when I tried to take it, her grip tightened. My gaze crashed into hers.

"Dawn, I respect you so much, but I can't do this. I can't pretend Noah's betrayal doesn't sting me nonstop, okay? And working here will make it worse."

"I've never seen him like this," she said.

"Yeah, well, I've never been this hurt before," I said without thinking.

Her eyes softened. "I didn't ask you here to fight with you."

"*Ask?*" I said pointedly.

She placed the check in front of me. "You got him to take down his armor for you, and then you left."

"Did he tell you everything?"

"Yeah."

"Did you know?"

"I would've kicked his ass if I had known," she said.

My mouth quirked.

"Rain, if I'm being honest, I wouldn't blame you for not getting back together with him. But he's my brother," she explained. Her voice caught on emotion. "You didn't see him fight for you."

"I saw the aftermath," I replied, trying to get out of this conversation.

"But you didn't see the fight. Both he and Rob went at it. They couldn't hear anyone yelling at them to stop. Noah didn't stop until Rob took a plate to his head."

I cringed. "I know, okay? Why are you telling me this?"

"Because I've never seen Noah care about anyone the way he does about you. Even afterwards, while he was bleeding, all he cared about was you. He begged Travis to call you."

"Stop," I pleaded.

"He didn't want to press charges, and in some messed-up way, I think he refused because he was scared that hurting Rob would hurt you. Don't you understand? To him, you're worth burning everything to the ground. If there's any hope for you two, can't you just...?"

"Get over him lying to me for months? Forgive him when I'm still putting the pieces together? Get his hopes up when I know I probably won't be able to see past it?"

Dawn nodded, slowly understanding where I was coming from. I wanted to forgive him. If I knew I could, I wouldn't be here talking to her. I may not have had a lot of experience being loved, but I knew how it shouldn't feel. This terrible stomachache and these never-ending tears weren't the signs of anything pure or remarkable.

Maybe my heart was like a bone that needed an extra break to be reset completely. Now, it could heal itself properly. Maybe the hand I needed to hold was my own, because it wasn't going to be Noah's, and I doubted it could be anyone else.

"I need to be alone, Dawn. All of this happened too fast."

"The morning after he showed up drunk outside your dorm, he told me how he felt about you. I asked him if he felt tricked into it because there was no way Noah would fall in love willingly. He's too scared. But I could hear it in his voice. He meant his feelings, and I know he's an idiot for what he did. But just how that's a fact, so are his feelings for you. Both can be true."

I chewed on my lip, not knowing what to say. I understood her need to go to bat for her brother. I didn't want to disappoint her. But he was family, and his happiness mattered more to her than mine ever would. Her testimony, although beautiful, passed through me like it was a murmur from a ghost.

"I just wanted you to know that, even if you don't see how much he loves you, everyone else here loves you, too." She pushed the check to the edge of the counter. "I'm sorry, Rain."

"Me, too."

I left knowing that at least he had her. She'd help him get back to being the old Noah, or maybe even a better one, and one day, this fiasco could just be a story not worth revisiting.

On the walk back, the streets were too crowded for how I was feeling. People weren't paying attention to me, but my anxiety convinced me they were. I wrapped my arms around myself, wanting to disappear. I thought about what Dawn had said. I believed her, but the glass wall between Noah and me had thickened. It didn't matter if people threw flowers or paint or beautiful words at me. They all slid away, falling to my feet.

§

Back at the dorms, I found Mikayla in our hallway, carrying our coffees. I jogged up to her. "Hey!"

She turned, immediately smiling. "Hey, roomie. Here's your coffee. Where'd you go?"

"I quit Dawn's."

Her face drooped. "Was it messy?"

"Oh, yeah. But at least it's over."

"Job hunting is the next thing on our breakup to-do list, huh?"

"Yeeeep," I sighed, opening the door.

"The tutoring center is always looking for help."

My brows arched. "Really? That sounds like it could be fun."

"It'd be amazing. You'd turn every poorly written essay into a work of art."

"Suure," I replied, unconvinced but excited. As much as I loved tattoos, I didn't have a future in it. With a job as a tutor, I could work with a subject I loved.

I grabbed my laptop from my bag and sent in an application while Mikayla and I sipped our coffees.

Afterwards, I held up my cup, prompting a toast. "To picking up the pieces."

"And to finding new ones."

§

A week passed. I was getting better at timing my breakdowns. For example, I purposefully played sad songs and induced the tears before heading out with Mikayla. The dried-out tear ducts helped me fake it.

174 | A N D R E A   C A S A N O V A

I went to dinner with Mikayla at a renaissance-themed restaurant. The waitresses were dressed up in gowns and the tables were set with candles and chalices. It was fun, but I was ready to fall into my bed and wallow the rest of the night.

On this side of town, strings of lights hung from tall cedar trees and the sides of buildings were canvases. We walked arm in arm, already planning what we'd do the following weekend. I clung to every moment I that wasn't thinking about Noah like it was the first breath of air after being dragged underwater. This drove me to saying yes to everything.

"So, next weekend it's either drive-in movies or the new hiking trail on the other side of campus. You pick," she said.

"Why not both? We can go hiking first and catch whatever movie is playing when we're done."

"Spontaneous! I love it."

"Mikayla, we're planning it right now. How is that spontaneous?"

"We could get stuck watching a horror movie! Not knowing what movie you're seeing is spontaneous," she argued.

I laughed against her shoulder. "Watching a horror movie at a drive-in might freak me out. Maybe we should check what they're showing."

"No way! It's funner this way."

"More fun," I corrected, at which she rolled her eyes.

We were walking around people going in and out of a bar. Suddenly, my eyes made contact with someone who was smoking. I stopped as if lassoed, as if the world had abruptly decided to work against normal gravity. My dress swung, and my long, dangly necklace bounced off my ribs.

My mouth silently formed his name, not having the conviction to actually say it aloud.

Mikayla reacted late, realizing who stood in front of us. He was a mountain I couldn't walk around.

"Oh shizz," she sighed. "No offense, Noah, but why the heck do you have to be here?"

He laughed softly. "Can't I say hi?"

Again, and without fail, anger came to me first. My gaze narrowed.

"Hi," I said.

Despite the disdain coursing through the single syllable, my acknowledgment visibly breathed relief into him.

I averted my gaze to his hands. "I didn't know you smoked."

He knelt, stubbing it out against the concrete. "Thought I'd pick up a bad habit since I have the free time now."

His smirk baited me.

"Lying is a bad enough habit, don't you think?"

He smiled like he had misconstrued my insult as a compliment.

"We should go," Mikayla said, interrupting our staring contest.

"Don't," he whispered, his façade cracking. "Fuck, can I talk to you? I just need one minute."

My feet sank in emotional quicksand. Time become a weird construct. I hadn't seen him in days, and I felt the weight of missing him. I had tried to forget what he looked like, but after one glance, I remembered exactly how his expressions worked. I could almost predict every jaw tick and lip quirk.

"Just one," I said.

"Tick tock, tick tock," Mikayla muttered.

I glanced at her. "I'll meet you back at the dorm."

"Positive?"

"Yeah."

Mikayla dramatically saluted him. "See ya, Tattoo Dude."

Eager to get this conversation over with, I held onto a nearby post for support, waiting for him to speak. Noah hesitated, looking at me with his lips pressed tightly together.

I didn't know what I was doing. The sadness kicked in, and it made me say stupid things.

"You're making this difficult."

"Good," he replied quickly.

"You're trying to hold on when you need to let go." I didn't know if I meant it, but it's what came out.

He smiled sadly. "Are you my Diego or my trolley?"

I let go of the post and stood in front of him. "What are you talking about?"

"Are we like Frida Kahlo's trolley accident? Running into each other was the impact, but the way you're looking at me is the iron rod impaling me, causing me a lifetime of afflictions. Or are we like Frida and her husband, Diego? Two people who caused each other nothing but love and pain?"

The glass wall began to thin, because the way he reached me through poetry was the same way I came to him in paintings. Yet, even under the admittance of our hearts beating in similar patterns, my mind picked up on how neither option was the happiest of endings.

"Frida Kahlo was in pain until she died. I don't know what you want me to do here," I said quietly.

"Love me back," he replied carelessly.

"You're handing me a knife when I already know what sharp edges feel like. I can't."

Ignoring my frown, he inched closer. His knuckles brushed across my jaw. "I'm begging. Please."

"Don't," I whispered.

"What am I supposed to do without you? You can't just dance into my life, make me want to spin you around forever, then expect me to walk you to the door when it's time for you to go. It's not fair, Rain."

I hit his chest, suddenly mad again. I didn't want to refuse him, but I couldn't let myself have him, either.

"And you can't give me everything I've ever wanted, then make me doubt you. You lied to me when I thought you were safe."

"You look happy," he mumbled.

I tucked my hair behind my ear. "I guess I can be good at pretending, too. I'm sad, I'm feeling untethered, and I miss you so much I swear I'm homesick."

His gaze darted from my eyes to my lips. "Rain…"

"Please don't."

He stepped in toward me and kissed me. My whole world shattered. I sought shelter by leaning my body into his. Immediately, he clutched my waist. My shoulders caved when our tongues touched. Betrayal mixed with love, and despite what had happened, all I could think was, *This can't be the last time I kiss him.*

A broken sob hovered between us, driving us apart. His hands were on my skin. Tears dripped onto my cheeks.

"I'm sorry," he said. "I fucked up. You have every reason to kick me out of your life." He backed away, stuffing his hands in his pockets. "I'm sorry. Just let me wait with you until you order an Uber or something."

I nodded quickly, not able to tell him what I was thinking. Three minutes later, a car pulled up.

I glanced at Noah. *I'm trying to forgive you. I just don't know how.*

"We fell at the wrong time," I said.

"You didn't say wrong person."

My lips twitched. "Take care, Colt."

"You too, Rivas."

Epilogue

Standing in front of the door, I double checked the address, stalling.

You can do this, Rain.

I raised a closed fist, riding on temporary courage.

The door swung open. Rob came into view. His hair was shorter and there were no bags under his eyes. His arms were stronger. He had gained some weight and looked good. Healthy. I smiled.

"Hey," he said.

"Hi."

My hair had grown longer and was dyed back to its natural, black-brown shade. I had on heavy makeup because I was nervous and needed confidence. I wore a black dress and an oversized jean jacket. My book earrings hit my neck.

"You look great," he said.

"Thanks."

"Do you want to come in?" He made the offer but didn't move.

"Uh…" I fumbled with my keys. "I just—to be honest, I don't know why I'm here."

His face didn't change. "Oh. I'm happy either way."

"Rob, we never lied to each other, right?" I asked, not knowing where I was going but blindly trusting myself.

He chuckled softly. "I think we fought because we were too honest."

"Right." I was growing more uncomfortable by the second.

"What's wrong, Rain? Is it Noah?"

I blinked. The conversation was too casual, too normal for it be us.

"I ran into him a while ago," I said. "I haven't heard from him since. That's not why I came."

"Oh," he repeated. "Then, why?"

I still couldn't answer that, so I word vomited. "My mom is in therapy."

His brows arched up.

"Yeah. Crazy, huh? She keeps saying that she's sorry. I feel like everyone is sorry for something." I tried to say it lightly, but we both knew what I meant.

He nodded. "All decent people are, Rain."

"I know I hurt you," I whispered, the words too heavy to be said at normal volume.

He smiled sadly. "I hurt you more."

"Did you hate me for being with him?"

"I hated how quickly it happened, and I think I hate him. But I can't hate you."

I nodded. "I know I've said it—and trust me, I've tried—but I can't hate you, either."

He studied my face, his eyes glistening. "Do you love him?"

I didn't answer.

He changed approaches. "Was it different with him?"

My eyes watered. "Yes."

"But you can't forgive him?"

"I want to."

He shifted his weight. "What are you doing here, Rain? Do you want anything from me?"

"I don't know, Rob." After all this time, this history, I hated being at odds with him.

"I've always wanted you to be happy," he said.

"I think what I've realized is that… happiness has to come from within first," I said carefully. It sounded like the sort of thing Mikayla would say. I was surprised when Rob nodded.

I smiled. "I should go."

"I know."

Neither of us moved. I wondered if he was thinking the same thought: *This is the last time I'm going to see you, isn't it?*

He pulled me into a long hug. I leaned my face into his chest. He didn't smell like the cologne I had given him. We both knew things were over, but my heart still twisted, missing what we used to be. He used to be my universe. Now, he wasn't even a star.

I gently pushed us apart and looked into his eyes. In a lot of ways, neither of us wanted this closure. In a lot of ways, both of us needed it. I looked at him, trying to take a snapshot of who he was, focusing on all the good and hoping to leave all the bad with this last glance. But, staring at those caramel eyes, I couldn't think of him without remembering both.

I reached down and squeezed his hand, then turned around.

We didn't say goodbye. We had already done that. I walked away. Without a fight. Without a twinge of my heart.

We let go.

§

On the way back to the dorms, I called Noah. He answered on the first ring.

"Rivas?"

I smiled. "You were right, Colt. I didn't say wrong person."

Acknowledgements

First, a million thanks to the Newfangle Press team! You came around right when I thought my work was condemned to live in my computer forever. I'm so honored to work with you. You made my pipedream a reality. Thank you, thank you, thank you!

To my husband, Ken, thank you for listening to every version of this story and for giving me the time and space to write. Your love, your support, your patience, and your belief in me are what kept me typing. I love you.

To my best friends, Melanie and Mariela, thank you for believing in me when this was just an idea during one of our phone calls. Your friendships are one of my safe places in the world, and, without trying, you both inspire so much of what I write.

To Cassie and Stephanie, my book friends! You two were whom I was most excited to tell! I had so many moments of self-doubt and insecurity, but you two listened to every worry and talked me down from every intrusive thought. Your excitement and support helped me find my confidence as a writer. Thank you!

Thank you to my family for encouraging me when I was getting my degree in English, and for loving me even when I hid the delicate parts of myself. I hope this book helps you see more of me, and I hope you like it.

Lastly, thank you, dear reader! Some people dream of being on the big screen, selling out stadiums, or even flying up to study the stars, but I always dreamed of this. I dreamed of writing and of my words finding you. Thank you for welcoming this story and my voice into your life. I hope we find each other again.

Andrea Casanova grew up in Brownsville, Texas and first fell in love with writing after her third-grade teacher assigned a creative writing prompt for class. What was supposed to be a scary story for fall became the start of her obsession with writing. Her love of writing led to her love of reading, and in college, she majored in English with the plans of becoming a English teacher. However, after getting married, she decided to give her dream of becoming an author a try. She's been writing while traveling with her husband who is serving in the military. She picked up her pen back in Clarksville, Tennessee, started this novel in El Paso, Texas, and finished it in Pyeongtaek, South Korea. You can keep up with her on Instagram, @andrea.casanova27, where she gives updates on books, writing, and the occasional post of her dog, Mocha.